THE HAUNTING OF
THE OWENS FAMILY

1969-PERR

THE HAUNTING OF

THE OWENS FAMILY

Patricia A. Perry

Patricia A. Perry

To order additional copies of this book, contact:
Xlibris Corporation
1-888-7-XLIBRIS
www.Xlibris.com
Orders@Xlibris.com

For Bob Hendrickson

Who had the heart of a dreamer
and the soul of a true writer

And whose spirit I can feel
with every word I write

I would like to thank my family — your love, encouragement, support, and faith in me mean more to me than you will ever know. Thank you for teaching me to believe in magic.

I would also like to thank the following friends who took the time to read my work and offer suggestions:

Carl Midura, Dave Apostolico, Veronica Manlove, Beth McAllister Kantu, Gail Germain, Maureen Montgomery, and Mary Catherine Donnelly. Thank you so much for your hard work. You will never know how greatly your confidence in me touched me. Sometimes it was the only thing that kept me going.

To Lisa Simon, Stephanie Patterson, Virginia Baker, and Diane Gottlieb — thank you for helping me with my journey, and for your wisdom and compassion when things got tough.

To Brian Jang — thank you for your dedication and hard work in getting this novel published.

To Bridget Mooney — thank you for your excellent proofreading skills and for being my first "official" reader.

CHAPTER 1

Movement in Sound

(The First and Third-to-Last Word)

The crispness of the air, in the air. It was the same as last year, and the year before that. As always. Soon, trick-or-treaters will be ringing bells and knocking on doors, asking for what is rightfully theirs. Masks of bright pumpkin will match the fruit sitting on stoops and steps, with hollow angled eyes and toothless grins glowing from an internal fire. And after receiving their bounty, the children will scamper away in their ghoulish cloaks and latest action-hero attire, ready for their next house. Meggie sighed. It seemed to her that she stood at the window longer and longer these days. Maybe it was just the season. Maybe it was just the sounds. She could hear them again, you know. The sliding, moving of furniture. That's really what it was this time. Oh, with Dan at his volleyball game and the kids at respective friends' houses, the library, whatever, she didn't have anyone to actually bounce this off of. She couldn't look over at someone while they all watched television in the re-done basement (well, the half that was re-done, anyway) and say, "Why, what do you think those noises are?" Well, maybe it was better that way. Then she wouldn't have to deal with looks of "Oh, Meggie," from her husband, even if he did have to, on more than one occasion, rearrange the furniture back to where it belonged. But no one ever admitted that anything was out of the ordinary. Well, she supposed she understood why her children were that way. After all, it is how they grew up, or are growing up since the oldest is now seventeen and the youngest seven. But she knew she could never accept what was in her house as ordinary. No, she's seen enough, been in the midst of enough, to know when something has singled her out, has singled her family out. But, you see, Meggie could also pretend if she put her mind to it. So, she shut the window in the room two of her daughters share and checked twice to make sure that it was locked, even though what she feared was inside. She wrapped the cord around the vacuum cleaner and carried the vacuum down the straight staircase which leads directly to the front door (and would also lead to the outside, where freedom reigned, with only the rustling leaves seemingly taking advantage of this). And, as she suspected, the noises grew quieter and less frequent as she approached. Oh, she could still hear the last scrape of one of the dining room chairs as it moved across her hardwood floor. And she could hear the dying movements of the hinged leaves of the table as they slowed themselves from flopping up and down. But she knew that when she would finally approach the room, all would be quiet. It always worked that way. So that for a split second you wonder if you had imagined the whole thing, if maybe you were just hearing things and that it was only the wind that had come in and rearranged your life.

It had started innocently enough. When the kids were younger and the youngest, Daniel Jr. and Annabelle, were little, real little, only the smallest of inconveniences had seemed to be attracted to them. Oh, for example, car keys found on the kitchen countertop when Meggie was sure that she had left them by the blue marble vase in the living room. Oh, and don't forget that time when Annabelle was throwing a hissy fit because she couldn't go out in the snow without her boots on. She couldn't have been more than five years old. She screamed and hollered, until the tears she wanted so badly for effect finally found themselves leaving wet tracks down her chubby cheeks. She ripped off her gloves (big girl gloves, not mittens) and threw them down on the floor, one at a time. The first fuchsia knit glove landed on the tips of its first two fingers (the index finger and the middle finger), balancing just so, as if it were posing at the end of an intricate dance, or gymnastic routine, waiting for the applause to come. Meggie couldn't help but say, "Oh, my!" with an open smile and a voice much too friendly if trying to battle the will of a stubborn five-year-old. Annabelle didn't even crack a smile, although she was fighting the urge inside. She simply ripped off the other one and threw that, too. And, of course, because of what was around them, what was in the air (why couldn't Meggie have seen it then?), the other glove landed neatly next to its mate, it too ready for the intricate balance and dance of life. Well, that was the end of it. Annabelle had to give in to the disappearance of her tears and laugh along in surprise with her mother and two sisters who happened to be passing by on their way out to a night of riding the snowy mountains (hills, really) of suburbia. A quiet town, really, when asking anyone who didn't know what else to say.

Well, then, bigger things started to happen. Like a rustling from the walls, or something, in the middle of the night when Meggie was finally free to think only of herself. She would hear the satisfied snores of her husband, glad that he was no longer on top of her. Sex. Maybe that was the sound. She didn't really enjoy it, you know. Never did. In fact, she half-wished that what her mother had told her on her wedding day was true—that a husband and wife "joined in relations" only when yearning to conceive a child. Well, she had had her four children (and four miscarriages, to boot). Did she really need it anymore? Well, she already knew the answer to that. But unfortunately, Dan wasn't on the same wavelength. No, he and his girlie magazines, trying to get Meggie to look at them once in a while. For educational purposes, he said. It's hard to know what's out there, what you're missing, if you don't open up your restricted little world once in a while, he said. I mean, really. Meggie would shudder when she would think of

some of the things he wanted to do, things that should be practiced only by newlyweds, if at all.

Dan. Was it really all his fault? Well, yes, it was, according to
Meggie. Except, of course, for the painting. Meggie supposed that
was her doing. Oh, she knew that it was Aunt Ruth, Dan's Aunt
Ruth, who passed away and left an attic full of antiques worthless
and worthy. But she was the one who said what a waste it would
be to throw away, or worse, give away, a perfectly fine painting.
Why, it would look just perfect above the marble mantelpiece.
Almost majestic in its colonial way. When was it painted? During
the Civil War? Was that Colonial Times? She'd have to look that
up. Oh, yes, she knew that anyone who prides themselves on working on furniture from a different century, stripping their skin with
chemicals never known to such a time, and who collects books
that are filled with cracked, yellow pages should know the facts
concerning her hobby, of her little diversion. The ins and outs.
But that would defeat the whole purpose, wouldn't it? It would
simply confine her to something she sought for little episodes of
freedom, right? Do you agree? Little of episodes of freedom. What
a strange way to put it. Were they necessary? Well, let's put it this
way. Right now in Meggie's life she felt that they were the only
things that kept her breathing. Those and her children. Oh, her
children helped her in a different way—they made sure she kept
taking those frantic worried little breaths, the kind that constantly
have you on edge. But that was okay, she wasn't sure if she knew
any other way, really. She'll admit. Maybe she does do it to herself
sometimes, like Dan says. But that still doesn't excuse what has
found her. Nobody deserves that.

All she did was keep her end of the bargain. She just did what
people were supposed to do. She just hadn't known that she had
made a pact with the devil. That's what a psychic had told her
once. "You made a pact with the devil," she had said, in those
exact words.

Meggie wasn't the type to reflect on her life too much (not the
kind of reflection that is self-identified anyway). Things just hap-

pened. They were often unfair, believe me, and she did feel the pain of being victimized, of even looking at it that way. Whether great or sad, moments did call on Meggie to participate but they rarely left their mark on her (remained as such). Oh, she would remember things alright, but she never (hardly ever) even thought of trying to step back somehow so that she would find herself in a moment that was too precious, too happy to give up. And she never tried to escape the torturesome moments, either (that's true). She just stood still in the middle of the road so that the wind could carry anything it wanted to her. Sometimes it turned her upside down and sometimes it barely lifted a hair out of place, but it always came to her. And she always stayed.

No, she supposed it wasn't in her nature to reflect on much. She had never anticipated anything happening to her. Or at least never had done so before Dan came along. Anticipation. Would it have somehow found her (happiness) if she stopped walking on bits of broken shell?

And the door (*where?*) lightly creaked as the wind from who knows where crossed the room.

The sound of Elizabeth's platform shoes hitting the hardwood floor snapped Meggie back without even a sting.

"Hi, Mom," Elizabeth said. Meggie turned and looked at her eldest daughter. Her black curls cascaded past her shoulders like a dark waterfall and the light coming from the streetlamp outside was reflected in the steel of her blue eyes.

"Hi, sweetie," Meggie said. Meggie touched her own dark hair, albeit much shorter than Elizabeth's, and then closed the door to the pantry after making sure the vacuum cleaner cord was safely tucked inside.

"When's Dad coming home?"

"Oh, I suppose around ten, after his game."

"Oh," Elizabeth said. "Hey, watch it!" she said when Annabelle raced in from the next room, almost knocking her over.

"Sorry," Annabelle said. "Hey, Mom, can I have a doughnut?"

"Sure, honey."

Annabelle opened the refrigerator and reached in. The door blocked most of her, with both her mother and her sister able to see only her ankles and feet.

"God, you're short," Elizabeth said.

"Elizabeth!" Meggie said.

"Well, I'm sorry. I just don't remember being that short at seven."

"You weren't."

"Well, then."

Annabelle ignored this exchange and smiled as she held up the chocolate-covered doughnut that looked two sizes too big for her and said, "Mmm," to an imaginary audience.

"You're so weird," Elizabeth said.

"Elizabeth!" Meggie cried again. "I wish you'd stop."

"I don't care, Mommy," Annabelle said. "I'm just ignoring her."

"Well, that's what you should do, honey."

"I'm going to bed," Elizabeth said.

"But it's only eight-thirty," Meggie said.

"I don't care."

"Did I do something?" Meggie asked.

"No."

"*I'm* not going to bed," Annabelle said.

"Big fuckin' deal," Elizabeth said.

"Elizabeth!"

Annabelle licked the chocolate that had found its way to her fingers and then resumed eating big chunks out of the doughnut, smearing more chocolate on her chin and back onto her fingers again.

"Well, goodnight," Elizabeth said.

"Oh, Elizabeth, I *feel* bad," Meggie said.

"I *just* want to go to bed," Elizabeth said.

"Oh, well, alright," Meggie said to the back of her daughter because by this time Elizabeth was already out of the kitchen, on her way to her room. Meggie tore a piece of paper towel off its roll and handed it to Annabelle. "Here, sweetie," she said. "You don't want to get that all over your clothes."

"Hey, Mommy, can we do my costume tomorrow?"

Meggie was now at the sink, trying to scrub the burnt bread crumbs from the pan that had held her meatloaf a couple of hours earlier. "What is it you wanted to be again?"

"Barbie," Annabelle said. "Remember?"

Meggie picked up the liquid soap and poured more into the pan.

"Remember? Susan Gallagher said that I couldn't be Barbie because I have brown hair and you said it didn't matter, remember?"

Meggie put back the sponge and picked up the steel wool pad. "Oh, yes, that's right. It doesn't matter."

"I *know*. That's what *I* think. I can be Barbie if I want to." Annabelle wiped one of her hands with the paper towel and then wiped the other hand on her purple t-shirt that was covered with peeling white flower decals. Meggie turned and looked at Annabelle. Her baby. She remembered so clearly the night when she was born.

Annabelle had been delivered in what you would call a perfect, textbook way. The only complaint, if it could be looked upon as that, was that it all happened so quickly. Seven years ago, in early May, Meggie had just finished doing the dishes from dinner and decided to rest in the den. Dan was upstairs tucking in the kids, Elizabeth, then ten, Grace, eight, and Daniel, Jr., then only three. Meggie looked at her watch and noted that only four hours remained in the day her doctor had said when the baby would come. Oh, well, Meggie had thought, it wouldn't be the first time when her baby would be overdue. Elizabeth had been two weeks late, and Grace almost a month. Danny (Daniel, Jr.) had come early, but that was different, he was a boy. Meggie knew she was going to have another girl. Oh, no one said as much. They couldn't, back then. But she knew. She knew by how the branches moved when she walked past the trees, she knew by the shape of the mist as it passed by the moon, and she knew by her dreams which had sent her visions of purple and blue. Right after Dan had come down from tucking their other children in for the night, Annabelle decided to come. And it started with such a small pang that Meggie wondered if this baby was trying to spare her the pain of yet another child coming into the world.

"Boy, that was easy, wasn't it?" the doctor had asked as he held the slippery baby in his hands. "This one came right out. In less than two hours, no less. You're lucky you got here in time." Meggie had smiled then, half-way remembering her hazy thoughts of Dan weaving in and out of traffic, telling Meggie to hold on as she held her abdomen, with the pangs and pulls and rips coming much too quickly for her peace of mind.

"So, what do you think, Meggie?" the doctor asked. "Are you going to have a couple more and make it half a dozen?"

Meggie looked up groggily and said, "What?", not focusing on anything, really.

"I said you had a girl, Meggie," the doctor said loudly. "Another beautiful girl."

"A girl," Meggie repeated sleepily.

"I think we should name her Annabelle," Elizabeth had said when she first saw her sister wrapped tightly in a soft, thin blanket, "after my doll from when I was little." The baby hiccupped right when Elizabeth finished saying this, so her big sister continued, "See? She likes it. I can tell."

Meggie and Dan looked at each other. Dan shrugged and Meggie kind of liked the ring to it, as if it were the name of a fairy that would hide in the brush until all would go away and then come out and dance and sing under the trees of backyard forests.

"Well, then," Meggie said and then brought her face close to that of her new baby, who had small blue eyes and soft dark hair that would soon give way to light brown. "Annabelle," she said softly.

CHAPTER 2

Elizabeth sat at her desk, writing down all of the things she wanted to accomplish in her life.

1. *Go to college.*
2. *Finish college* (as best she could, which is what her mother always told her, a sentiment that was comforting, even though she did get mostly all A's).
3. *Get a job and buy my own house.*
4. *Write a book.*
5. *Win an Oscar* (something she only told MaryBeth, who sits next to her in physics class).
6.
7.
8.

Elizabeth stared at her list wondering what came next. She just wasn't sure. Maybe it's . . . But then again . . . This wasn't like her. More realistically, it wasn't like the part of her she liked to show, to admit (to show), to anyone, really. She used to hem and haw and pause, looking at the flat sides of things, contemplating humps and bumps and the edges where all meet. Like Grace in a way. But Elizabeth didn't consider this a strength. Not at all. Not when her friends would stand, lips pursed in mocking amusement, hips bent with hands on top, waiting for the next hesitation, willing it on, so that they can say, "Elizabeth, really, make up your mind." And sometimes, "It's almost as if you're hysterical. Look at you." And she did. She would run home and look in the mirror that was starting to make its own frame out of chipped rust. The smell of mildew would overcome her and she would see the lumpy outline of her personality, take on things, with hesitant rises there and change-of-mind dips over here. So that all she could see was the pink of her unsure flesh, not knowing if it should stretch here or there, still making up its mind as its reflection sighed in exasperation, not knowing what else to do but to mirror back a lump of clay.

But, you can get hurt only so many times, a sentiment she found out much sooner than her mother would spout, thinking it's her own, with Meggie trying to help her daughter, and herself, in I suppose about a year from now, with clear sad eyes. And so, Elizabeth stood up straighter, steeled her jaw and heart, and sharpened the edges of her soul, telling her friends and the world that no longer would they be able to trounce upon any softness, whittle through open gapes. She was firm in her decisions, even if that was to go back and visit hesitancy again and now, with one time resulting in a friend saying, "Elizabeth, you shouldn't say, 'I *think* I'm going home now.' You should be stronger than that. Just state the fact, what you're going to do." With Elizabeth responding in a locked gaze that squeezed her friends' eyes with its hinges, took her friend's breath while she answered, "No, Carol . . ." with a purposeful, iron pause in between, with gates high and large, fending off, hurting even, anyone stupid enough to attack. "I said," with clear, slow pronunciation on the "d." "I *think* I'm going home now," with a sour announcement to the world of strength a long time in its coming.

But, as with all who roam, wonder, walk, I suppose, when alone, relaxed, it would sneak back up on her again, so that after a few minutes she would find her spine curved, shoulders hunched, and clay beneath her fingernails.

Elizabeth put down the pen and shifted her focus from the unfinished list to the window. It was dusk and she looked at the soft, blurred images outside. Pigeons flew and glided from one rooftop to another until their wings and bodies meshed with the oncoming night and nothing could be seen of their flight but dots of grey that people strolling outside thought were just shadows in their own eyes. Elizabeth should have felt peace at this time. She always had when she had been younger. Like the time when she had been playing Baby in the Air with Stacey Lewis, Susan Nicols, and Timmy Beatty. She remembered how Timmy Beatty had thrown the ball up in the air and how they all ran. But she hadn't stopped, even when Timmy said "Stop!" as he caught the ball. She ran across her front lawn, past the side of the house, and into the backyard where the night was magically creeping into the trees. She saw the soft grey envelop the backyard, with the black of the night not far behind. Here she stopped, and she stood with her hands down at her sides, breathing in the new air that seemed to accompany the newness of nights. Twilight, the time of neither night or day—one could surely lose themselves in this mist. And Elizabeth tried. She sat down on the wet grass and breathed deeper than she ever had. She stared into the trees until her eyes glazed over with tears that wanted release, but she refused to blink. She stared and stared and listened to the far-off sounds of the swoosh of an occasional car driving by the front of the house and the clanging of a pot coming from next door where Mrs. Kane was starting dinner for her husband and herself, and of . . . (were those her friends laughing, calling her name?). But, soon the sounds grew louder, and Elizabeth blinked, resulting in two streams of tears running down her cheeks.

"Elizabeth are you alright?" Stacey Lewis had asked from behind. "We couldn't find you." Elizabeth turned while wiping her eyes.

"Yeah, I'm alright," she said.

"But, you're crying. Did you fall?"

"No, no, I'm not upset."

"But you're crying."

"I was just sitting. I'm not upset."

"Well, alright," Stacey said, unconvinced.

"I wasn't crying. It's just that sometimes it's nice to get away."

But how could you explain this to a little girl who lives in a normal house with normal walls with a normal roof? At least compared to the Owenses' house.

Elizabeth sighed and picked up her pen again.

6. *Maybe get married, if*
7.
8.

"I just need my flute," Grace said as she opened the door and tentatively crossed the room to the closet.

"Whatever," Elizabeth said as she put down the pen with more force than necessary.

Grace stepped back out from the walk-in closet.

"I mean, I . . . , you know, this is . . . this is my room, too," Grace said, trying to be assertive, with the red rising on her cheeks as she clutched onto the thin black case that held her flute.

"Did I say it wasn't?" Elizabeth asked sharply. "God, I'll be glad when I'm out of here."

Grace took a breath. "You know, Elizabeth . . . " she started. Elizabeth looked up from her desk and stared at Grace. Grace clearly got thrown off track and asked, "What college are you going to anyway?"

"I don't know," Elizabeth said. "I'm hoping for USC or University of Texas."

"They're so far away."

"I know."

"Sarah Wilkins," Grace said. Elizabeth looked at Grace as if this held no meaning to her whatsoever.

"Sarah Wilkins," Grace said again. "She's going to Rutgers."

"So?"

"Well . . . "

"I'm not Sarah Wilkins, whoever that is."

"I think she's in your math class."

"Oh." Elizabeth shut her notebook and got up out of her chair.

PATRICIA A. PERRY

She walked over to her bed, turned the covers back, and climbed in right on top of the beam of light from Old Mr. Kane's spotlight. Everyone knew it was supposed to be angled toward his own house, but he insisted on keeping it turned toward the night, so he could have peace of mind by telling himself he can see anything that would dare to approach.

"I don't know where I'm going," Grace said.

"Well, you don't have to worry about that now. You're only a freshman."

"Well," Grace said. "I guess I'll go practice in Danny's room."

"Turn out the light on your way out."

"Okay." And Grace turned out the light and shut the door, leaving Elizabeth in a room that held no light except that coming from a scared old man.

Grace opened the door to Danny's room. Dinosaurs and soldiers were over there in mid-battle in that corner, rolled-up dirty socks and crumpled gym shorts were by the open closet, and scattered comic books and those two plastic horses Danny loves so much, the tan and black ones with manes of what seem like real hair, were right there by his bed. Grace went over to the bed and moved aside the torn sleeping bag so that she could place her flute on the bare mattress. She then went to the closet and opened the door even further. She looked at herself in the full-length mirror and remembered when, before all the bedrooms had been shifted around, this had been her room.

"A pact," her friend, Elsie, had said when they both had been about Danny's age, ten. Elsie, Hillary, June, and Grace had all agreed, right in this very room, to be best friends forever, sealing their agreement with a trip into the secret world that can be entered only by travelling through the mirror right here, found in Grace's room.

"Our friendship can only be destroyed," Elsie continued, "if this piece of paper is put back together." And Elsie completed the

symbolism, as the others somberly looked on, by shredding a blank
piece of notebook paper into tiny little pieces.

"Alright," she said. "Now it is time to go into our secret world."

"Will we be able to come back?" June asked.

"Of course," Elsie said. "All we do is slip through the mirror
and then slip back whenever we want to come back."

Hillary was the first to stand. She broke from the group and
then slowly and gracefully walked toward the mirror. She then
lifted her right leg and meshed it to the mirror, bringing it back
down again. She repeated this with the other leg and then turned
around when the journey was complete. She walked away from
the mirror and held herself as if she were a wise old nun, looking
around the room as if it had been her first time there. She ignored
the other little girls as if she were the only one in the room and she
looked out each window, taking in all the vantage points this new
world had to offer.

"Me next," Elsie said quietly, clearly excited. And Elsie followed Hillary's footsteps, with June going next, and finally, Grace.
When they had all entered the secret world, they held hands and
smiled and hugged. And right at the time when they had all agreed
that the next step would be to go and explore that new wonderful
backyard that looked like Grace's, but really wasn't, Grace's mother
yelled up the stairs that June's mother was on the phone, breaking
all spells.

"Oh," June said. Elsie sighed and Grace looked down at the
floor like it was her fault.

"Well, that's alright, I guess," Elsie had said.

"What time is it?" Hillary asked.

Grace looked at the alarm clock of that little yellow bird from
the Snoopy cartoons and said, "Five thirty."

"Oh, I should go," Hillary said.

"Yeah, my mom's on the phone," June said.

"Well," Elsie said. And they all walked toward the door, but
then Grace said, "Should we go back through the mirror?"

"Oh. Well, I guess we should," Elsie said, and in the same

order they had so slowly and gracefully entered their magical world, they one by one quickly and clumsily lifted their feet to their reflection, smearing the glass with their sneakers.

"Well, thanks for coming over," Grace said.

"Yeah. We'll see you tomorrow," Elsie said.

Grace looked at her reflection now and carefully watched the grey eyes that stared back at her. When she had been younger she would sometimes look in this mirror and scare herself, convinced that her reflection had smiled a little when she hadn't, or had winked when she had had her eyes open wide the whole time. But now, it was just Grace. She knew that. It was just her with her shoulder-length blonde hair and her soft, clear skin. Her blonde hair that had been jet black with a streak of white down the back when she had been born, causing the nurse to say to her mother, "That's a good omen," as she handed Grace over to Meggie. "It means this child is gifted. She can see."

And over and over Grace's mother had told her daughter how she had felt when her second born had been handed to her. Reliving words, Grace remembered her mother saying, "It was so calm. I just felt so calm. Different from the other children, you see. When Elizabeth was born, I felt all mixed up. Excited, scared, sentimental. Oh, yes. And love. Pure love like sugar. My sugar baby, she was. But, you . . . I loved you just as much. I loved all my children just as much," Meggie would say as if the time was already gone and she was an old woman standing on a porch lightly swept by prairie wind, her children removed from her by the door swinging one way or another. "Yes, with you, I felt only calm," she would say. "I was on a waveless ocean that was as clear as glass when they handed you to me. Clear as glass, my baby." And Grace's mother would look into her daughter's eyes at first with the purity of what comes from canes in a field, just like with the others, remembered through Elizabeth, but then with a curiosity expressed by a tilt of the head, an inquisitive squint of the eyes, trying to look into the pool, and then a quick, "Hmm," not dismissing but acknowledging that some things you just can't figure out.

And as Grace grew into toddlerhood, her jet black gave way to a soft dark blonde, and as each year passed, her hair grew lighter and lighter, until (years later) the day when it matched the mark of her gift of sight and all was blended so that nothing special could be seen, or remarked upon, by anybody. But her eyes stayed the same. Grace was born with grey knowing eyes that saw through anything, and these eyes would and will keep their color—through grade school when other children would gaze into her eyes just a fraction of a second longer than they did with others, through high school when teenage boys would fall in love after asking to borrow a pen or if there was going to be a quiz that day, through adulthood when cashiers would give her the wrong change wondering why they couldn't take their eyes from hers as they reached into the till, through death when her future grandchildren would look down and shiver from seeing such beauty that was surrounded by old and weathered skin.

Grace wasn't as tall as Elizabeth, but she tried to hold herself as if she was. She wasn't successful all the time, however. Her shoulders often slumped, causing even her own mother to say, "Really, Grace, you should try to straighten up." She wondered if Elsie, June, and Hillary remembered, or ever thought of, their secret world, which had been entered only two other times. Grace wasn't even sure what had split them up. Something about David Cassidy. Elsie and Hillary had fought over who would marry him. Grace couldn't even remember now what T.V. show he had been in. But, Elsie and Hillary had fought as if his bones and flesh were going to enter their town that very night and sweep up only one fair bride-to-be out of her bed and into his strong, protective arms. And soon, fictional men gave way to real boys and other concerns to pre-teens who think they'll be all grown up in about a year or two. Oh, they all still said hello to each other, talked once in a while, and even sat next to each other during lunch sometimes, but it wasn't the same. They each had their own lives now and other, more important friends.

Grace closed the closet door and walked back to the bed. She opened the black case and traced the soft red felt of its inside. She then took out the body of the flute and attached the mouthpiece and then the tail end. At first, Grace had chosen the flute because it looked the prettiest. And you looked the prettiest playing it. Your cheeks didn't stretch more than twice their size, looking as if the painful air would have done anything for release, as when playing the trumpet. And your teeth didn't jut to the forefront, looking as if you suddenly had been transformed into a beaver searching for something to sharpen your long dull teeth on, as when playing the clarinet. Grace played her flute every chance she got and some she made herself. It helped to lull yourself. That took you away sometimes, or better yet, took the others (things, more than that) away while you sang. Peacefully. Knowingly. It's okay, you know. She lifted the flute to her mouth and then began to play the theme song to M*A*S*H, which she knew by heart.

Meggie had just gotten the last of the dried meatloaf off of the pan when her husband came home. He was six feet, three inches tall, which lent to the drastic comparison between him and Meggie, who was only five-foot three. He had dark hair like Meggie, but his was now speckled with white, something that wouldn't happen to Meggie for at least fifteen more years.

"We won," Dan said as he put his gym bag on the chair in the corner. Meggie lifted her forearm to scratch a soap bubble from her nose, bending her hand away so that the wet yellow glove wouldn't touch her face.

"That's great, hon," she said.

"Is there anything left over from dinner?"

"Yes. There's a plate for you in the refrigerator." Dan opened the refrigerator door and had to bend to one-half his size to reach in. He took out the plate and unwrapped the cellophane.

"Do you want me to heat it up for you?" Meggie asked.

"No, I'll eat it cold. I'm starving."

"Oh, Dan, let me heat it up for you," she said as she went over to take the plate from him.

"Meggie, please. It's alright. I just need some silverware."

"Here, let me get that for you." And Meggie scurried over to the pantry and opened the door and reached into the green plastic flatware holder.

"Thank you," Dan said as Meggie handed him a fork and a knife. "I'm going to go eat this in the dining room."

"Okay."

Dan turned back toward Meggie. "Did you eat yet?" he asked, carefully holding his plate out in front of him.

"Yes, I ate with the kids, but thank you."

"Well, I'll be in the other room."

"Okay. Oh, Dan?" Meggie said, causing her husband to turn back again. "Do you want me to bring you the paper? I can."

"No, no. I'll get it myself later."

"I can."

Meggie by now had ripped the dishwashing gloves off of her hands and was drying her hands on a dirty dishtowel.

"Sure," Dan said, sighing.

"Okay. I'll bring it right in."

Meggie went through her and Dan's bedroom to the living room. (Their bedroom used to be a den before Annabelle came along and forced her parents to scratch their heads and wonder where they would put her—so they doubled-up Grace and Elizabeth and gave the new baby her own room, right next to Daniel Jr.'s room and they moved downstairs.) The heels of her feet banged determinedly on the floor as she looked to the ground in concentration and swung her right arm. She had always walked like this. When she was little, her mother had to often yell, "Margaret, over here!" when Meggie would walk with her bottom lip curled back over her teeth and her eyes squinting in concentration. One time, when they had all (Meggie, Meggie's parents, Meggie's sister, Emma, and her brother, Alfred) taken a trip down to the shore, Meggie had walked straight ahead, without realizing that her family had made a right turn. She walked and walked, looking down at the boardwalk and swinging that right arm, that had it not been for the safety rail at the end of the pier, to this day Meggie's mother swears her daughter would have found herself in the Atlantic Ocean, still in her own world, squinting at the bottom of the sea.

Meggie crossed the living room and picked up the paper that sat on the colonial blue, high-backed chair. She felt the eyes staring at her again, but she refused to turn around, not right away anyway. She opened the paper and browsed through the living section, which she had already read that day; she skimmed the headlines on the front page and in the first section; and she even turned to the sports page, pretending to be interested in the local football scores. But when the hair on the nape of her neck started to rise, she realized, that, yes, she probably should turn around. And there he was. Same as always. Uncle Ezra. Poor Uncle Ezra who was murdered on Halloween night. Shot right in the back. The killer was never found. He was looking at her now. Oh, his grin looked a little more mischievous now than on other days (sometimes it varied), but his eyes still managed to follow her, didn't they? Uncle Ezra, who was the subject of many slumber party ghost stories, with her own daughters telling their friends that his eyes were really alive. Just walk anywhere in the room and you could not escape the gaze from this painting. Meggie sighed. It looked as if someone had reached up and pulled down one of the corners of the painting, so that it now hung in some sort of pathetic, crooked display. How on earth did he ever find himself hanging from this position? She walked over, stood on one of her antique chairs she just completed re-finishing (she wished all those antique dealers would quit calling her) and reached up to straighten the portrait so that it hung in the way it was meant to all along, the way the anonymous painter had envisioned his art to be displayed when he had worked so painstakingly with each stroke back in the times during the Civil War. Well, maybe not, Meggie thought. It was more likely that the artist had been commissioned to paint this portrait, yawning at every turn of boredom, just like a photographer who has dreamed of Pulitzers but settles for blushing brides who have no business wearing white. It frightened Meggie to be this close to Uncle Ezra, but she felt she had no choice. Nobody else would do it. She steadied herself by grabbing onto the mantelpiece and then stepped off the chair back to the floor, with Uncle Ezra watching her the whole time.

"Here's your paper," she said to Dan as she handed him the newspaper, with the sports section neatly folded on top.

"Thanks," he said as he tried to gather up the last of his crumbs onto his fork.

"I could get you some more," Meggie said.

"No, no, that's okay."

"But if you're hungry . . . "

Dan didn't answer, but instead opened up the newspaper.

"Uncle Ezra was crooked again," Meggie said.

"Hmph," Dan said and Meggie wasn't sure if this was in response to the latest trade in the world of sports or to her.

"I just stood on a chair and straightened him out," Meggie said.

Dan looked up and for a moment blankly stared at her through his glasses. It finally seemed to register and then he said, "Oh, well, that's just the house settling."

"Dan?"

"Yes?" her husband answered as he was back to reading the paper.

"How long does it take for a house to settle?"

"What?" he asked as he turned the page. "Oh, well, they can do that for a long time."

"Oh," Meggie said. And she stood up and went into the kitchen to try to work out that rust stain in the sink that seemed to have been there forever.

"Mom, how did you and Dad meet?" Annabelle asked while

her hair lifted up and then down again as she swung back and forth and held onto the bar. Meggie was on the other side of this see-saw type swing, facing Annabelle, and also held tightly onto the bar as the night air swept through her hair as well. Annabelle was in her Barbie costume—a pink, netted skirt with tights underneath and a matching shawl that wrapped around her pink t-shirt that had a smiling teddy bear close to her heart. Her short brown hair had been swept up, or at least the effort had been made, into a large, white barrette sitting at the very top of her head. Large clumps of hair had fallen from the barrette and were now covering Annabelle's ears.

"We met at a dance," Meggie said. Annabelle giggled. Meggie smiled back and lost herself in the rhythm of the swing, almost until her daughter disappeared, until she hadn't even been born yet.

"Well, he *does* have brown shoes," Meggie had said to her best friend Bea as she stood at the edge of the sea of chiffon.

"Honestly, Meggie," Bea said. "The things you say. He's also kinda cute. And he's staring at you." The song was "Stardust Melody," and in years to come, it would always bring Meggie mixed feelings. The tall boy, man, really (I suppose), walked across the gym. Oh, he was self-conscious about it alright, pushing his glasses back up on his nose when they weren't even sliding off, bumping into embraced couples dancing—things like that.

"Gee whiz," he finally said. Bea and Meggie giggled. He turned red. "Um," he continued. "Would you like some punch?" looking at Meggie.

"I'll see you later," Bea said, with a wink.

Meggie was aloof without trying to be—the only way it worked. She just didn't care about this type of thing. Boys and diaries and boys. Who had the time?

"No, thank you," she said. "I already have some." And then,

"See?" with a smile as she held up her crystal punch glass, because she felt sorry for him.

"Oh, yes, well, um," he said.

"So," she said, because she could, because she could feel that she was at some sort of advantage. In an odd way, at least in this setting. Not caring, I mean. The power of it. Really. "Do you go to Haddon Township High?"

"What? Oh, no, um, I did. But not now. I go to Drexel."

"The business school?"

"Yes. College. Yes."

"College," Meggie said.

"Yes."

"I Only Have Eyes for You" was now playing, but the dancers didn't seem to notice the change in song. They kept swaying to the same slow beat and holding each other tightly, occasionally being joined by converts who before had pretended to be satisfied just watching and sitting on the bleachers, with the other flowers that had been cut out and pasted on the walls behind them. Until, of course, they had gotten up the nerve, by themselves or on a dare, to ask that girl over there to dance or had decided not to look away so quickly this time when that boy looked this way again.

After he formally introduced himself, after he told Meggie that his name was Dan Owens and that he had grown up in Haddon Township, a couple towns over from Haddonfield where Meggie lived, he held out his hand and asked for a dance.

"Only if you want to," he said.

"Of course," Meggie responded, taking his hand ever so lightly, enjoying the role she had put herself in. And she, too, became one of them. Swirling around in her strapless, pale yellow gown (with the stiff netting) that would not see its first tear until her granddaughters would discover it hidden in the attic, in about fifty years from now.

Was she in love? She didn't think so. But that still didn't stop her from marrying him and having four babies. Babies—they did make her smile. And her husband smile. And her parents smile.

And her friends smile, her new friends with babies of their own and who would ask her and Dan to join their bridge groups—friends, who, when the troubles had begun, had deserted her; friends who had said, "Couldn't you ignore it? For the children," and then followed their own advice and turned the other way when spotting her at the . . . , in the . . . , anywhere, really.

"Did you *like* him?" Annabelle asked, blushing in her own cheeks. Meggie crinkled her eyebrows, narrowing her eyes, and contemplated this seriously.

"Well," she said. "I liked the fact that he had brown shoes and wore glasses." Meggie tells this story once in a while and when Elizabeth and Grace hear it, Grace just looks at her mother in a puzzled sort of way and Elizabeth says, without fail, "That's ridiculous."

"And a college education," Meggie added. "I did want someone with a college education."

Annabelle looked up at the sky and removed one hand from the bar so she could try to tighten her barrette. It was getting darker now and the cool October air had a sort of eerie feel to it.

"Mommy?"

"Yes, sweetie."

"Sheri says that if a man's penis touches a woman down there, then that's fuck."

"Hmm," Meggie said, not shocked, or at least not showing it, at all. "Well," she said, giving this the same amount of contemplation as she did the question of how she and her husband had met. "I *suppose* that's a form of . . . of fuck."

"If someone pressed in one of your boobs would it hurt?"

"Oh."

"Does it hurt to have them?"

"No, no, it doesn't. It's just something that happens gradually. You get used to them."

"Oh," Annabelle said. And soon Annabelle grew bored and let

the swing slow so much so that Meggie dropped her feet to the ground and Annabelle followed, jumping off the swing before it was fully stopped.

"Tomorrow's Halloween!" Annabelle screamed excitedly as she bounced into the back screened-in porch. Meggie laughed.

"I know, honey," she said as she started to follow, with her eyes looking down and her heels brightly pounding into the dirt, her arm swinging up and back, propelling her forward.

* * * *

Dan stood in the dark, his hands down at his sides, his eyes squinting, half trying to get adjusted to the dark and half challenging anything he couldn't see that wanted to invade, mark. Mischief Night. Rotten kids with eggs. Toilet paper. Soap. Laughter in dark clothes and movement like graceful, black skeletons behind bushes and under streetlights on deserted corners. Full moons and howling dogs as these teenage skeletons, boys, race by. Cats that hiss and arch their backs as the boys dance, strewing their mischief. The dark crisp made its way to Dan, into his lungs. He accepted it, breathing. There's something to be said for a cool, fall night. Especially when safe, dark magic comes with it. Kind of fun. Oh, he knew those kids didn't mean that much harm (most of them, anyway). But, he did need to be out here, in the dark. Bats flew and the ghost in the tree shook (the one he and his kids hung that very night). The beam of a flashlight crossed. Roots, the siding, and then Dan's feet.

"Oh," Old Mr. Kane said. Old Mr. Kane who was about seventy-eight, his hair now only sides of grey, his eyes taking in as much they could from the sidelines (his choice).

"Hi, Joe," Dan said.

"Gotta watch those kids," Old Mr. Kane said in a conspiratorial tone, looking from the shadows on his left to those on his right.

"Yup, yup," Dan agreed.

"They'll come and get you," Old Mr. Kane whispered, with an eerie whistle of the wind agreeing, lightly shaking leaves, disturbing mist around the corners of both their houses.

"Well, now," Dan said.

"They will. Aarrh, they will," Old Mr. Kane said, leaving, taking his weak beam of light with him. Laughter came from the bushes across the way. Down the block, footsteps with no bodies (it was too dark) clopped quickly across the street, toward here and then again down that way, far-away devilment causing hair to rise, bumps to form on the skin. A rustling from outside the house on the other side of Old Mr. Kane's.

"Just some good ol' fun," Dan said, to no one in particular. Reassuring himself. Now sitting on the front step with his own flashlight in hand, a warding off, a staking claim in his mind.

* * * *

Meggie wiped the end of the dining room table with her sponge.

"Mom," Danny said. "You're going to get that on my candy."

"What?" Meggie asked distractedly, studying the mini Snickers bars and Dum Dums. "Oh, no I'm not, see?" she said as she made one last wipe, accidentally hitting a Hershey bar.

"*Mom*," Danny said, frustrated. He was sitting at the table with his Insect Man costume still on, with his cape sadly slipping to one side and his rubber antennae drooping on top of his head as well.

"Oh, honey, I'm sorry," Meggie said. "But I didn't get anything on the actual candy. I only touched the wrapper, see?" she said as she held up the candy bar.

"Don't *touch* it," Danny said. "You've just been cleaning. You might get some of those chemicals on it," he said. His eyebrows were crooked, worrying, forming two jagged lines, and one of his antennae bounced to agree with this sentiment.

"Oh, I think you're tired," Meggie said.

THE HAUNTING OF THE OWENS FAMILY   35

"I'm not . . . "

"I bet I got more," Annabelle said as she bounced into the room holding a pillow case full of candy. She was looking as bright as she did the night before and she held her sack upside down as what seemed like pounds of candy spilled forth onto the table.

"I got Reeses," she said, pleased with herself as she started to silently count all of the chocolate bars she got.

"So? I did, too," Danny said, trying to relay that he was not impressed with his little sister. He, too, started to count his candy, occasionally looking over at Annabelle, with worry seeping into his eyes whenever he thought she was ahead of him.

The front door opened and Elizabeth walked in, turning around to wave at whoever dropped her off. A car horn was heard and then the sound of tires streaking the street, and Elizabeth turned back, with her smile turning into a scowl as quickly as the car had pulled away.

"I got Reeses!" Annabelle shouted.

Elizabeth ignored her and walked over to Meggie.

"Where's Dad?" she asked her mother.

"How come you came in the front door?" Danny asked.

"He's downstairs watching T.V.," Meggie said.

Elizabeth sighed.

"Did you have a good time?" Meggie asked.

"It was alright," Elizabeth said as she dropped her pocketbook onto one of the chairs.

"When I get older," Annabelle said. "I'm still going to get dressed up for Halloween."

"Yeah, well, you have a scary one on tonight," Elizabeth said.

"No I don't. I'm Barbie."

"Well, that's what I . . . "

"Elizabeth," Meggie warned, as best a mother like her could.

And Elizabeth must have been in some type of strange mood, for she didn't argue and she didn't indignantly leave the room. She just pulled back one of the chairs and sat down with her brother and her sister as their mother went back into the kitchen for something or other.

"Don't touch my candy," Danny said.

"You can have one of mine," Annabelle said, handing her sister a small Peanut Chew.

"Those rip my teeth out," Elizabeth said.

"They do?" Annabelle asked, retreating her offer and inspecting the candy.

"Mom, where's Grace?" Elizabeth shouted into the kitchen.

"Oh, she's at Rebecca's at a slumber party."

"Where were *you?*" Annabelle asked as she started to pile up her candy, one on top of the other.

"So, what's everyone doing tonight?" Elizabeth shouted again into the kitchen.

Meggie walked out of the kitchen into the dining room, wiping her hands with a paper towel.

"Oh, I don't know, honey," she said. "I still have some cleaning to do. Why?"

"This house is never clean," Danny said.

"Well, sure it is . . . " Meggie started. "I . . . "

"No, it's not. It's not like John McGowan's house. His mom . . . "

"Oh, Danny, you're tired," Meggie said.

"No, I'm not," Danny said, frowning.

"I'd send him to bed if I were you, Mom," Elizabeth said.

"Shut up," Danny said. He then reached out his arms to bring all his candy further toward him.

"Oh, Danny, I think you should go to bed," his mother said, concerned.

"I'm not *tired! Mom!*"

Off in the kitchen, the side door creaked. Made an awful sound as if coming from, for, the dead. And they all turned their heads. After a long pause, the door shut and footsteps came. Toward them slowly as if navigating through a fog, but being those who chase. A light seemed to flicker (did it?) and so did eyes. The bang came from another room and shoulders and thighs, knees and elbows, jumped. Scared was there. With eyes wide. Lips pursed. Unsure. And, like the other times, the pulse was true and hard, telling whoever wanted to know that they were just going to have to wait and see.

And then Grace came into view.

"What?" she asked, becoming frightened herself when she saw them. "Is something going on?" she whispered, looking to the windows, to the doorway across the room, and then ultimately, but not willingly, behind her.

Meggie let out a breath.

"Whew!" Annabelle said.

"Oh, get real," Elizabeth said. "It wasn't anything. It was just Grace."

"You were scared, Elizabeth. I saw you. I *saw* you," Annabelle said.

"It wasn't anything," Elizabeth said.

"Hi, honey," Meggie said as she went over and gave her daughter a kiss. Grace blinked and then hugged her mother back.

"Mom, you said Grace was spending the night at Rebecca's," Danny said.

"Wow, look at all this candy," Grace said.

"Mom," Danny said, increasingly becoming upset.

"Oh, yes," Meggie said. "Both Danny and Annabelle spent hours out there, getting it all. They're exhausted."

"I'm *not* tired," Danny said. "Grace, why aren't you at your friend's house?"

"Where's Dad?" Grace asked.

"Oh, he's downstairs," Meggie said.

Grace's eyes seemed even more clear now than they had ever been. She was slightly flushed and her camel-colored mock turtleneck seemed out of place, too light of a color for someone whose cheeks had been lightly, coolly, burned by the fall wind.

"Where were you?" Elizabeth asked.

"Oh, I was at Rebecca's."

"Why didn't you stay?" Annabelle asked. "Mom said you were going to stay."

"Oh, I didn't want to," Grace said, almost too casually as she reached for a candy bar.

"Why *not?*" Danny asked. *"Mom . . . "*

Meggie looked at her son. "Why didn't you want to stay, Grace?" she asked.

"Um . . . "

"*I* know why," Annabelle said. "Remember? She came back last Halloween, too."

Grace busied herself with opening the wrapper of another candy bar, even though she hadn't even taken a bite out of the first one.

"That's right," Elizabeth said. "She did."

"They were telling ghost stories and she didn't like it," Annabelle said matter-of-factly. Grace looked up sharply.

"Well . . . " Meggie started.

"I wouldn't like that," Danny said quietly as he looked down at the table.

"They don't even wear costumes, and she got scared," Annabelle said.

"Annabelle," Meggie said.

"What?" Annabelle asked, thinking her mother was simply trying to get her attention for a further statement. Elizabeth let out a strong sigh and then put her head in her hands.

"I don't have to like ghost stories if I don't want to," Grace said.

"No, you don't," her mother agreed.

"I can't even believe you're all talking about this. There is no such thing as ghosts," Elizabeth said.

"Well . . . " Meggie started.

"Mom," Elizabeth said sternly. "Stop this."

Footsteps through fog. What about the noise? Well . . . isn't it enough to explain one thing at a time? It is for them. But no time for this. Not now. Another's coming (breaking?).

"Daddy!" Annabelle screamed when she saw her father.

"Hey, guys!" Dan said to his children.

"We're telling ghost stories," Annabelle said as her father came over and playfully picked her up. "Swing me higher," she said as she laughed.

"Ghost stories!" Dan said playfully. "You shouldn't tell ghost stories on Halloween, that's too spooky," he said as he lifted Annabelle as high as he could without hitting her head on the ceiling.

"Why?" Danny asked.

"Well," his father answered with a wry smile. "That's the one day a year when all the ghosts do come out."

"That's today," Annabelle said, her eyes dancing as well.

"I don't like this," Grace said.

"Grace got scared at her slumber party and had to come home," Annabelle said as she slipped back into her chair.

"Nothing happened. There are no ghosts," Elizabeth said.

"Well, you know, Uncle Ezra was murdered on Halloween back during the Civil War," Dan said.

"*Mom*," Danny said.

"I don't like this," Grace said again.

"I can't believe this," Elizabeth said as she let out a groan.

"Dan, maybe you shouldn't . . . " Meggie said.

"What? Oh, it's fine. We're just playing around . . . "

"Yes," Meggie began. "But, sometimes . . . when you concentrate . . . on something like this," with breaths in between. The others looked at her. "It finds you," she finished in a sharp whisper (no indecision there), looking only at Dan.

"Oh, don't be ridiculous," Dan said with his usual mixture of good-nature trying to mask bubbling on the edge because really this is very frustrating. (Why does she have to say things like this? Be like this? Causing the kids to be scared and, more importantly, more frightening, causing them to be more like her than just a color of the eye or strand of hair.)

"That's what that psychic told you, isn't it?" Grace asked, mimicking her mother's whisper.

"Oh, just . . . " Elizabeth said.

And, of course, synchronism is a strange thing. They've all come to know this now (through both dark breath and light eyes), this punctuated by another large bang coming from the living room, as if something had fallen or had been thrown. And each member of the Owens family stopped their thoughts and movement, frozen, with only their eyes moving to that person or this, waiting to see into what direction someone else is going to take this.

"*Dan*," Meggie finally said, almost in a pleading tone. Dan quickly recovered from his own initial response and resumed his appointed position of head of the family in times like this. Even the expression on his face gave an air of, "I'm sure it's nothing." He walked, heavy-footed, into the living room. His wife followed, with each of their children following her, not wanting to go, but not wanting to be left behind even more.

Uncle Ezra invited them all in with his eyes, connecting to each one of them. Even Dan couldn't help but first look at the portrait before assessing the rest of the room.

"Oh, my," Meggie said when she saw the crumpled pages of the open book on the floor, right below the painting. Dan bent down to pick the book up and straightened out its pages before closing it.

"Did that fall off the shelf?" Danny asked.

"How could it?" Annabelle asked. "The shelves are way over there." And it was true, the book shelves were across the room, built right into the walls.

"Do you think it was Uncle Ezra?" Meggie whispered to her husband.

"Oh, Meggie," Dan said, annoyed, the bubbling surfacing, popping, pricking his skin. He walked over to put the book back on the shelf.

"The book's red, just like the one he's holding in the painting!" Annabelle said.

"Oh, Meggie," Dan said again, blaming his wife for her

daughter's voice. He turned from the shelves before he reached them and put both arms down at his sides, showing his disappointment.

"I didn't do anything," Meggie said like a child.

"I'm going to bed," Elizabeth said, and she turned and started to walk up the stairs.

"I think that's a good idea," Dan said in his father voice. "Up to bed. Everybody up to bed."

Grace turned and followed Elizabeth, and Danny hung his head as he moved closer to his mother. Annabelle took Meggie's hand and led her and Danny toward the stairs.

"The book just fell," Dan called out after them. "It just fell."

And the bubbles continued their sizzle, and Dan continued to stand by the book shelf (still holding the red book in his hand), and Uncle Ezra continued to hold Dan's gaze with his own of speckled grey and black.

CHAPTER 3

Danny zipped up his bright red windbreaker as he sat on the grass and watched the moving truck. He watched as the other little boy wheeled his own bike, which looked almost like Danny's, out of the truck and down the platform. He saw the boy's mother come out of the house and shake her hand and tell her son to leave that to the moving men, that he could hurt himself. Danny stood up and picked up his bike that had been lying in the grass next to him. He got on and rode up and down the street, doing his wheelies and making his skid marks without looking at the other boy, but making sure that the boy could see him.

"Hey," the boy called out. Danny hit his brakes and then looked over, brushing his blonde thick bangs from his forehead.

"Hey," the boy called out again. "I have a bike."

"What kind?" Danny asked.

"It kinda looks like yours."

Danny stared at the boy, squinting away from the sun.

"Are you going for a ride now?" the boy asked. He looked to be about Danny's age but he was shorter and stockier. He had thick, dark hair and his skin was darker than Danny's.

"Yeah," Danny said. "Wanna come?"

And the little boy ran to get his bike, hopped on, and rode down the hill of his driveway to meet Danny.

"I'm Vinnie," the boy said.

"Danny."

"What school do you go to?" Vinnie asked.

"Sycamore."

"That's where I'm going to be. Fifth grade."

"That's my grade," Danny said and they both started to ride down Second Avenue. And as blades of grass swayed in clean molecules (found only, mostly, outside) and as the crisp air smacked Danny's skin, releasing toxicity, Danny expanded his cage of ribs as he rode further and further from his house, relaxing in talk about how they may be able to find leftover pumpkins to smash that had already been injured on Mischief Night three days ago.

✳ ✳ ✳ ✳

"My goodness, four children," Vinnie's mother said as she poured Danny another glass of milk. "Your mother must be at her wit's end."

Danny stared at Mrs. Angelucci. She wasn't like any other mother he had ever seen. She was curvy and wore tight clothes to show it and her dark hair was long and wavy. She was wearing gold-colored shoes that looked like slippers and her long fingernails were painted the same color gold to match.

"That poor woman," she said with a laugh. Danny just continued to stare and drank his milk, with each swallow making a gulping sound he was sure even the sparrows in the backyard could hear. He wiped his mouth with the sleeve of his jacket and started to get up out of his chair to leave.

"Oh, no, sweetheart, here, use a napkin," Mrs. Angelucci said. She grabbed some paper napkins from one of the many boxes in the kitchen and handed them to Danny. Danny panicked. What else had been in that box?

"Here, Danny," Mrs. Angelucci said, puzzled. "Take them."

Danny looked around the room. Brown thick tape and cardboard boxes hid everything. How was he supposed to know what to do?

"Um," he said. "Um," he stalled.

A large, sweating moving man came in, asking where she wanted the sofa.

"Oh, my," Vinnie's mother said, putting the napkins down on the table. "We really should put that one downstairs." And she scrambled off to tell the movers to put this there and that here.

"When do you start school?" Danny asked Vinnie.

"I guess tomorrow," Vinnie said.

"Okay," Danny said. "See ya."

"See ya."

And Danny walked out the front door and picked up his bike from the cement walkway, brushing off his hands on his shorts before he touched the handlebars.

"I know," Mrs. Jeffries from next door said. She was holding a Bundt cake and stood outside while she talked to Mrs. Angelucci, who was standing in the doorway. "I certainly wouldn't want to do anything to hurt any of the children. It's just that I thought you should know."

"Know what, Mrs. Jeffries?"

"Well, that, that the family is a bit . . . different." Mrs. Jeffries had lived in Haddon Township for about forty years now, ever since her new husband carried her over the threshold of their one-story rancher, when she had been only twenty. He had puffed and heaved and huffed, joking by asking how would he ever be able to help her move around when she became pregnant. But, the years went by and the children never came and in perceived disappointment her mouth became thin and cracked, with her bright red lipstick often bleeding up into the thin branches of her dry skin.

"Well, thank you for the cake," Mrs. Angelucci said.

"Well, you're quite welcome. I felt it the proper thing to do." Mrs. Jeffries brushed some imaginary dust off of her black blazer and then turned to leave.

"Oh, Mrs. Jeffries . . . "

"Yes?"

"I am sorry I can't ask you in, it's just that . . . "

"Oh, believe me, no apologies are necessary. I know what it's like to be a newlywed and move into a new house."

"Oh, no," Mrs. Angelucci said, letting out a small laugh. "Vincent and I have been married for about eleven years now."

"Oh, yes," Mrs. Jeffries said as she reached a bony hand up to her greying hair. "I remember." The older woman looked her new neighbor up and down, as if making a mental note of her outfit. The younger woman took a breath.

"When you said *different* . . . " she said.

"The police have been there on many occasions," Mrs. Jeffries finished and then sharply turned on her heels, as if lending punctuation to an official piece of proof.

* * * *

Danny couldn't remember when it had started, the toilet flushing that is. There it would be, before he went (three times), sometimes while, and after (only two, but maybe it should be three because that's how many times he did it beforehand, four to make sure, five for good measure, six for security, seven because he lost count, eight because he was stuck, nine because he couldn't get out, ten because he was scared, eleven because something might reach up and grab him if he didn't get it good, twelve because . . .)

"Danny, are you alright in there?" his mother would ask. He could see her right now, you know. Oh, not so much for real, but in his mind. There she was, on the other side of the door, with other or something in her hand, a sponge, a dust rag, a broom with a broken handle, props to ensure her place even though the walls would always be covered with streaked, thick dust, the floor with invisible mites that sometimes latched onto your skin, the sink, countertop, toilet (oh, no) with unimaginable horrid things sprouting from imaginable layers of mold because they were spreading, turning colors, right before your very eyes. (Oh, it was real, alright. The slime, the dirt. His mother was an awful housekeeper, you know. Ironic considering how much of a ceremony she would make out of it all. "I'm ready! I'm ready to clean!" she would announce to the world and then scurry off, come back proud, with nothing free from ooze, muck, and scum. Oh, it was in his mind, alright. It may be a little dirty, but busy, busy, busy is what it does! Others, having no time to act, to allay fears; his mind, having only time to act, seeing [creating?] things sprout.)

"Danny, is all that necessary?" his mother asked, exasperated. She had had enough but he didn't care.

"Yes," he said through the door.

"Well, can you come out soon?"

"Yes."

"Why don't you come out now? Do it just one more time and then come out."

Danny then reached for the handle one last time (that visit), not telling himself it was the last time because he just couldn't handle endings very well.

It didn't matter that it had started with a closure, folding in of his own skin upon his bones. He didn't mark that as any special occasion, something for future incidents to be measured against. No wonder there. He only wondered when the toilet flushing had started. When swirling water against bacteria-laden rims had caught his attention, his morbid attention that was both repulsed and attracted to dark stains that didn't seem to go away. It didn't matter that preceding this (he may not care to document, declare, but I do), his breath had threatened to take his life, first torturing him with particles spiked with ammonia, alcohol, fluid meant to strip away what was bad but really was bad of and in itself, and then traveling to his organs, interrupting even intervals of pumping, pulsing, trying to ignite abrupt, unforeseen, deliberate seizures, a frying of the mind. He didn't wonder, stop to think about, his need to wash his hands every fifteen minutes. He didn't wonder, stop to mentally comment on, his ritual before each time he left the house (each right shoe must be lined up higher than the left, that way good will prevail over evil—it's a fact). He didn't wonder, stop to see the incongruence, of wiping away harm that can't be seen and keeping the chaos of a room strewn with a ten-year-old boy's paraphernalia (he did need his toys after all, he wasn't dead). No, he was just mildly alarmed at this new symptom, wondering if it was taking him away much further than he had intended.

Vinnie had wanted to sleep over. How could that happen? He didn't mind sleeping at Vinnie's. Over there, the wall came down somehow. The air was fresh, the molecules tinier, not large enough to threaten. Closed windows weren't such a bad thing over there.

"Why can't I sleep over your house?" Vinnie had asked as Danny leaned up against his bed, reading a comic book. Danny pretended to be too intent on the story line to answer his friend.

"Danny."

Danny looked up, keeping his finger pointed to where he had stopped reading.

"Huh?" he asked.

"Why don't we sleep over here tonight? We've slept at my house the last two weekends."

Danny got up and tossed the comic book on his bed.

"I don't know," he said as he started to put his sneakers on. "You wanna go for a ride?"

"Nah," Vinnie said as he sat down on the bed. "It's getting too cold."

"No, it's not."

"Yes, it is."

"Well, what time do you want me to come over tonight?" Danny asked.

Vinnie made a face like he wasn't sure what he wanted to do and then said, "Do you want me to come *here*?" Vinnie did like Danny but he had an ulterior motive for wanting to spend the night. He had heard things at school and wanted to see if they were true.

"Be careful," Kathleen Meyers had told him. But, he didn't mind. He was a man of danger. You can't change a man's nature. He might have actually said that to Kathleen. You just can't, he said. "My mom says to stay away from them, from there," Kathleen said. "Not to associate," with the word "associate" clearly trying to copy sounds from another's mouth.

"Aww," Vinnie answered, half feeling bad for his new friend Danny and half trying to play up his own bravery by playing her warning down.

"I don't feel well," Danny said and took off his sneakers again. He sat on his bed so that he was leaning against the headboard and his feet rested straight out in front of him. He picked up his comic book and started to fiddle with its pages.

"Maybe we shouldn't have a sleepover tonight," he said.

Vinnie studied him. There was something going on alright. He *did* look like he was hiding something and he even looked a little scared. It must be awful living in a house like this, Vinnie thought, but, it still must be pretty cool, at times.

"You know, Joey Greerson says that . . . " Vinnie started.

Danny quickly turned his head and stared at Vinnie. Vinnie felt his heart pump and he looked down at his sneakers.

"He says that your house is haunted," he blurted out.

Danny took in a labored breath and he stared at the bottom of the bed, with the muscles in his face taut. He knew he shouldn't even begin to think how many particles of dust were on the posts of the bed, surrounding him, but he couldn't help it. His eyes moved to each post, knowing the grey film was thickening right this very moment. He shuddered, thinking that maybe the particles got tired of where they were and jumped off onto his bedspread. He wiped his arm against his pant leg to remove any unseen bacteria, reaching for his comic book as an excuse. Vinnie started playing with his own shoelaces and snuck looks at Danny from time to time as the silence surrounded them both. Danny was reading his comic book with a frown.

"Insect Man's going to get killed," he said.

Vinnie looked at him and shifted his weight.

"Nah," he said. "They wouldn't do that. Where d'ya see that?"

Danny moved over so Vinnie could see. "Right here," he said as he pointed to the page where Earl, the evil scientist, was about to start the Dynamic Deathly Disintegration Machine he had invented. Insect Man stood inside its special unbreakable glass walls, seemingly trapped.

"Nah," Vinnie said again. "He'll get out of that."

Danny took in a breath and then surveyed the room to make sure all of his windows were open—that way any dangerous smells or fumes that might have found their way here from downstairs (oven cleaner, glass cleaner, lemon wax finish his mother sprays on her wood furniture, even his sisters' aerosol deodorant fumes from the next room) could escape to the outside, leaving him safe.

Danny turned so that they could each sit on the edge of the bed and read the comic book together. And soon, for a few moments anyway, he forgot about the dust long enough to find out that Insect Man did indeed have the power to break the walls by spitting his special insect saliva, causing his cage, not himself, to disintegrate.

CHAPTER 4

Grace looked at her breasts. How had they gotten like that? It was disgusting. She was standing naked before her bed, the first time she had allowed herself to do so without immediately reaching for her underpants and bra, feeling safe in their stretched cotton armor. The naked body was a disgusting thing. At least hers was. Her fleshy mounds tipped with puckered brown. Her coarse, dark, curly hair between her legs, spreading to the insides of her thighs. Her white stomach that had the nerve to be sexual in the way it curved in at her waist and then seductively rose on her tummy, just a little, between her hips. If she had a knife, she'd cut off her breasts, shave off her pubic hair with its sharp edge. That's what she would do. Who said that she had been born with clear, grey eyes? She forgot.

CHAPTER 5

Annabelle knew it didn't matter very much. She just sat in her chair and folded her hands on top of the desk. Mrs. Brown was standing at the head of the classroom, with her heavily rouged cheeks turning a softer pink as she contemplated the situation. "I don't know," the teacher said. "That doesn't sound like Annabelle."

"She did, though, she did," little Cathy Carpenter cried. "See my arm, see?" she cried again.

"Well . . . " Mrs. Brown began, averting her eyes to Annabelle. "Annabelle?"

"I didn't do it," Annabelle said. Mrs. Brown's heart went out to her. She looked like she was a kindergartener trying to see what it feels like sitting at a third-grade desk. Her feet didn't even touch the ground and her head looked like it would retract any minute between her shoulders that were hunched because her elbows had to reach high to rest on the desk. But there she was, folding her hands like a little lady. Oh, she was a tomboy, alright. Hating to wear dresses, her mother had said, hanging from the monkey bars from her knees better than any boy, and being the feistiest soldier during games of King of the Hill. And, oh boy, was she fast. Little Annabelle. How had this all started?

This Tuesday afternoon, Mrs. Brown had stayed late after school to finish taking down Halloween decorations by the moon of the back bulletin board—cut-out black goblins with no eyes and orange witches with no faces. But she couldn't find her stapler remover, so she left the room to go to the supply closet down the hall. Her heels clicked and clacked on the floor and their echoes filled the empty hallway. She smiled as she saw the children's drawings hanging on the walls. Crude pictures of deer with white spots grazing by unsturdy fences with a too yellow sun coming up through over-sized mountains hung here and those of a small house with slanting sides and a chimney that blew bouquets of daisies rather than smoke hung there. She went into the supply closet and reached for a stapler remover, two boxes of staples, and a large blue marker. No matter how many times Mr. Patterson cleaned this closet, it still smelled of musty childhoods. Manilla folders, construction paper, white thick glue, crayons, colored chalk, two discarded chalkboards all joined forces to create a scent that would bring even the oldest of the old back to the days when they wore pigtails in yellow ribbons and ran through mud in their Mary Janes. But, Mrs. Brown thought, the children are right. This closet is a little spooky. If a teacher was in this closet and the door was ajar, passing children on their way to the lavatory or special reading class would peer their heads in, only being able to slightly make out shapes and sizes in the shadowy, dark room. They would report back to their peers that they saw poor pretty Miss Josephs get caught in the labyrinth of shelves and cabinets that at first moved apart to welcome her and then swallowed her whole as she made the mistake of bending forward toward the cobwebs to reach for a pair of rounded-edged scissors. They would talk of how they saw old Mrs. Beetle smile at them before she entered the closet and then how she closed the door almost all the way, but left it open enough for Joey Priest to see. If you gave him your brownie or browned apple tart, he would tell you how he saw her turn into a witch and then escape through a hole in the floor so she could fly and screech and cackle and scream all through the secret underground maze that held captive children who had committed the unforgivable of shooting spitballs or laughing during a book report of *Little Women*. And now, now they were forever held captive within the maze, not permitted to see the light of the day or to ever grow old. Though, once in a while, if the moon is shining right and old Mrs. Beetle is feeling generous, she might let a couple of kids out just for the night so that they can swing on the swings and hang from the bars under the dark sky that cloaked them all. Suzy Phillips said that once she and her parents were coming home from her cousins' house and at first she fell asleep but then she woke up and they were passing her school. It was close to midnight and she wiped the fog from the window and saw, out of the corner of her eye, kids who looked like ghosts sadly playing hopscotch and hanging from the monkey bars with such a defeated look in their eyes as if they knew they would never escape.

Mrs. Brown smiled. The imaginations of children, she thought. But she supposed they *were* right in a way. Shadows are a funny thing and for some reason Mr. Patterson never put in a lightbulb that gave this old closet more than a shadow.

"It's haunted," a voice came from the other side of the grimy-covered window. Mrs. Brown jumped and then walked toward the window after moving over a couple of boxes that were sitting on the floor. She moved the heavy once-red, now-pink curtain and saw Annabelle outside on the playground focusing intently on her big, blue, sparkled-covered ball she was bouncing.

"It's haunted," Cathy Carpenter said to the other children, Lisa Weller, Ralphie MacKenzie, and Dolores (named after her mother) Robbins. The other children stopped the game they were playing and stared at Annabelle. "My older brother is in Annabelle's sister Elizabeth's class and he says that he knows someone who knows for sure." Annabelle just kept bouncing her ball, but now she was trying to bounce it off of her knees before it hit the ground again.

"Did he see anything?" little Ralphie asked hesitantly, looking over at Annabelle. She was only about two feet away, but she ignored them all.

"I think it was a girl," Cathy said.

"Oh," Ralphie said. "Well, did she see . . . "

"Oh, she sure did. She saw a ghost."

"A ghost?"

"Yeah," Cathy said. "Standing in the window, just looking at her." Lisa and Dolores stood with their eyes wide, changing their focus from Annabelle to Cathy back to Annabelle again. Dolores looked a little torn, as if she wasn't sure if listening to this was somehow betraying her friend whom she liked to sit next to in music class and share a book with as they sung "She'll Be Coming Around the Mountain" together.

"Yeah," Cathy continued, but now with a sort of mock tone that took pleasure in whatever she was trying to accomplish. "His face was all evil and mean and he lifted up his hand and did this with his finger as if he wanted that girl to come in the house." Lisa gasped and Ralphie said, "I have to go home now." Ralphie had to keep from dropping his books as he walked faster and faster over to his bike.

"See ya guys!" he called out when he reached his bike, and then "Uh, bye, Annabelle," as if he felt badly for her.

"Um, I should go, too. Come on, let's go, Dolores," Lisa said with a look that gave way to the whiteness that was spreading on her face. Dolores hesitated and moved closer to Annabelle.

"Annabelle, are you okay?" she asked. Annabelle was now bouncing the big ball from one thigh to another, occasionally taking a few steps to retrieve it from the ground when she would miss.

"Let's go, Dolores!" Lisa said.

"Well, okay," Dolores said to Annabelle. "I'll see you Monday in school then," and she left with Lisa, occasionally looking back to see Annabelle still playing with her ball and Cathy standing right next to her with a twisted look of victory on her face.

When the other children had gone, Annabelle stopped playing with her ball. She placed the ball on the ground, stood up straight, and then said to Cathy evenly, "My house isn't haunted." Cathy gave out a little sharp laugh.

"Well, something is going on over there," she said.

"My house isn't haunted," Annabelle said again, looking straight into Cathy's eyes. Cathy averted her eyes and then said, "Well, the police were over there the other night. What was all that about?" Annabelle didn't answer. "My mom *said* so. She said that when she was taking Aunt Emily home that she drove by and saw them there and your mom was crying right by the front door. 'They had the front door wide open,' my mom said. She said, 'Why would they do that? Have the front door wide open like that?'"

"Don't ever say my house is haunted again. It's not the truth."

Cathy tried to look braver than Annabelle, but she couldn't pull it off. Her eyes wavered and her lip quivered.

"I don't care," Cathy said with mock courage.

"Well, I do," Annabelle said with real courage. Cathy looked down at the black asphalt and twisted her foot back and forth. She looked up and squinted at the setting sun and Annabelle could have sworn she saw Cathy's hand tremor a little when she lifted it to brush an imaginary wisp of hair away from her eyes. She looked like she was going to say something and then changed her mind. Then finally, she said, "I'll race you for it."

"Race me for what?" Annabelle asked.

"I'll race you for it. If you beat me, I promise never to talk about your house again."

"You should never talk about my house anyway."

"Are you afraid?" Cathy asked, feeling her nerve build.

"I'm not afraid," Annabelle said.

"Well, then."

Annabelle put down her ball and both little girls walked over to the white line (now chipping) that had been painted on the playground to be a boundary for kickball and whiffle ball games.

"Up to the fence and back, okay?" Cathy said.

"Alright."

And both little girls hunched over, firmly placing their right foot in front of their left, their stance ready for the contest.

"I'll say it," Cathy said.

"Alright."

"Ready, set," and Cathy was off before she even said "go." But Annabelle didn't protest, she just took the deep breath she usually takes before her races and moved faster than the wind. Before trees had the chance to sway back and forth even once, before mothers stopped at red lights could turn around and wipe the noses of crying toddlers in the back seat, before the cat across the street sitting on the uneven steps could finish his yawn, Annabelle had raced up to the fence, grabbing it with her whole hand, and then flew back to the white, chipped starting line. Cathy was still making her way to the fence when Annabelle finished, catching her breath. At the fence, Cathy stopped and turned, first looking on either side of her as if wondering where Annabelle had gone. When she looked up and saw Annabelle standing at the finish line with her arms crossed, Cathy narrowed her eyes and walked slowly toward Annabelle.

"Chicken," Cathy said.

"What?"

"Chicken. Why didn't you want to race?"

"I did race. I won."

"Yeah, right," Cathy said as she bent down to pick up her book bag. "You're a coward."

"I'm not a coward. I won. I raced and I won."

"Oh, yeah? How did you do that? Were you invisible? Did you turn into a ghost like the one in your house?"

"Shut up."

"You're all crazy. Everyone in your family. Owenses suck." And the little girl went over to the bicycle rack to unlock her Schwinn she had gotten last year for Christmas. And Annabelle felt the sickness in her stomach spread. She's not crazy, she thought. And what does "suck" mean anyway? She'd have to ask her mother. She looked at Cathy and wished for every bad thing she deserved to happen to her. And that's the moment when Cathy's feet decided to slip on the dry pavement beneath her and she landed on the black top on her side with a thud. Annabelle started to smile slightly and Cathy started to cry. But then Mrs. Brown came rushing out of the back door and over toward them.

"I didn't push you," Annabelle said quietly to Cathy, not know-

ing the reason herself why she said this except that she was starting
to get scared. Cathy wailed.

"She pushed me!" Cathy cried to Mrs. Brown as she reached
her side.

"Oh, my," Mrs. Brown said, helping Cathy up. Cathy was
still crying after she stood and Mrs. Brown said, "Girls, why don't
you both come into the classroom for a minute." And that's where
Cathy cried even louder and Annabelle stayed quiet, looking first
at Cathy and then at Mrs. Brown.

"I didn't do it," Annabelle said.

"She did it!" Cathy cried. "She had her ghost do it!"

"Her ghost?" Mrs. Brown asked. "Oh, Cathy . . . " Mrs. Brown
sighed. "I think that this is just an emotional time," she said, not
sure herself what that meant. She calmed Cathy down and then
they all went back outside again. She helped Cathy get back on
her bike and then turned to Annabelle after Cathy had ridden off
occasionally lifting her right arm from the handlebars to wipe her
nose with her sleeve.

"Annabelle, are you alright?"

"Yeah."

"I know that you didn't push her."

"I know," Annabelle said. Mrs. Brown sighed. She had heard
rumors about Annabelle's family life, just like mostly everyone else
had. But how could she even begin to approach this with Annabelle?
She was just a child. And look at her, with every muscle in her
little body tense, ready to fight for herself at any given moment.

"Annabelle, you know that you can talk to me whenever you
want, right?" Annabelle looked puzzled. "I know," she said, but
she looked at Mrs. Brown with blank eyes that had no desire to
reveal anything.

"Well, I suppose you should be getting home to your parents.
We wouldn't want them to worry."

"My dad doesn't get home until seven," Annabelle said innocently.

"Oh. Well, we wouldn't want your mother to worry."

"No."

"Alright then. Do you have your bike?"

"No, I'm going to walk home."

"Oh. Alright. Well, be careful and I'll see you tomorrow."

"Goodnight, Mrs. Brown."

"Goodnight, sweetheart," and Mrs. Brown's heart broke a little as she watched this tiny girl walk away from her, standing as straight as she could to fight off whatever made her want to run as fast as the flutter of a hummingbird's wings.

* * * *

Elizabeth stood hugging herself as the cracks of fire flew by her hair. She moved because twice now a tiny spark had landed on her cheek, causing her to feel a small pinprick burn.

"Hey, Elizabeth," her friend LuAnn yelled. LuAnn was tall, almost as tall as Elizabeth, but her limbs were spindly and lanky, with her shoulders, hips, and knees all providing sharp angles for others to focus on. "Are you coming with us?" she asked. She was wearing her cheerleading uniform, as well as Ricky Landon's varsity football jacket. Her face seemed to be more flushed than usual, probably a result of Ricky Landon occasionally wrapping his arm around her, a gesture telling the rest of the team that she was his girlfriend. It was windy and Elizabeth's hair blew across her face. She raised her hand to brush a few strands out of the way and LuAnn walked over to her, out of breath.

"Are you coming?" LuAnn asked again. Elizabeth looked over at Ricky Landon, Craig Manning, Pat O'Donnell, Cindy Krauss, Megan O'Riley, Ellen (LuAnn's best friend), and the rest of the gang and wondered why she felt so much older than them. They were all laughing and Pat O'Donnell had just now dropped his marshmallow stick in the fire, causing Cindy Krauss and Ellen to raise their hands to their faces and everyone else to laugh that much harder. Elizabeth took a breath.

"Where are you going again?" she asked LuAnn.

"I told you. Pat's Steaks. In Philly," LuAnn said.

Elizabeth looked up at the night sky and grew uncomfortable because she couldn't see any clouds or stars. All she saw was black; the only light slightly touching it was the dull glow of a dying bonfire coming from below.

"Who's driving?" Elizabeth asked.

"Bob."

"Bob Delaney?"

"Yeah," LuAnn said as she looked over to their friends, who seemed to be getting ready to leave. "Come on, Elizabeth, why don't you come?"

"I don't know," Elizabeth said, feeling the uneasiness grow inside her. "I just wish I had my own car."

"What?"

"I'd go if I had my own car."

LuAnn looked at her friend as if she had lost her mind.

"But you don't, Elizabeth. What are you talking about? You always used to love to go out with us." At this point, Ellen had noticed LuAnn and Elizabeth talking and had started to walk over.

"*Bob* can drive," LuAnn said again.

"Hi, guys," Ellen said.

"Elizabeth's going to come with us," LuAnn said.

"I never said that," Elizabeth snapped just as one of the last flames cracked, causing everyone to say, "Ooooh!" and move back.

"What's wrong?" Ellen asked. She also had on her boyfriend's varsity jacket and her hands were stuffed in the pockets while one hip jutted to the side, lending to her stance that she had a right to know.

"Nothing," Elizabeth said the same time LuAnn said, "She wants her own car."

Elizabeth just stared into the fire and LuAnn said, "She said she'd go if she had her own car."

"Oh," Ellen said. "Well, *I* would go if . . . I had my own beach house." LuAnn bit her lip and looked down as if trying to suppress a laugh. "But we can't always get what we want, Elizabeth," Ellen added. Elizabeth looked away from the fire and toward Ellen and LuAnn. It was clear that tears were forming in her eyes, but the night and the flickering fire hid their cause—a passerby could easily think they were coming from the smoke.

"Well," Ellen said and LuAnn cleared her throat. "It's alright," Ellen said, the tone of her voice not revealing if she was sincere or not. "You know," she continued. "I had an uncle like that." Both Elizabeth and LuAnn looked up at Ellen. "With that problem."

"What?" LuAnn asked. Elizabeth hugged herself tighter and constricted her heart. The wind now seemed stronger and Elizabeth could feel her lips crack in the cold.

"Claustrophobia," Ellen said. LuAnn looked at Elizabeth.

"I don't have that," Elizabeth said.

"Well why won't you go?" Ellen asked.

"I don't have to explain that to you."

"I just think that you can deal with things better if you just bring them out in the open," Ellen said.

"I don't have *claustrophobia*," Elizabeth spit. "Why don't you just leave me *alone*?" And she turned and walked angrily away, lifting her hand only once to wipe the stream of tears that had decided to come.

"Well," Ellen said. Someone from the group yelled, "Where's Elizabeth going?" and Ellen answered, "Who knows? She's got problems." And everyone laughed.

Elizabeth first cut through the Headley's, then the Moore's. She then reached the back fence of the new people, the Angelucci's, and decided they wouldn't mind if she cut through their yard, too. She bent down to fit between the two thick wooden rails and snagged her jacket on a piece of splintered wood. The matter splintered and split. Oh, no. It was starting again. And at such an obvious time. Her head became light and she now began to see stars of her own making. She managed to pull herself to the other side of the fence even though her hands were now traitors, giving into the tingling that wasn't meant for laughs. The wheezing now came, making her face contort, its odd shape mocking her for fearing like this out in the middle of nowhere. For fearing the middle of nowhere. For fearing. If all you have to fear is . . . well, then. You're pretty unlucky. Her fingertips were now the wax kind Annabelle likes to wear on Halloween. Her hands were barely connected to her wrists by a weakening rubberband some gnome of the night kept snapping, snapping, accentuating her gasps. Her legs. Forget it. They were shaking, with her knees knocking, not stopping, unforgiving, really, until someone answers. The sky now held dangling blades of grass, upside down ant hills and the ground held a crescent behind some mist, all the while she stood upright. She's a standing uprright kind of person, you know. When it was over (intermission, really), she began to cry.

"Shit," she said. And the sparrows that had been hiding in the nearby bush flew away and a small mouse scurried past her feet. "Oh," she said, still being able to be surprised after all this. Her shoulders then slumped in some kind of defeat and she sat down, right there, still breathing heavy, leaning on the fence in the Angelucci's backyard. No one could see her. She was sure of that. This time. The brush was too thick and the trees too tall. And way back in this corner, not even the small animals of the night remained. It was just her. For now. She brought her knees up to her chest and wrapped her arms around them. She opened her hands, feeling her own fingers again. She stretched out her legs, feeling the odd calm that usually comes afterward, a reveling in knowing that the worst sort of *did* happen. Well, almost. But the rewards of the purge are short-lived and she began to cry again. She cried because she really did want to go out with her friends but couldn't. (Who could risk *this*? Was this claustrophobia? Is *that* was this is? Was something else wrong with her? What was *wrong* with her? Wrong, wrong, wrong. All Wrong. All Weak.) She cried because she wasn't sure where her life was taking her, and she cried because it just wasn't fair how her veins became lax in purpose and confused, panicking at the wrong moments, stopping all flow of blood and then unwinding, lingering at times when what she needed most was alert protection. Why? All this? She lifted her head and looked up to the sky. Giving it one more chance. But the only glimmer she could see was coming from the light that was going bad above the Angeluccis' back door.

* * * *

Grace sat on the steps by the lake, the ones that ended abruptly before the water, as if someone had planned to build a path but then realized that a large lake stood in the way and they abandoned their effort. She could hear the children playing behind her on the playground. "Hey, come on, Justin!" she heard one little boy yell. "That's not fair!" she heard from another. The sounds were soft and dull, as if they came from children with blurred edges whose faces had no discriminate features but had been smoothed out with an eraser. She pulled her denim jacket tighter around herself and looked out at the water. The geese were still there, silently floating and then flapping their wet wings when on shore, like someone running from the smooth, cool ocean, making a fuss bumping into beach chairs and overturning bags, trying to find their towel. Sometimes after band practice, Grace would come to this park, waiting for the next time of day to start. Sometimes she walked around the lake, ducking beneath the branches that hung here and there, often stopping to sit on that log or run her hand down the bark of this tree. And sometimes she sat on the bench by the playground, watching the children steer their magic ship (which was really the sliding board) or see who could jump furthest from the swing. But usually she sat right here, on the unfinished steps by the lake. She liked places like this, solitary, yet not too far removed. It reminded her of a more special place, even, the one she and Elizabeth had found about five years ago.

"Wow!" Elizabeth had said. It had been the middle of the summer and sweat was dripping from her hairline onto her face. She squinted and wiped the sweat off with her hand and then said again, more quietly, "Wow."

Grace had been following Elizabeth, walking her bike through the thick brush, not even fully realizing when she had reached the clearing, with her hand still reaching out in front of her waiting for the next tree branch to move aside.

"Oh," she said when she realized that they were no longer in the midst of the woods. She walked over next to Elizabeth and looked down to the bottom of the hill.

"What's that?" Grace asked as she gently laid her bicycle on its side.

"I think it must have been some sort of pool at one time," Elizabeth said. "Maybe for the Romans. Look at all those steps on the other side."

"The Romans? Here?" Grace asked.

"Well, maybe for someone like them."

Elizabeth and Grace started walking down the hill, toward the empty cement pool that had both large and small cracks filled with moss and weeds. Large cement steps, football stadium bleachers for giants, sloped up the other side.

"It must be almost as big as a football field," Elizabeth said.

"It sure looks that way," Grace said.

"And look, they even look like bleachers. I can't even see where they end," Elizabeth said as she pointed to the steps.

They reached one of the sides of the pool and Elizabeth sat down, swinging her legs over the side.

"Elizabeth, what are you doing?"

"I'm climbing in," she said. And she balanced herself with her hands and then pushed forward, landing on her feet on the cracked floor. "Umph!" she said as she landed. "Grace, come on!"

"Oh, I don't know," Grace said.

"Come on."

"Maybe one of us should stay here to help the other one out."

"Well, alright," Elizabeth said and she started running, over the moss and through the weeds, moving her arms like she was swimming.

"Elizabeth!" Grace said as she laughed. When Elizabeth returned, Grace grabbed her hands and helped her out of the pool.

"Let's climb the stairs now," Elizabeth said. And Grace followed her older sister as they lifted their legs high to climb the bleachers seemingly made for Romans to sit upon as they drank wine and watched sacrifices be made to the kings of the jungle below. The top step led to a well-cared-for lawn and Elizabeth and Grace stepped onto the grass as quietly as if they had planned to be trespassers.

"Wow!" Elizabeth said. The lawn had hills of its own, rolling here and rolling there, and straight ahead, now looking as tiny as a playhouse, was apparently the owner's house, looking stately and proud.

"That must be huge," Elizabeth whispered.

"They must be rich," Grace whispered back.

"Ssshh. What's that?" Elizabeth said.

"What?" Grace answered.

"*That.*"

Grace now heard the trickle and drizzle of a far-off brook, and when she turned her head toward the sound, she could have sworn that she felt the mist of an ancient stream on her face.

"It's water," Grace whispered.

"Let's go see," Elizabeth said as she started walking toward the sound.

"Oh, I . . . " Grace started to say, but then she moved her face more forward toward the mist and followed her sister.

"Grace!"

"Oh, my!" Grace said. And they both stood with their arms down at their sides and their mouths open as they looked at the elaborate fountain that had angels sitting on the side looking down at the giant goldfish that swam below.

"Are those real?" Grace asked.

"Yeah, they are," Elizabeth said. "Look, they're swimming."

"Wow," Grace said. She sat on the edge of the fountain and lightly dipped one of her fingers into the water. Two goldfish came rushing to her, opening and closing their round "o" for a mouth.

"They must have a garden somewhere here," Elizabeth said.

"We should come back," Grace said as her fingers slowly and gently grazed the water. "To see the flowers."

And when Elizabeth and Grace rode their bicycles home that afternoon, not even the sounds of the passing cars and trucks or the dust-covered traffic lights took their magic away. They rode home in silence, each thinking about their find. And when they reached their driveway, they hurriedly parked their bikes against the garage door so that they could run in and tell their mother. But as it turned out, their mother found them, opening the back door before they even had a chance to reach for the outside doorknob. Her eyes were red, her mouth contorted, and her blouse ripped.

"AAAAAHHHHHH! AAAAAHHHHHH! HHHHHAAAAA!

HHAAAAAAHHHHH!
nOOOOOO!!!!!!!! nooOOOOOO!!!!! NOOO!!!!!!!

NOOOO!!!!!! Heyyyyyyyy!!!!! Whyyeeeeeeee!!!!!!!!

HEAVEN HEEEEELLLPP!!!!!!!! STOOOOOP!!!!!

HAAAAAAAA!!!

OoooooohhhhhhhhhHHHHHHHHHHoooooooohhhhHHHHHHH!!!!!!!!!!"

"Oh, girls!" she sobbed. "He's a monster! He's such a monster!"

"MEGGIE!" their father screamed as they heard his footsteps
pound toward them. "MEGGIE! STOP THIS!" he yelled as he
came closer. Elizabeth's eyes grew wide and Grace bit her lip and
when their father reached them, he simply said, "Girls, get inside,
dinner will be ready soon."

"Oh, you're a monster!" Meggie cried. "LOOK! LOOK AT
WHAT YOU'VE DONE TO MY BLOUSE!"

"MEGGIE, I DIDN'T DO THAT! GIRLS! GET INSIDE!"

Elizabeth and Grace maneuvered their way past their parents but
only made it as far as the kitchen before the monster turned. On his
wife . . . on . . . There's a monster, here, you know. His face was red,
his skin flapped with angry bones, his stumps stomped the ground,
with roots giving him more than enough leeway. Liberty is good. His
sacrifice sacrificed. She played, too. Wasn't this fun?

"Ooohhhhhhoooohhhhhooohhhh!" It was her turn, afterall. She
swayed in ritual, her sobs becoming monstrous. There's a monster
here, you know. On her knees, her wrists banging against ankles, not
her own. "Pleeeeeeeeeeeeeeaaase!! Pleeeeeeeeeeeeaaase!!" is the added
chorus, the tragedy. The tree's feet drew back and kicked her arms out
of the way.

"CUNT!! YOU FUCKIN' CUNT!" aS hE hiT thE walL. eveRythInG ouT of kilTeR. where'S thE kilTeR??? As it traveled to where God had intended to bless these daughters with the future, but the tree re-named it as evil when it should have been a gift. The girls ran up the stairs to their room. And followed where they had been before. Eliza-beth reached for the book on how to be an actress she had gotten from the library and sat on her bed, scowling before she opened it up. And Grace picked up her flute and began to play. The notes sang, not caring about wails that tried to crush, crushing that tried to howl, roars that followed the crowd. Not caring . . . which carried her. The graceful and the strong were now here. Stopping the bite below. Smoothing and dodging at the same time. Swimming in and out, above and below. Them. Had some of the ancient mist been kind enough to follow them home?

* * * * *

What about when Elizabeth and Grace had first come along? Well, it had been there even then, during first this and thats. (It did not initially appear from blue, waiting for a day of magic when they were half grown. But, of course, you knew that.) Oh, it sometimes hid behind picture frames, books on shelves, and the large antique stuffed chair that sat in the corner of the living room. But it had been there. Even then. Under each braided throw rug (the one that lay in the middle of the hardwood living room floor and the one in the upstairs hallway), behind every flower pot, and in the downstairs closet that held old cans of paint and a ragged dust mop. And if someone had told Elizabeth and Grace when they had been little girls that there was a strange force in their house, that other houses didn't have candles that took a lighted match to their own wicks, shadows that walked, light switches that you could actually see go up and down causing a storm of electricity greater than that of any ac-companied by thunder; if someone had told these two little girls in a language they would have understood, they simply would have looked at that person with a child's acceptance of what they've known and then turned their heads to look at their new baby dolls that drank from a small bottle and wet their cloth diapers just like a real baby does. Chaos doesn't have the same meaning if you've been born into it. And this is something that Dan and Meggie would never understand, for all of a sudden finding yourself in a life like this is nowhere near having it be waiting for you before you even take your first breath.

* * * * *

"I am fine. I am kind. I am fine. I am kind. I am fine. I am kind," the fairies told Grace to tell herself over and over again.

* * * * *

Gasping. Elizabeth.

CHAPTER 6

Danny watched the dead leaves hanging from the tree dance. It really was a sight, you know. As if suspended from bands too short but they decided to forego the disappointment and bounce in happy surprise. But they were dead. Couldn't they see that? How can you look on the bright side of things if your very being has already become brittle? Brittle being. Believe. Bet on it. Oh, well. But, wait . . . They were just filling in gaps. Of the picture. Taken when ghouls crush the earth, from their perspective, roofs, from the other side, opening graves. Rotted seeds filled the air. And a turbid sense of it all filled in the background. My.

"I'm scared," Danny had told his father once. His father had been working, sawing, blowing freshly made dust off of something. The burring had made an awful noise.

"I feel weird," Danny said. His father looked up. "Like, like I'm not here or something," he added, then looked down toward his feet (were those *his*?).

His father kept staring at him. Not knowing how to talk to someone who doesn't know how to take up his own space? Maybe.

His father moved old rusted screws, tools, washers here and there on the old rusted workbench that stood in for a table. Looking through the mismatches wasn't an easy job, especially when you had no plan.

"Well," his father finally said. And then, "I'm glad you're here helping me," as he handed Danny an already used piece of sandpaper. "Just slide this back and forth over the top," he said. Danny took the sandpaper and slid it back and forth over the top, like he was told. Back and forth over the top. Coming back. At least for a while. For a few minutes.

"How is it, Danny?" his father asked.

"I think it's okay," he answered. And with that, his father went to look for that new box of nails he had just gotten at the hardware store that very morning. And with that, Danny continued. Back and forth. Over the top. With the sawdust embedding itself under his fingernails, latching onto the tips of his fingers, giving him prints.

CHAPTER 7

"Well, who am I to take away his dreams?" Meggie asked. She was surrounded by blank, open envelopes and was in the middle of addressing one.

Burt Reynolds
Blue Jay Drive
Hollywood, CA

"This isn't sane," Dan said. He had just come home from work and was standing in the doorway between the foyer and the dining room. His overcoat was still on and he was still holding his briefcase. "He's a grown man, for God's sake."

"Grown men have dreams," Meggie said quietly as she wrote the return address in the upper left-hand corner.

Alfred J. Lee
3182 Avondale Avenue
Haddonfield, NJ 08033

"Oh, for . . . " Dan said as he left to go change his clothes, scratching the back of his neck with his right hand.

"Mom," Grace said. Meggie jumped.

"Oh, sweetie," she said. "You have to think of some way to let me know when you're here. You're so quiet."

Grace pursed her lips and looked thoughtfully at the envelopes.

"Are these for Uncle Alfred?" she asked.

"Yes," Meggie said as she licked the envelope she had just finished addressing.

"Do you think Burt Reynolds will write back?" Grace asked as she pulled up a chair and sat down. Meggie sighed.

"Oh, I don't know, honey. Maybe."

The back door flung open. "Mom!" Danny shouted.

"We're in here, Danny!" Meggie shouted back as she craned her neck and looked sideways toward the kitchen. Danny ran to them, out of breath.

"I just went for a bike ride with Vincent," he said, panting.

"That's nice, honey," Meggie said distractedly as she started to count the envelopes.

"His mom wants to meet you. She's real nice."

"Who?" Meggie asked, first looking at Danny and then Grace.

"His mom. She's real young and pretty and she says she wants to meet you."

"Oh, that would be nice," Meggie said as she bent forward and gathered all of the envelopes with both of her arms. "Danny, honey, could you start getting the plates out for dinner?"

"Okay," Danny said as he walked back into the kitchen.

"Wow, it looks great, Mom," Danny later said as he began to lift his fork to the chunks of potatoes and carrots.

"Yeah, it does. I'm starved!" little Annabelle echoed and then proceeded to eat only three bites before declaring, "I'm stuffed!"

Elizabeth started describing the perfect college campus she wanted to go to in two years, with no one really listening because they were involved in mini conversations involving, "Of course you can have seconds," "I can do it myself," and "You just don't understand the state of the economy today."

Dan told Meggie that his boss and his wife were going to have a dinner party next weekend, that they were expected to attend. Annabelle said she hoped a scary movie would be on channel 29 that night, that the "spooks are that much scarier when Mom and Dad aren't home." Elizabeth said she was sure she already had plans that night, that she shouldn't be expected to stay home and babysit. Grace said she wouldn't mind. Danny asked if he could have some more stew. Then the sound of sulfur about to be stirred, struck. Meggie asked what the ladies would be wearing, if she should wear that powder blue pants suit or perhaps the dress with the polka dots. Annabelle said she hoped the movie wouldn't be the one where the tree comes alive because "it was stupid and you could tell it was a guy dressed up to look like a monster tree." Elizabeth didn't say much of anything at this point. Grace asked if someone could sign her permission slip to go on a school field trip to the Franklin Mint next week. Danny asked if that was a candy factory. Then a step from above, making one of the floorboards creak. Dan told Meggie whatever she wanted to wear would be fine. Meggie smiled and seemed to readjust herself on her seat as if content. Annabelle announced she'd like to make her own horror movie some day, one with "lots of goo and scaly creatures." Elizabeth rolled her eyes and Grace asked Annabelle what did she mean by "goo." Danny made a frown and tried not to think.

And the air rose and fell and travelled sideways until it hit the walls with a crack so silent it didn't even register as a self-attributed pop in the middle ear. And normalcy gave way to its own punctuation of slashes, ellipses, crooked commas, and lopsided colons. The balance of things. It has to be done, you see. Who needs to be comfortable? Safe? That is most frightening of all, don't you think? Especially if it had never run its course with you, staying, developing its permanence. Especially if its break had already created its place, its role, in the jagged pattern with smooth edges, in the smooth pattern with jagged edges, in the smooth jagged, jagged smooth of all things that pump, move, breathe in this house.

It has to start somewhere.

At least to the perception of others (for memory's sake, stories told later, pinpricking a start).

And so, Dan cleared his throat and his eyes casually darted around the room, finally settling on Meggie. He reached for his glass of milk and then said, "You're looking skinnier, Meggie," without emotion. The resulting silence crept up on the table. "Are you on another diet?"

Meggie looked down at her plate, feeling the apprehension crawl up her arms and across to her chest. She looked at her children with eyes that looked shinier, more vulnerable, under this light, under this dull roof. The children looked down at their plates also.

"Um, what?" Meggie asked as she dished out even more stew for Danny, even though he hadn't asked for any.

"You are," Dan said as if he were the only judge whose opinion mattered.

"I'm . . . I'm *what?*" Meggie asked, feeling as if she should've thrown in, emphasized some other word to make her look more innocent, which of course, she was.

"You're getting skinnier," he said evenly. "*I* know. Meggie, why don't you go into the kitchen and get us some of that pumpkin pie you picked up at the Penn Fruit today?"

"Oh, I'm not so sure . . . " Meggie started.

"I'll eat some," Annabelle said in a small voice. Meggie looked over and her heart went out to her daughter whose head barely came up over the table.

"But Danny's not done his dinner," Meggie said, taking the napkin off of her lap and slowly weaving it in and out of her fingers, feeling, somehow, the change.

"Oh, that's okay," Dan said. "Just go get it. The kids want some."

Elizabeth and Grace exchanged a look, and Elizabeth gritted her teeth and stared at the center of the table while Grace looked down and spread her hands on her thighs, looking at her long fingers.

"Ssshh, kids, watch this," Dan said as he quickly got up out of his chair and smiled conspiratorially. Danny looked up at him and offered a weak smile back, not sure what to expect. When his father came back with the long, cardboard skeleton that had been hanging on the front door, he said, "What are you going to do with that, Dad?"

"Ssshh. Just watch." And Dan pulled back Meggie's empty chair and sat the skeleton in it, holding it up by pushing the chair all the way in and placing its paper bones for arms on top of the table, as if it, too, was waiting for the pumpkin pie. The children could hear the clinking of mismatched pie plates as their mother made a small stack of them and they looked at their father who looked like he could barely contain his laughter.

"Alright," Meggie said as she entered the room. "Here are the . . . " but when she saw the skeleton in her chair, her arms lowered the plates and her body slumped as if already knowing it would give in to defeat.

"Oh, Dan," she said as her brow furrowed, her eyes worried, and her mouth frowned. She put the plates on the table with a sigh and then said, "Oh, Dan," again.

"What?" Dan asked, laughing slightly, even then still trying to hold in more laughter.

"Do you *have* to do this? Do you *have* to do this in front of the children?" she asked, lifting her hand up to her forehead.

"What?" Dan asked again, looking innocently around at his children.

"Oh, you're cruel," Meggie said. "You're just cruel."

"I think you look pretty," Annabelle said in an even smaller voice than the one she used before.

"Oh, thank you, honey," Meggie said as she walked over to Annabelle and brushed her daughter's hair with her hand. Meggie sighed and tears started to well. "Your father is just, well, he's just *cruel* . . . " she said as she started to cry.

"She doesn't look pretty, kids. She looks like a skeleton. Look at her," Dan said as his face grew into more serious lines and his eyes gave no impression of granting a stay. "Danny, when I married your mother, her breasts were at least two sizes larger than they are now. They used to fit in my hands like this," he said as he held up one cupped hand. Danny looked up for a second, his face horrified that he might somehow be responsible for this. The other children still looked down at their plates, but their moving shoulders exposed their labored breaths. Meggie was now sobbing openly, with her mouth contorted, and her hands twisting a napkin, showing the world her suffering.

"Elizabeth," her father said.

Elizabeth looked up hesitantly, with the look of a child in her eyes.

"What size bra do you take?"

Elizabeth felt her stomach lurch and the bile start to travel to her throat. She looked back down at her lap, feeling her chest tighten.

"I bet it's bigger than your mother's."

Meggie took in a big sob, so much so that no sound came out. When she finally found her voice, she stood up, taking her fingernails to her face, crying, "You're just cruel! You're just cruel!" all the while scratching her own skin until it started to bleed.

Dan pounded the table with his fist and his neck swelled with red rage. Elizabeth and Grace jumped and Danny spilled milk on his sweatshirt. Annabelle just seemed to grow smaller, until she could barely be seen . . .

"GODDAMMIT, MEGGIE! WHY DO YOU HAVE TO BE LIKE THIS?!"

"BECAUSE I AM, ALRIGHT? I AM! I'M JUST STUPID, ALRIGHT? IS THAT WHAT YOU WANT TO HEAR?"

"THAT'S RIGHT, I MARRIED A PRETTY GIRL WHO ALL OF A SUDDEN THINKS SHE HAS A BRAIN!"

"OH, ALRIGHT, ALRIGHT! JUST STOP IT! YOU'RE CRUEL! JUST CRUEL!"

"FUCK YOU, MEGGIE. WHORE."

And by this time, the children had already scampered and scurried, familiar with escape routes, but they were still close enough to hear their father lunge for their mother, striking the wall (yes, on purpose, but does it matter?) instead, with the dining room table being pushed and shoved, and glasses of milk being turned over, and plates of beef stew sliding and slipping, with at least two crashing to the floor, and their mother, almost purposely throwing herself in his path, knowing she had a penance to pay.

Annabelle got under her covers, hoping that this would warm her and stop the shaking of her legs. Each FUCK YOU! and HOW COULD YOU! and MEGGIE, GET BACK HERE! shook the walls and found their way beneath her skin, causing her muscles to spasm. She reached down to massage her legs, thinking that maybe that would make them stop, make them hold still so that at least she would be able to take in normal breaths again, but that didn't work either. She looked over at the superball she had won in school last week. It was sitting right there on her desk and she had won it by being the first one to complete the multiplication tree Mrs. Brown had made. She felt the pounding getting louder, climbing the walls, making the floor of her room shake, and she looked around her like a victim of an earthquake wondering if she had time to go and grab the ball before everything came crashing down on her. She took the chance and pulled back the covers and raced over to the table, right when YOU FUCKING SLUT! bellowed from below. She jumped, then picked up the superball and crouched down next to the desk. And she separated her knees as her little hand started to bounce the ball between her feet and she recited in a shaky voice, "Nine times *one* is nine, nine times *two* is eighteen, nine times *three* is . . ."

Danny sat on his bed, held his head in his hands, and rocked back and forth. He moaned—soft, quiet, scared, child moans. After moments, minutes, hours maybe (does it matter?) he looked into the corner and the pasty, sticky flesh of his organs almost collapsed in exhaustion, grabbing onto bones and gristle with thin stretched pink punctured with dots of dried red, dying with patches of yellow-brown. The dark dirty corner gave way to his dark dirty room and he barely was able to swallow as he realized that, yes, he was responsible. He must have failed in ritual somehow. And he thought he had been so careful. Not enough. He stood, his insides not wanting to follow, dragging below, beneath his skin, his intestines in balled, bunched-up clumps. He walked to his closet, then the window, then back to the bed, not sure where to start, his own feet confusing each other as they bumped into, stepped upon, circled one another, trying to follow the erratic instructions of an erratic brain not even quite fully developed. He walked to the window, then his closet, then back to the bed, not sure . . . he walked to his closet, his bed, then back to the window . . . the window, the closet, the bed, there must be more than this, but how could he handle more? the closet maybe he could hide there for a minute too much to do the window could be opened but it is the bed underneath too much to deal with he couldn't get to the vacuum now the curtains didn't seem that way before he only has a top sheet where could he get a bottom sheet the one with elastic at the corners did they even have those he'd have to wash it himself he'd have to . . . he'd have to . . . he'd have to . . . the list was growing which also needed to be dusted, disinfected too . . . And chemicals slumped when they shouldn't have, raced, causing hues to blur, when they shouldn't have, and sat by, propped up, watching, when they shouldn't have. You would have thought a child would have been exempt.

Grace went to her closet and reached for her flute. Occasionally, she would jump when she heard her father scream, YOU'RE SPENDING ALL MY GODDAMMED MONEY! and when her mother would wail, "I'VE DONE MY BEST! I'VE DONE MY BEST! I'VE DONE MY BEST!" But, as long as she could get to the magic that slim black case held, she would be alright. She flipped back the metal latches and then opened the case. It was so beautiful. There it sat waiting for her, with its silvery body stretched out along the red velvet as if it were upon the softest sand of the most beautiful beach in the world. She picked up the body of the flute and then attached the mouth and then the tail end. She lifted the instrument to her mouth and began to carefully blow, making sure her mouth formed the perfect "p" sound for the notes to come alive. And they did—around her, in her, above her. And her lids lowered in peace and her fingers moved in grace as the beauty of the notes took her to other worlds.

YOU CUNT! YOU FUCKING CUNT! IS THIS WHAT YOU WANT? and HOW DARE YOU SCREAM AT ME LIKE THIS! HOW DARE YOU TREAT ME LIKE THIS! I DON'T DESERVE *THIS* MUCH! punched the air below. Elizabeth sat at her desk, with her face tight and drawn as she heard her mother's knees hit the ground as part of her dramatic pleas. GET UP! she heard from her father. NO! THIS IS WHAT YOU WANT! YOU WANT ME DOWN HERE, LIKE THIS! she heard from her mother. The voices started to intermingle and overlap, until the shrieks and bellows became one. DON'T BE RIDICULOUS! OH, I'M RIDICULOUS? YOU'RE STUPID! WELL, I DIDN'T HAVE THE MONEY TO GO TO COLLEGE, *MY* PARENTS DIDN'T . . . *SLAM!* (the dining room table back against the other wall) . . . *POUND!* (a fist through the wall) . . . *CRASH!* (the milk pitcher to the floor) . . . OH! . . . WHY? . . . YOU MAKE ME DO THIS! YOU DRIVE ME FUCKING CRAZY! FUCK, FUCK, FUCKING CRAZY! YOUR LANGUAGE! THE CHILDREN! FUCK! Elizabeth picked up her college catalogues and started reading, "The atmosphere of this collegiate town fosters an education filled with more than just . . ." "Our students are known for their academic achievements . . ." "With a degree from our university, graduates are ensured a future filled with . . ." "That will never be me. That will never be me. That will never be me. That will never be me. That will never be me. That will never be me. That will never be me. That will never be me. That will never be me. That will never be me. That will never be me." And

Elizabeth lifted her hand to dry the word that blurred with her tear, the only one she allowed to escape.

Meggie never quite got used to the roaches scattering, the sea that had parted simply because of a flick of a light. There they all went, scurrying, hurrying, fitting in between sticky cracks filled with grease, crumbs, old hardened, old-fashioned dirt. Across countertops, the gas range (into the pilots even), down sides, up to escapes, and sometimes up on hind legs, a twirling around once, a confusion, and later mostly regret (if caught) of taking the time to take stock of things. This washing of the yellowed, greyed floor simply by an exodus was not to Meggie's liking. (And apparently she wasn't the only one. Wasn't it just the other day when Annabelle had come screaming to her, crying that a big, black roach had quickly ran up her arm, straight out of the sleeve of her rain coat she had been so happy to find again? I believe so.) Oh, well. What were they to do? They tried sprays, traps. And sometimes it looked as if they would work (at first). One time she had even found Grace sitting on the front step, watching quietly as all of the baby roaches lined the front walk, covering it from slate to slate, marching away, forced out. But, only the babies, toddling away to begin their life somewhere else. "Where are the big ones?" Grace had asked. "Aren't they going to go, too?" Apparently not.

Meggie poured herself a cup of coffee and went into the dining room. It was three o'clock in the morning and she couldn't sleep, not after her latest fight with Dan. She could feel the tightness of her cheeks where her tears had dried. And when she moved her hand to her face to feel their tracks, she could also feel the dried blood with (caused by) her fingers. She sighed and hung her head. She remembered how he yelled and how his face got all red and his spit seemed to be made of fire, burning anything in its path. She remembered how she took her fingernails and dug paths down her cheeks. She just felt she was getting deeper and deeper into her own hole. She really isn't worth much. She really does deserve it. She *has* to scratch her own skin as he pounds the walls, shaking the house. Thank God the kids were asleep, Meggie thought. They didn't deserve to see that. I should just leave, she thought. Pick up and leave. Elizabeth has been trying to get her do that for years. Meggie smiled. She remembered how Elizabeth, she couldn't have been more than eight, had cut out a letter to Dear Abby from a woman who had left an abusive relationship (that's what it said, "an abusive relationship"). The woman had written that, yes it had been difficult, but she did survive and it was the best decision she had made. It saved her life. Saved her life, Meggie thought. That's what she needs.

Meggie started to further contemplate her life, her future, her past. She would have wondered why she even married Dan, except that she already knew. It was strange, Meggie thought. How things turn out. How the power in relationships changes. At first, Meggie couldn't have cared less about this seemingly awkward and shy business student. She had had other things on her mind. In her heart. It's funny, she thought, how when you don't even know certain things exist, that's when they come and find you. But when you start seeing yourself in those things, when they become a part of you, that's when it gets dangerous.

And for lack of a reason except that Meggie really couldn't imagine any other kind of future for herself, she allowed what hadn't even existed before to come and claim her. And then things just started to build. And the balance shifted. She started feeling out of place in her parents' home and thought of having her own. She thought of putting up curtains and having her own telephone and her own bathroom to spend hours at a time in if she wished. She thought of the diversion of children (at this time, before she had any, she naively thought kids would be the diversion to the main event of life, not the other way around) and how nice it would be to sit on her very own porch on summer nights and rock them to sleep as the fireflies dusted specks of the soft black sky with the blinking of their beings. And before you knew it, Meggie had a lot more invested in this awkward and shy (seemingly) business student than she had ever intended. But she was lucky (she thought). Because sometimes when the balance shifts, the other person leaves, frightened of their newfound power and the prospect of defining anything for anyone else. But Dan embraced this power. He stood up straighter, looked other men in the eye, and took heavier steps, telling the world with each one that this was his time and he owned a little bit of the very earth that was found beneath each stride. And on his graduation day, the sun shone from above and the air stirred with promise, and he proudly posed for pictures, first with his parents and schoolmates, documenting his past, and then with Meggie, securely holding her shoulder with his large, thick hand, pressing her close to him, owning the future.

But Meggie's thoughts were interrupted by her coffee mug that decided to cross the table to the other side on its own.

"Oh, no," she said quietly to herself as she took in a breath. It stayed on the other side, motionless, until Meggie decided to stop staring at it, that it was best to leave, and she started to slowly get up out of her chair. The mug then started to turn in circles, making a wet ring on the table and then it began to clank from one side to the other. Meggie gasped and covered her mouth with her hand. The mug then rose from the table, suspended in mid air, and Meggie could feel the buckling of her knees. "Oh, no," she said again. And the mug came rushing toward her, only slightly missing the side of her head before it crashed into the wall, leaving Meggie with the pounding of her heart and dark, bleak stains that travelled down the antique white of the walls.

CHAPTER 8

Meggie walked up to the small, yellow house, first straightening her hair with one hand while she balanced the envelopes in her
other arm. She walked past the tall, tied wheat stalk and the stuffed
pair of pants her father had placed upside down on the lawn (topping the ends of the legs with an old pair of workboots) for the
effect of this scary lawn swallowing a man from the waist up. In
the spring, her father's garden would be filled with strawberry
foxglove and hyacinths, and in the summer it would hold rose
bushes, morning and evening belles, and hollyhocks of white,
maroon, yellow, and pink. But now it held the last bits of black-
eyed Susans and straw-colored, dried-up bells of Ireland, readying
its graveyard for the perils of winter. Her father had always loved
gardens, since he had been a little boy and lived on a farm in
Marlton. Back then, he had spent more time following his father
around while he pruned and snipped and dug and planted than
when his father would feed the animals and work in the cornfield.
Oh, Meggie's father had still liked to milk the cows and raise the
puppies and sometimes sit next to his father on the tractor as it
plowed through the field (sometimes his father had even let him
steer), but he didn't fully feel at peace unless he was surrounded
by the beauty of the tall delphiniums and the sweet smell of the
pink dianthus. And Meggie's first memories of her father were
how he would set her down on a blanket next to the terrier puppies that were playing in the front yard and work in his garden as
his little ones licked and cuddled and played with each other. And
when Meggie had been old enough, she would kneel right next to
her father, planting and digging as best a child could. She remem-

bered once how she was flipping through his seed catalogue and how she had come across the morning glories—*Morning Glory Heavenly Blue, Morning Glory Tall Mix, Moonflower Giant White (fragrant), Cardinal Climber (attracts hummingbirds)*, and *Thunbergia Susie Mix*—and how their colors of bronzy purple, magnificent sky blue (with white throats), rich crimson, and mix of white, yellow, and orange (some with dark eyes) and the promise of huge flowers, balloon-like buds, and vines almost reaching the moon made her clap her hands with anticipation and ask her father, "Please, Daddy, can we plant them? Can we plant them right by the back porch? It says that they'll actually climb up and around porches." But her father had scratched his nose, looked up at the sun, and said, "Nah, they have pretty flowers, but we have pretty flowers right here in our garden. Morning glories grow everywhere. If we plant them, they'll just take over." And Meggie had slumped her shoulders with disappointment, silently promising herself that someday she'll have her own house and then she'll be able to plant them anywhere she wants, not knowing that her future husband wouldn't be too keen on being overtaken by flowers, either. (Besides, Meggie thought now, they really didn't have the type of porch or any kind of trellis for the morning glories to latch themselves onto anyway.)

"Hi. Here are your envelopes," Meggie said to the small man who answered the door. He was about five-foot six and balding, and a new red color seemed to be spreading across his face—from the middle of his forehead to the bridge and tip of his nose across to the bulge of his cheeks.

"Did you address all of them?" Alfred asked. Meggie started to drop the envelopes in Alfred's arms, but he seemed to get too nervous when she had gotten to about half of them, so she walked over to the kitchen table and dispensed the rest there.

"Yes," she said. "Are Mother and Daddy home?"

"You have the one in there to Burt Reynolds, right?"

"Yes, I do," Meggie said.

"To the address I gave you?"

"Alfred, I did what you asked."

Alfred started to breathe a little harder and his face seemed to get even more red.

"I just hope some of them write back, that's all," he said.

"I'm sure they will," Meggie said, as if placating a child.

"Man, they better. Or call. I wouldn't mind that. You put my phone number in, right?"

"Yes."

"Man, I'm sick of this. Maybe I should just give up."

Meggie looked thoughtfully at her brother. He had a stout paunch of someone who was mildly overweight, yet he held himself in a nervous, rigid way, always darting his eyes and lifting his hand to the balding of his scalp, as if constantly trying to check if his hair was still gone.

"Are Mother and Daddy home?" Meggie asked again.

"No, they went to go get some . . . " and right at that moment Meggie's parents were at the side door, as if proving their son wrong, with her father fiddling with the doorknob and his wife standing in her walker, yelling, "Hurry up, Norman!" in a screechy tone.

Meggie's mother, Addie, had lost her hearing almost thirteen years ago. She and her husband, Norman, had gone to the shore for their summer vacation. And on August 2, 1962, Addie woke up in that two-room (not counting the screened-in porch) house up on stilts, with not so much as a flutter in her ears to let her know she was in the world of the hearing. The sun shone silently through the window, with no chirping of the birds or fresh laundry cracking in the wind below. She had pulled the silent covers off of her and put on her silent slippers. Then she walked down the short, narrow hallway into the other room where her husband was sitting at the table eating his corn flakes. He hadn't realized his wife was in the room yet and he held his spoon in the bowl for a moment and turned his face toward the sunlight coming in through the open window. He smiled as if alone and let the passing breeze rustle back the few hairs he had left. She tried to say something, but caught her voice in her throat because she was afraid not to hear sound that came even from herself. Her husband must have heard her trying to say something, for he broke his spell and looked over and began to talk himself. He was smiling and talking and gesturing a little as if talking to someone who was hearing him say why don't you sit down and I'll get you a cup of coffee. But she just moved to the sofa, sat down, put her head in her hands, and began to cry. And her husband rushed over and sat beside her and stroked her back.

They never did find out what went wrong. Each doctor and each specialist would scratch his head and then start to tell Addie that they couldn't find . . . but, then they caught themselves and redirected their attention to Norman, telling him that they couldn't find the reason for such a thing, leaving Addie with not only her silence but her newly assigned place in the world. But, in the beginning, she bore it well. At first, she held her head high and walked with a slow purpose, proud of her own stoicism. But, nobody else noticed—anything. Oh, they tried to include her, saying "H E L L O" and "G O O D B Y E" with patronizing smiles whenever she would enter or leave another's home, the doctor's office with her husband, or the pancake suppers held in the rectory's basement after church. But, of course, that just wouldn't do. She also needed to be included in the in-between time. So, she stooped over a little more, willed her hair to turn even more gray, and talked her bones into becoming brittle before their time. She would shake people's hands with fingers found to be barely covered with flesh and smile at them with old teeth that were too big for her face. "Norman!" she would yell with every ache, every second into old age, "Come help me!" and her husband would scurry and run and rush and serve and lift her and sit her down. And people rolled their eyes and whispered what a shame that this nice man has such a manipulative wife, but they never forgot her again. Not while she was in their midst.

"I'm going to catch my *death* standing out here!" Addie yelled to her husband. She leaned further on her walker, causing the look of determination on her face to grow more severe.

"Oh, Addie, for Pete's sake," her husband answered as he fumbled with the keys, realizing that he had inserted the wrong one. "Huh?" he said as he looked up through the window. "Oh, look, Meggie's here. Well." Meggie walked over to the door and opened it for them.

"Hi, Daddy," she said. Her father smiled.

"Hi, sweetheart," he said. He, too, was a small man, barely taller than five-foot seven. Meggie smiled when she saw him wearing the bright purple, short-sleeved collared shirt the kids had given him for Christmas last year. He was slightly hunched over, but looked to be still as fit as when he played point guard for the local basketball league in 1922.

"Norman, *move*," Addie said as she tried to maneuver her walker up the small step.

"Mother," Meggie said as she reached over to give her mother a hug.

"My treasure," Addie said as she brought one bony hand up to touch her daughter's face. "Are the girls with you?" she asked too loudly as the walker clopped along the kitchen floor.

"No, no, it's just me," Meggie answered back, also too loudly, with her lips exaggerating each word and her hand pointing to herself as if she were speaking to someone who didn't understand English.

"And Danny? Is he here?"

"No, mother," Meggie said even more loudly. "He's at school."

"Oh, Norman, *help* me," her mother said as she tried to maneuver herself in front of the scalloped-back arm chair in the living room. "Is Danny at school?" she asked after plopping herself into the chair.

"Oh, *Addie*," Norman said sharply as he took the walker away and put it by the bay window. "She just got finished saying he was at school. He's at *school*. It's Wednesday. A school day."

"You treat me like a pile of twigs."

"Well," Norman said while he started to smile. "If you'd pay attention once in a while maybe I wouldn't have to."

"I've been deaf for over fifteen years," Addie said indignantly.

"Oh, Addie, it hasn't been that long," her husband said.

"I hope this *never* happens to *you*," she said as her eyelids lowered and her lips pressed together to become one thin line.

"Oh, *Addie*."

"Meggie got all my letters addressed," Alfred said. He was standing close to Meggie, in the doorway between the kitchen and the living room and he had his hands tucked awkwardly in his pants pockets.

"Well," his father said uncomfortably. He turned on the television and then sat down in the rocking chair next to Addie. "Dutchess, *move*," he said to the Lhaso Apso that was following her owner's feet wherever they went.

"She thinks they're going to write back," Alfred said as if Meggie wasn't in the room.

"Well," Norman said as he picked up the T.V. Guide. "I don't know. Writing to movie stars . . . "

"They're not *fan* letters," Alfred said. "I just need one of them to look at my screenplay."

"Hmph," his father said while he thumbed through the magazine. "Ellery Queen is on tonight," he mouthed to Addie.

"Oooh, good," she said.

"Dad," Alfred said and then looked down at the worn carpet.

"What time do you go into work?" Norman asked his son.

Alfred took a breath, looked up at the drawn heavy drapes and said, "I work the night shift tonight."

"What time's that?" his father asked.

"I go in around eight," Alfred said. And then he turned, walked over to the sofa and sat down, defeated.

"Dutchess, I said *move*. Go lay down!" And the dog whimpered and slowly walked across the room to the corner to her very own scalloped-back chair, which was a little more worn and a little more faded than the one Addie was sitting in.

"Daddy, I'm thinking of leaving," Meggie said.

"Leaving?" Alfred asked. "You just got here."

"Well, I mean . . . "

"Meggie's going now," Norman mouthed to his wife.

"Going?" Addie said loudly as she looked over at Meggie and then back to Norman.

"Well, I wasn't *going*," Meggie said.

"I guess she has to go home and start dinner," Addie said. "Norman," she continued, "Is that a Negro?" she said as she pointed to the television. Norman rolled his eyes.

"Yes, Addie," he said.

"That's a *Negro* on television?"

"Yes, Addie! Yes! It's a Negro on the T.V.! Oh, for Pete's . . . " he said as he slammed the T.V. Guide shut and threw it on the T.V. tray next to him.

"Well, I'm . . . I'm going," Meggie said.

"What?" her father asked as he turned his head. "Oh, that's right. You have to go home and start dinner.

"Yes," Meggie said.

"Well, goodbye, sweetheart. Are you all still coming over for dinner Sunday?"

Meggie stood up from the sofa and pressed the front of her slacks with her hands.

"Yes," she said. "We still plan to." She walked over to her father and gave him a hug. "Goodbye, Daddy," she said. Then she moved to her mother and bent forward so that her mother could give her a hug without getting up out of her chair.

"My treasure," Addie said, holding onto Meggie tightly. "Bring those babies next time."

"I will, Mother," Meggie said and then she walked back through the kitchen and out the side door, passing where she had wanted to plant the morning glories.

* * * *

That night, Meggie lay in her bed and felt the force again. The one that had a torso, arms, and legs. The one that would creep up onto her after Dan had fallen asleep and try to suck the life out of her. The first time it had happened she had been in her last months of pregnancy with Danny. She had climbed into bed and pulled the sheets up around her mound of a belly. She could hear the even breaths of Dan's snores and rolled onto her side to both escape the smell of her husband's sleeping breath and to obtain a more comfortable position. She fell asleep that way and when she awoke a couple of hours later, in the middle of the night, she was on her back and it felt like someone was sitting on top of her chest, trying to stop her beating heart. The first couple of times, that was all she felt—the pressure of all that weight on her chest. She had gasped and tried to move her frozen arms to wake Dan, but it was no use. Whatever this was was more powerful than her. Whatever this was had won in its quest to stun, overcome her. And all she had the power to do was to allow the tears to come from the corners of her eyes and run down the sides of her head, wetting her ears. She didn't mention this to anyone, hoping that daylight would convince even herself that it had been a dream. But then the next time it had gotten even worse, with Meggie waking to a force that now had legs pinned to her own, arms that held hers down, and hands that sometimes first caressed and then wrapped their fingers around her throat, causing her to gag on the night fog. Then, she would tell Dan what had happened.

"Dan," she had said after the first time. "I felt a funny pressure on my chest last night." Dan was sitting in the den, fiddling with a toaster they had gotten for a wedding present long ago but which was now turning out toast that was much too dark.

"Hmm?" he said.

"I said I felt a funny pressure on my chest last night." Dan picked up the screwdriver and started to take the toaster apart.

"Are you sick?" he asked absentmindedly.

"No, it's not that," Meggie said. "I mean, I feel fine now. I don't know. Maybe it was a dream," she said as her voice trailed off.

"That's probably it. You are pregnant after all. Your system will probably go back to normal after the baby is born." And then Meggie went to go answer five-year-old Grace who was calling for her and Dan continued to fiddle with the toaster. But it hadn't been a dream and Meggie knew this. But, just as she was taught (somewhere), Meggie tried to look for the good in this. And all she could come up with was that it didn't happen every night. Sometimes it happened only once a month, once a week, or five nights in a row—but it didn't happen every night. Oh, for some, that might be worse, not knowing when to expect it. Some might say "Bring it on every night! That way at least I'll know what to expect!" But, Meggie would take any kind of reprieve there was, even if she didn't know when to expect that either, even if it was mixed in with dots of something forever trying to take her breath away.

And on the night Danny was born, that force felt only in the darkness had been stronger than ever, and just when Meggie was about to give up, when she almost stopped breathing in defeat, her water broke. Dan collected the girls and Meggie put a few last things in her suitcase. They then opened the front door and stood as the heavy mist and vapors of the night covered them from head to toe.

"Oh, my," Meggie had said.

"Mommy, I can't see!" Elizabeth said.

"It's alright," Dan said. "It's just the fog." And little Grace stood wide-eyed and still as she saw through the fog and into the night that was waiting for them all. She saw shadows and ants and beetles scurrying by. She saw small, dark things scamper and scuttle through the tall blades of grass. Swoosh, swish, swoosh, they went as they weaved in and out, over and under the wet blades. She saw the branches of trees bend down to see what they could find and the tips of their twigs get nipped by the creatures below.

"Oh, my," Meggie said.

"It's alright," Dan said. "It's just the night." And he loaded
his family into the navy blue station wagon, cleared the front and
back window shields with a crumpled up tissue he had found on
the floor of the car, got back into the car, and started their way to
the hospital so that his wife could deliver their third child, a son.

CHAPTER 9

Daniel, Jr. tries, tries, tries, tried. True as a try. Try as he might. Might is stronger than the kid. Kid is blue as true. Normal. Slips on shoes like others. Slips by unnoticed. Sometimes. If druthers are what he had.

"My mom stays home and my dad works at a business firm," is his answer in school when his turn comes to offer information about home and hearth. "I have three sisters and I'm the second to the youngest," tips it off in a swirl. "I don't know what I'm turning into," is what he doesn't add, but still surrounding it in quotes in his mind. I'm afraid of what I'm turning into, is what is peeking around soft tissue protected by cranium, only showing the first couple of words for now. I'm afraid, simply—is what he says to himself when about to sleep, inviting nightmares during twitches and sucking of the tongue and roaming of the balls undering fluttering lids. Such times of the night. During which. The car accident, yes. On Dead Man's Hill. He was asleep. It wasn't real. No. But he did see the victims propped up and covered in cellophane from dead head to dead toe. No body bags in this horse of the night. This one-horse night that galloped and halted at the bodies, long enough for Danny to see the nice man and nice woman sitting on lawn chairs near the dell, drained of their blood. What did that *mean*? When he awoke, things were much better. Recesses of the mind were now minding. Much better. Good. Time to call Vinny and act like a little boy. His mom wants to meet your mom, remember?

CHAPTER 10

Meggie looked across the table at her neighbor. My, she was pretty, Meggie thought. And so bright, from her deep turquoise blouse (which matched her earrings and bracelet) right down to her lipstick.

"Anyway," Maureen Angelucci said right before she threw back her head to finish her last drops of tea. "That's how Vincent and I met, and to this day I don't know whether to thank my brother or kill him," she said as she laughed and took out her compact and checked her make-up. Meggie kept quiet and looked around her own dining room as if she were a visitor admiring the wallpaper. She didn't know why, but this woman made everything seem so new. Maybe it was because it had been a while since she had had a visitor in the house. Oh, when she and Dan had first married and moved in, they had had lots of friends over, for card parties and cocktail parties, filling Meggie with wonderful anticipation of what married life was going to be like. But then, slowly, things had started to change and it got to be that her friends didn't call her anymore and had only polite, rushed smiles when Meggie would approach them in the bank line or at the local department store, tapping them on the shoulder and saying sweetly, honestly, "I miss you." Why was that? Meggie thought.

"How did you and Dan meet?" Maureen asked.

"What?"

"You and Dan."

"Oh. At a dance."

Maureen smiled. "You must have been very young," she said.

"Oh, yes, well. I suppose by today's standards, not back then."

Maureen poured herself some more tea, clearly getting comfortable for more of a discussion with her new neighbor. Meggie looked up surprised, not fully believing that her history could be that interesting to anybody.

"I was twenty-four," Meggie said.

"That's how old *I* was."

Meggie smiled. "I suppose I thought it was time."

Maureen looked at her thoughtfully. Meggie continued.

"I remember hearing my parents talk and how my mother had said `Oh, but he'll never *marry* her.' A part of me wanted to show her. That and, like I said, I thought I was getting old." Meggie looked down at her tea cup. "I suppose those are stupid reasons for getting married."

"I've heard worse," Maureen said sympathetically. "I know someone who married her husband because he was number twenty-three in the bank line."

"Excuse me?"

"Number twenty-three. She was a teller and, like you I suppose, she thought she was getting up there, except she was. She was almost thirty." Maureen checked the bottom of her high heel for something and then continued. "Anyway, she had just gone to her umpteenth baby shower that weekend and she said to her friend, Clarice, 'Clarice, I'm gonna find me a husband if it's the last thing I do. And I'm going to set my sights right now. I won't be picky and I won't be close-minded. In fact, if he's available, and, of course, a man, it's going to be my twenty-third customer today.'"

Meggie laughed. "My!" she said, bringing her hand to her cheek.

"And sure enough, she did. Oh, he was about forty-five and was thick in the middle, but to this day he treats her like a queen."

"My," Meggie said, tracing the edge of the cup with her fingers.

"Your son Danny is a treasure," Maureen said, studying Meggie.

"Thank you. I hope he hasn't been a bother."

"Oh, no, no." Maureen took another sip of her tea. "Little Vinnie loves having him over for sleepovers. They play G.I. Joe, I think."

Meggie smiled and leaned forward, putting her elbows on the table. "My little boy," she said. "All my kids are special. Every one."

"Yes, they are," Maureen agreed with a smile. "Meggie, may I use your powder room?" she then asked.

"Oh, of course. Here, let me show you."

Maureen followed Meggie toward the stairs. "I hope you don't mind using the upstairs one," Meggie said. "The one by the kitchen clogged today and I just can't seem to get it unstuck. Dan will have to fix it when he gets home."

"That's alright," Maureen said.

Meggie showed Maureen to the bathroom and then walked back down the stairs to start cleaning up their dishes from their tea. She started to sing "There's Got To Be a Morning After" as she cleared the china saucers.

Maureen studied herself in the mirror. Just a few lines at the corners of her eyes, she thought, nothing to worry about yet. She turned and looked at the shower curtain that was almost completely covered with mildew and shuddered a bit. She carefully pulled back the curtain and looked at the tub. That, too, didn't look like it had been cleaned in months. Well, she *does* have four kids, Maureen thought. That must be tough. But this house was strange. In some places it was meticulous—the living room looked spotless with its antique cream sofa and the classic, writing desk looking dignified and formal with its high back pressed against the wall. And that portrait—Vinnie was right, it was spooky, but it also lent a certain elegance to this room, as if people dressed in their evening clothes [good black trousers (uncreased, without cuffs) and vests (brown or black, blue even, with various tapestry patterns) over shirts, dresses made of silk, satin, and poplin with hoop skirts to boot, and elaborate hats (high-top hats for the men, thank you very much)] could waltz the night away in this tiny room, not feeling a bit out of place. But, the dining room had looked all cluttered and confused, with the drawers to the sideboard open and flustered and puzzled papers peeking out, tangling and bending their corners with and on top of each other. The kitchen's walls had been streaked in black here and there (probably grease from cooking), and the blender and toaster, as well as parts of the countertop, had been covered with grime and gook. But, Maureen didn't care. She still liked Meggie. There was just something so kind about her. But, it was more than that. She also seemed so open to something, like she couldn't help it. It was as if she was trying to protect herself from something, but couldn't help but run up to whatever she was trying to flee and say "Here I am, see?" as if she were a small child who clearly didn't understand the rules of hide and seek and would loudly say "I'm here!" while snuggling in a back closet, answering her opponent's false pleas of "Where *are* you?"

And this was a nice house, with its three large bedrooms upstairs and a downstairs that went round and round with no end. The dining room led to the living room which led to the bedroom (Meggie and Dan's) which led to the kitchen which led back to the dining room again. Meggie had said how the kids used to ride their tricycles for hours, following that route, never having to stop or change direction, except when they would scrape a scab off one of their knees by accidentally bringing it up too close to the handle bar. Maureen opened the bathroom door and peeked out into the hallway. Meggie must be downstairs, she thought. Meggie had already showed her the upstairs, but Maureen wanted to see it again, more closely. She walked into Danny's room and smiled because it didn't look any different than her Vinnie's. His bed was unmade, a haphazardly thrown sleeping bag covered the otherwise bare mattress, and toy soldiers, old comic books, and G.I. Joe's new moon terrain vehicle lay scattered across the floor. She closed the door and walked toward Annabelle's room. This was a room that was caught between the stages of childhood. Annabelle's bed had been neatly made, with a Barbie sleeping bag pulled neatly up over the pillows. But, a crib sat in the corner, filled with stuffed animals, a box of Colorforms, and an Etch-A-Sketch, as if only the child had known when it had been time to move to a big girl bed, filling the crib with things she still uses because she didn't want to hurt her parents' feelings. Two soft pastel clouds hung on one wall, as if in a nursery, and a poster of Leif Garrett hung on the opposite wall. Four pairs of worn out sneakers lined themselves up under the bed, and a small stack of school books sat on the chair by the desk.

Maureen went to Elizabeth and Grace's room next. The door had already been ajar, so she just lightly pushed on it, with her hand on the latch (each door had a black, old-fashioned latch instead of a doorknob), and heard the soft creak as it opened itself up. She walked in and looked around. No sheets or blankets were on either of the beds, again only sleeping bags, with one bunched in two mini mountains, resting on the corner of the mattress, and one pulled up neatly, like Annabelle's. Sheets of music lay scattered across this bed—theme songs to the movies Ben, the Sting, Rocky, and M*A*S*H. The bed that hadn't been made at all held open books entitled, *How To Be a Success in Show Business, Making Your Dreams Come True, and Five Easy Steps To Getting What You Want.* Maureen smiled.

She supposed every young girl wanted to be an actress.

Maureen was about to reach for one of the books when she heard a small noise. *Click, clack, click, clack* came from behind. She froze her outreached hand and then slowly turned around, toward the noise. But there was nothing. Just her mind. Just her nerves. Oh, look, there's a little door to behind the eaves of this house. Cute. *Click, clack, click, clack.* Must be for storage. *Click, clack.* No harm in opening it, right? No harm will be done. Maureen bent to reach for the latch that matched the other, more important (supposedly) doors. She just didn't expect the laughter to be so hollow or at all. Her heart did jump. Her skin did numb, as her mind, matching the cold rain that was beginning to spray, fall onto the selfish ground which was lapping it all up. She didn't expect to actually feel the tips of fingers that didn't belong to her (or anyone else she could see) caress behind her knees, but as if someone were reaching up, not down. Oohh. Was all she could manage. Her mind? My nerves.

Maureen slowly backed away toward the door, consciously lifting each leg, feeling as if white thick bricks had replaced her bones, and then she turned around, forcing her feet to take her to the hallway. Once she reached the hallway, the bricks disappeared and she ran down the stairs toward Meggie.

"Meggie," she said coarsely, out of breath.

Meggie turned from the kitchen sink and was holding a sponge.

"What's wrong?" Meggie asked with her brow furrowed.

"I was just upstairs . . . "

"Did the toilet overflow?"

"No, no . . . Meggie," Maureen started. She then walked over more closely to Meggie, as if they had been confidants for years. "Your house . . . "

"Oh, I know," Meggie said, somewhat ashamed. "It's not as clean as I'd like it to be. It's just so *hard.*" And she started to cry. She put the sponge on top of the stove and started to cry. "I just, I just don't know if I can take it anymore."

Maureen was confused. She didn't know whether to take the time to comfort Meggie now or get out of that house for her own . . . (safety?). Sanity. Sanitary thoughts.

"Meggie," Maureen said in a hushed tone. "I *heard,* I *felt* something upstairs. It must have been . . . It must have been . . . " was where she seemed to be stuck.

Meggie looked at her new friend confused.

"I *thought* I heard . . . I *thought* I felt . . . Maybe it was just a breeze," Maureen said, with a quick sigh, an embarrassed laugh. A smile made to pass on this.

Meggie sighed and sat down on the chair in the corner. "I don't know," she said. "This house . . . "

"What?" Maureen asked.

"This house . . . " Meggie said again, looking at the spots on

the floor that needed to be cleaned. Maureen felt her head grow
dizzy and she held onto the refrigerator door for support.

"Has this happened before? Have *you* heard anything?" Maureen
asked.

"Oh, here and there," Meggie said.

"What?"

"Here and there."

"Have you . . . have you . . . *seen* anything?

A sigh. "Well, you know."

"Meggie, this is not normal."

"Oh, I know," Meggie said as she pulled her feet in under her
chair. "I know it's not."

No other sounds could be heard from the house except the
sporadic humming of the refrigerator. Maureen looked up at the
ceiling and saw that the paint was peeling. She all of a sudden felt
very claustrophobic and she pulled at her already unbuttoned collar to make it seem like she was giving herself some more room.

"You mean to tell me you've been living with this . . . this kind
of thing all of these years?" she asked.

"Off and on."

"Why do you stay?" Maureen asked this while she looked
straight at Meggie but Meggie was still looking at the floor.

"I think it's Uncle Ezra," Meggie said.

"Who?"

"Uncle Ezra. He's hanging in the living room. Well, his portrait. But he's hanging around as well. I believe it's all him."

Maureen let out a breath.

"Dan's great aunt died right about the time we got married
and she left a whole attic's worth of stuff to his sister and him,"
Meggie said. "They wanted to throw the painting out, but I asked
if we could keep it. I kind of liked the look, you know?" Maureen
didn't answer and Meggie continued. "So, I paid to have it re-
stored—out of my own money. I worked back then. I was a secre-
tary. I can still type over fifty-five words a minute."

Maureen was now looking at the magnets on the refrigerator,

as if right now needing to be distracted herself while listening to Meggie.

"Anyway, right after we hung the portrait up, strange things started to happen."

Maureen looked at Meggie.

"Oh, like . . . just things. The other day, I could've sworn the desk in the living room had been slightly moved."

Maureen swallowed.

"Have the children seen anything?" she asked.

"Oh, no. I don't think so."

"Meggie, why don't you take the portrait down?"

Meggie looked thoughtful. She looked Maureen right in the eyes and said, "I don't know. I still kind of like the look, you know?"

And this was a nice house, with its three large bedrooms upstairs and a downstairs that went round and round with no end.

* * * *

Grace first saw the man when she was a baby. She couldn't have been more than six months old, lying in her crib, being lulled to sleep by Winnie the Pooh and Piglet as they hung from above on copper-colored wires and danced in the air to tinny music. Her lids had become heavy and her lashes had fluttered with the closing of her eyes. Soft, white cotton clouds had floated right through the glass of the windows and into her room. Ordinary pigeons had turned into smiling bluejays and talking sparrows as they, too, danced and flew into her room, following the clouds. Daffodils sprung from the carpet and a small, whistling brook flowed softly from beneath her crib. She smiled as she saw Pooh and Piglet release themselves from their wire and jump from the edge of her crib to the meadow that had sprung up next to her toy chest. They ran and played and jumped, and balanced themselves on the tiny rocks of the prattling brook. Even the choo-choo train on the wallpaper came alive, opening its sleepy eyes and clearing its stack, taking a running start to race off of the wall and onto the track that ran around and up and down in the middle of the room, with nothing holding it except the sail of a dream. But then Grace saw the latch of her closet slowly rise. And the wildflowers of all kinds stopped swaying and the brook hushed its waters. Pooh and Piglet looked up, covered their eyes, and then bumped into each other trying to escape. The train stopped mid-flight, frozen in the interruption of its destination. And Grace also closed her eyes, not wanting to know what would scare even the things of childhood dreams. It was still, almost so that she could hear the clouds slowly evaporate and the resulting dew on the ceiling form tiny droplets that would soon drip into the fading meadow below. But then she felt his breath on the soft down of her cheeks and she had no choice but to open her eyes. Strangely enough, he wasn't *that* scary. He had dark hair and a pleasant enough face. Black clothing covered his arms, but his body was translucent. She could see the train shivering on its tracks right through him. He smiled a closed-lip smile at her and lifted his hand to his maroon-colored ascot that wrapped around his throat, placing his finger on his chin as if contemplating what to say. His eyes flickered and he studied the baby as if she were his own. This was a strange but fine dream, Grace thought. No harm done, right? But something didn't feel right. It was small—a needle's eye, a pin's point, a flash, but it was there—a quick to the cut, an imp's smile. Even babies could tell. And Grace wailed and screamed and howled and threw her tiny fists and kicked her tiny feet until her mother rushed through the door into the room that held no live choo-choo trains, no singing brooks, no smiling bluejays. And no stranger with ways of his own who had made his new home in a house that held even more than he knew.

"My, Grace, what is it?" the mother asked of her infant. "Oh, poor Grace. Did you have a nightmare? Poor thing." And the mother picked up her baby and held her close to her body, rocking back and forth, picking up the dry terry cloth washcloth nearby and wiping the perspiration off of her daughter's face. And Grace whimpered and hiccupped and clumsily rubbed her eyes with the back of her fists. Then she stuck her thumb in her mouth and laid her cheek against her mother's shoulder, all the while with her eyes wide and hesitantly searching the room for the man who had soaked up the stream of the brook with the weight of his soul.

Was it a nightmare? Maybe. How about the hangers in the closet that decided to sway back and forth, almost causing a tangle, the baby clothes that fell to the floor in a shuffle, a surprised pile, right before Meggie came in? Well, those were real. How about the shadow of a man that would walk back and forth in the hall, right outside of Grace's door (at least three times in her life) when her parents were safely asleep downstairs and her siblings also in their own dreams? Actually, he was real, too (seen, at least).

Why describe her dream (?). Because, ever since then, Grace has been able to see things others don't. When she had been a baby, she saw breezes of soft green-blue flow through the house and lightly lift the strands of her mother's hair as her mother rocked her to sleep. And she saw a piece of this breeze travel to her father and make him smile while he held his babies and also rocked them and sometimes even gently threw them into the air, catching them with a laugh and a love. While her mother would read to her and her siblings, she saw pink swirls emanate from warmed lightbulbs underneath lampshades with patterns of angels tucking children into bed. And sweet-smelling sighs came from her and her sisters and brother as they sat on the bed and listened in comfort as their mother's rocking chair creaked with her every other word. She saw playful bees with smiles and clapping hands fly from the worn ears of her brother's stuffed donkey. And on summer nights, she saw fireflies collect their sleepy children from their beds of summer green leaves so that they could all fly and dance under, above, and in between the stars and moon. Every sound, every sigh, every word, and, later, every thought had its own face. Oh, she learned how to control her sight. Otherwise, she would have been lost to other worlds (which may not be such a bad thing if the timing is right).

Bloom where you're planted she remembered reading right off her very own refrigerator, well, her family's refrigerator. Her mother had bought that magnet at a garage sale. Grace had been with her and remembered seeing the hazy memories that came from each item. She remembered looking at the card table with mismatched salt-and-pepper shakers, a propped up hand-made Raggedy Ann with half a stitched smile, and a deck of cards whose scrawled sign had boasted that each card was there, even if half the deck had one-eyed fish on one side and the other half had dark castles almost hidden by their own moats. And above each item were clouds of memories. Housewives cleaning, wiping, cooking, singing while snapping the sheets above their children's beds in front of open windows; a little girl, who now has children of her own, hugging, kissing, and dragging her doll by one arm as she runs across her backyard to meet her friend for yet again another tea party among the sticks and dirt and grass; and young sailors, who are now grandfathers, playing poker in the new bar that opened up in the town they are visiting on their two-day leave—they all mixed and mingled and grew sharper and grew dull as patrons of this backyard sale picked up and examined and put down and paid. Her mother had bought an old washstand (another antique to add to her growing collection) and had spotted the magnet at the last minute as the man started to lift the washstand to the car.

"Hmm," her mother had said. "What do you think, Grace?" Grace looked up at her mother with wide eyes, still not quite used to all that she saw. "What do you think?" she asked again and then said, "'Bloom where you're planted,'" and smiled and then added, "I like it." But her mother must have realized what it really meant because she seemed to grow sad on the way home. And when Grace looked over at her mother driving, in her own world, Grace saw the roots grow straight from her mother's tears until they went straight through the floor of the car and through the asphalt of the road, wrapping around the black rock of the earth. Grace knew then that her mother had realized that blooming didn't mean anything if what was around you was cracked, barren earth. But, Grace couldn't help herself. She took hold of that magnet herself and put aside the vision of an old, dying woman shopping in a seaside town (the magnet's first owner), a woman who liked the sound of a saying that held hope for someone who had never fulfilled their yearning to roam, and Grace created her own vision, that of gardens and ripeness and beginnings and promise. She thought of low white fences that rabbits could jump over and chipmunks that rolled and played with laughing children. All this she thought of while she heard the rain beginning to atap tap tap on her window and the groan of her mother's self-made roots as they twisted and tangled below.

And on some nights, when she had been about six, Grace had been able to see her breath float in the air. She had often let the cloud get as big as it could and then she would quickly suck it back in again. She had done this over and over, not for the sake of breathing, but to make sure she was still there. You see, sometimes she disappeared. Not always, but sometimes. Sometimes she willed it on her own like on the nights when her mother would take the cot from the hall closet and then place it next to Grace's bed. Just for a break, her mother would say. Just to get away for a while, she didn't mind did she? Grace would always shake her head no, she didn't mind. In fact, in the beginning of the night, when sleep hadn't yet come and she could still hear the neighbors drag their trash cans down their cement and gravel driveways, when dogs are taken for one last walk and cats are let out, when the world is still filled with the activity of others, of normal people in safe worlds, it's kind of fun, like a slumber party almost. And Elizabeth, who seemed to always sleep, would lend her snores as her approval, as if not caring whether their mother joined them in their room either. But then the blackness comes. It seeps and hides and slithers and crawls, slowly making its way toward Grace's (the one who's awake is the one who counts, right?) room. Grace often heard its breath as it pounded against her door and then as it was next to her, breathing in its heavy dark way, as it found its way into her father's voice.

"Come on, Meggie," he breathes, the stench, the stench, the stench. "You gotta let me feel your tits," he breathes, he breathes, he breathes, the mask of the blackness of it all unveiled because the sun went down hours ago, the drops of its wicked breath spraying onto the six-and-a-half-year-old little girl only two feet away who can barely survive where she's planted.

She would open her eyes and then close them. Open them and then close them. His back was to her. He was crouched down, holding a towel in front of him, which was strange because his audience was not in front of him. Did he know that? He was bare in the back. It was dark, but she could see. She opens her eyes and then closes them. What are those strange sacs between his legs? As he holds a towel in front, modest in the wrong place, here, doing this, at the worst of times. Her mother resigns herself, not even putting up that much of a fight. "Oh," her mother says, drained, sighing, drawn out, cut in between. Heavy breathing from two souls, one trying to hold onto arousal with black nails and grunts, the other wishing it were over. What about the third breath? Oh, never mind her, she'll never remember.

Grace couldn't bear to see it, but she couldn't bear to just hear it, either, which in its own way makes it come even more alive. So she disappears. She starts with her own breaths, causing them to become shallow and light. She then freezes her arms, her hands, her chest, her torso, her legs, her feet—until the blood stops, until there is no feeling, until she is floating above. Oh, she knows she can't leave the house. She's chained there with her mother for some reason. But she can roam the rooms, her own room even, touching things with her mind—her new pencils with the big colorful erasers that are too pretty to use, her plastic swimming pool for her Barbie that can be filled with actual water, the board game she got for last Christmas that has pieces that actually glow in the dark, her small, toy organ she just learned how to play "A Bicycle Built for Two" on. *Daisy, Daisy, I'm half crazy, all for the love of you*, Grace sings to herself as she roams, travels in her disappearance. And before you know it, morning is here and she can hear the dog being taken for a walk, the cat let in, and fathers saying goodbye to their wives and children as they leave for work.

* * * *

Danny had first seen the man about two years ago, when he had been eight. On that night, he had pulled the covers up to his chin as he listened to the sounds.

CUNT!

SLUT!

CUNT!

His
YOU CAN'T PUT ANYTHING YOU WANT ON THE CREDIT CARD! cut through the walls, ceilings below.

WHO THE HELL HELL HELL DO YOU THINK YOU ARE?????????

and Hers
Hooooooow CAN YOU DO THIS TO ME? I'VE DONE NOTH-ING BUT . . . OH, HOW COULD YOU? made the victim pound her own skin, almost drawing blood.

WHO THE HELL HELL HELL DO YOU THINK I AM???????????

Just like home

Danny's skull had numbed and his body had frozen, as if, ironically, positioning itself so that it could keenly hear every word, every breath. But, strangely, the content didn't matter much. This time it was about the Visa bill, like it had been the month before. What had it been about in between? He couldn't remember. The other times the bellows, pleas, shouts, and wails thrashed and trounced from below, battering any speck of life in its way, Danny had closed his eyes so hard that the trail of stark moonlight coming in through his window and crossing his face was reduced to nothing but dots of muted shadows. He had squeezed his hands so hard that the tips of his knuckles became as white as the bone beneath them. And he had clenched his teeth so hard that when he first bit down, the flesh of his tongue had been pierced and a slow, thin trail of blood slowly made its way out of the corner of his mouth onto the white pillow case marked with a tiny periwinkle in each corner. He never quite got used to this. And he never quite got used to what would follow either. On this night, as on the others, he listened to the other sounds. Oh, not the ones from his parents. The other ones—the ones that would start after his parents had gone to bed—the opening and shutting of drawers, the opening and closing of the kitchen cabinets, a candlestick holder being thrown across the room, sometimes a chair being turned upside down. The laughter. The trickling of fingertips down a wall.

On this night, when the sounds seemed to have stopped, Danny decided that since he was growing up, it was time for him to become more brave and at least investigate. He got out of bed, grabbed the aluminum baseball bat his grandfather had given him for his birthday two months ago, and opened his door. He walked down the short, dark hallway, feeling his way with his one free hand. He grabbed the top of the railing and then started to slowly walk down the stairs, trying to take even breaths so that he could hear more than just his pounding heart. The second he stepped onto the first floor, he felt something was different. His chin pointed a little outward and upward, as if readying him that much more for the sounds of other worlds. And his sock-footed steps were lighter, as if trying to sneak by something that shouldn't be there to begin with. Max was growling. Max, the family dog of many breeds, often slept in the kitchen, right on the rug by the side door that led out to the driveway. It was a low growl, which is probably why Danny's parents were still asleep in their bedroom next to the kitchen. But, there was no mistaking the intent of that growl. Someone had broken in. Someone was trying to take something, or at least cause a stir. And just like how soon-to-be victims in horror movies keep walking—slowly, hesitantly—toward their terror, even though audience members shout and scream, "Don't be stupid! Run for the door!", Danny allowed his steps to go uninterrupted, taking him to from where future nightmares would grow.

He couldn't see his eyes. He knew the man was looking at him, but Danny couldn't see his eyes. He felt dizzy. Everything around him seemed to be so . . . Blackness. This kind came with some nights and stayed away from others. How did it discriminate? Mortals could guess, but hardly get it right. The light of the moon, though, that was still there. Hushed. Quiet. But there. So that it shone a thin path straight through the kitchen window until it blended with the darkness of the room, its stream gone, without a fight, by the time it reached the linoleum floor. But, the dust of its light was enough for Danny to see him—the man by the back door. He was tall, taller than Danny's father and he seemed to be heavily cloaked in some type of clothes, but Danny couldn't tell what kind. The whole time, space of this encounter seemed to be from a different place. Later, if someone were to tell Danny that he had stood there exchanging blinded stares with this stranger for five seconds or five hours, he would have believed either one. When Danny had first entered the kitchen, the man turned his head and looked at Danny, right into his eyes. Danny could tell, even in the blackness. The man pulled back his arm, as if he was about to open the door but Danny had interrupted him. The way this person (?) had allowed his arm to lightly bounce back against his side was not human, but Danny couldn't accept this right now. The way this man's darkness pulled Danny toward him wasn't from this world. But Danny couldn't accept this now. The way the house seemed to start to shake but then Danny realized that, oh, it was just his heart, pulled him away from what he had known.

Practicality of thought broke the spell. Oh, the man was still there alright. As real as the moonlight shining (blending, really) in. But, Danny was able to move now, and divert his gaze. His feet obeyed when he ordered them to move, one by one, across the kitchen, out through the dining room, and then race through the living room to his parents' closed bedroom door. He knocked and knocked. His parents answered. They rushed and rushed, grabbing robes, slippers. They traced backward the racing steps. They found the black room empty, with no dust, specks of anything, to show that any kind of soul had been there. And they looked at their son like he was a sleepwalker, one of the rare times they were united in thought, wondering what type of moonlight had drifted in from his window and seeped under his eyelids to cause him to dream such things.

And Max? Oh, they had to get rid of him. Ever since that night, you see, he had been unreliable. Barking through all nights, sounding off, scratching at cracks, urinating in corners, in warning and in fear, when nothing was really there.

* * * *

Elizabeth didn't see such things.
How could she?
But sometimes she remembers the happy times.

* * * *

Annabelle heard the voices in the woods when she was about six. Danny was lining up sticks on the ground, one by one, as if he was taking inventory of all backyard twigs. Strangely enough, Danny didn't mind the dust and dirt when it was found outside. "It's more natural. That isn't bad," he explained to Grace once. The breeze was strong for the month of June and their mother went inside, "Only for a minute," she said, to get Annabelle's sweater. "Watch your sister," she said to Danny as she turned and walked up the back porch steps. Danny had looked up from his sticks and then went back to lining them up on the soft dirt. Annabelle watched her brother for a minute and then lifted her face to the sky when the clouds parted and felt the sun and wind come to her at the same time. The breeze felt as if it had gone right through her very bones. She shivered and smiled as she felt it travel up the sleeves of her blouse and tickle her arms.

"Mom's getting your sweater," Danny said without looking up.

"I don't care," Annabelle said as she felt the sun on her cheeks and nose.

"Well, you should. You're shivering," Danny said as he placed the long, gnarled twig next to the smooth, short one.

"What are you doing?" Annabelle asked as she bent over, placing her hands on her thighs. A strong wind passed through the trees and the rustling of leaves sounded like the wings of a flock of geese flying in circles. Danny looked up, slightly squinting from the sun that was now going back into the clouds.

"What's it look like I'm doing?"

"Mom said you shouldn't be smart with me," she said.

Danny looked at his sister. She was small for her age—he had heard his mother telling the neighbors this and he had heard some of the teachers at their school say the same thing, while they smiled and became all doe-eyed, as if they all of a sudden had come upon a baby bird that needed a gentle lift back into its nest.

"Fuck you," Annabelle said.

"Oh, Annabelle."

"I mean it. Fuck you."

"What if Mom hears you talking like that?"

"I don't care."

"Well, you will if she comes back and punishes you."

"Mom doesn't punish us." And how could Danny argue with that? It was true. Meggie never punished and she rarely scolded. Oh, sometimes she might raise her hands to her head and roll her eyes to the skies, displaying her displeasure. But, it almost never came out as sharp as disapproval, but as, "Annabelle, you really shouldn't . . . , Danny, why don't you . . . , Grace, honey, next time you should . . . ," with an occasional "Oh, Elizabeth!" thrown in often (most times), filling Meggie's self-requirements of discipline.

Annabelle stared at her brother, trying to lure him into some unspoken game of will.

"I'm not doing that," Danny said as he went back to his sticks.

"Doing what?" Annabelle asked.

"That stupid staring contest thing you do."

"I'm not doing any contest."

"Yeah, whatever," Danny said as he cleared some stones from his work area.

"I'm going exploring," Annabelle said. Her brother didn't answer her and just kept smoothing the dirt over and over with the palm of his small dirty hand.

"I said, I'm going *exploring*," Annabelle said again.

"So?"

"Well, when Mom comes back, tell her I'm back in the trees."

And this time Annabelle didn't wait for an answer and turned on her heels as she lifted her chin, leading the way for the rest of her body. And as she approached the clump of trees that the Owens children called "the woods" in their very own backyard, the day got even cooler and the surroundings even darker. The many branches bunched and combined and separated, so that Annabelle felt like she was in some sort of giant tunnel with a roof of green leaves that also shivered in the breeze, occasionally allowing small streams of sunlight to pore through into the forest. Annabelle walked over to her favorite tree and sat down, leaning against its trunk. She put her hand on the ground and sifted the dirt between her fingers.

"*Annabelle*," the voice from the branches said.

Annabelle jumped, reflexively clenching her fist around the small pebbles that had been in her hand. She looked to the sky, but saw only the leaves as they seemed to grow thicker and darker, not allowing even the smallest of sunbeams through. The dark coolness shut out all seasons and Annabelle sat still, except for turning her head every which way, looking for the person who had called her name.

"*Annabelle*," the voice said again.

"Danny?" Annabelle asked meekly as she retreated back into herself, becoming almost as small as one of the knobs on the tree trunk she was resting against.

"*Annabelle, Annabelle, the belle of the ball*," the leaves sang.

"Stop it!" Annabelle cried.

"*Oh, poor Annabelle. Don't you want to be the belle of the ball?*"

"Danny! Leave me alone!"

The leaves now began to rustle like they had when she had been watching Danny play in the dirt, and she wrapped her arms around herself, crying, as she rolled herself into a ball. "Stop it!" she said again, but now in a muffled tone because her voice couldn't get past her own limbs.

"*Poor, poor Annabelle*," the voice said as the earth became dry and the clouds loomed in the trees.

"Mom! Mom!" Annabelle shouted, hoping that her mother would somehow be able to hear her.

"*Mom! Mom! Annabelle needs a prince for her ball! Please hurry and come find her a prince for the ball!*"

"Stop it!" Annabelle cried.

"*Oh, no prince for the ball? Are you already spoken for?*"

"I'm only six!" Annabelle screamed. "I'm only six!"

And right then Annabelle heard the faraway sounds of the porch door slamming against its frame and her mother's footsteps as she ran to her daughter while the surprise of thunder crashed from above. Annabelle lifted her head and opened her eyes, too upset to take in anything around her, while her frantic mother raced to her, thinking that she was rescuing her daughter from only a summer storm, not her own daydream (which, of course, it was, a nightmare in the day, that's all, not Danny, not a backyard monster, oddity, or mutation, and deep down inside Annabelle knew this). How about the shadow of a man that would be half hidden by the trees when Annabelle would look outside (other, later times) to her own backyard? The one who didn't talk or sing. Him. Oh, he was real (seen, at least). Twice in Annabelle's tiny life.

CHAPTER 11

One time.

A few times.

"I want some more Hawaiin Punch, Daddy," Annabelle said.

"Me, too," Elizabeth said as the canoe tied by the bank swayed in its cradle of liquid rifts.

"Okay, okay," their father laughed, squinting away from the sun, walking toward the cooler. He reached in and pulled out the large jar and unscrewed its top to pour the drink in Dixie cups.

"Dad, can I go swimming?" Danny asked, so serious. The orange life preserver already on made him look as if his neck had been stolen and he had to go through life with still, somber arms down at his sides and an outlook to match.

"Sure, Danny. Stay by the canoe," his father said. And with that cut of a ribbon, Danny marched, head and shoulders above his usual, looking straight ahead, to the edge of the water. He waded in, then kneeled down on the slippery stones and pushed off with his toes, awkwardly jutting chin and preserved chest first, sputtering and grimacing as he paddled like a dog.

"Daddy," Annabelle said. "How come you like camping and Mom likes the shore?"

"I'm not crazy about the shore," her father answered as he swatted a fly, smacking his own skin.

"I *know.* How come you don't like the same *things*?"

"Well, people don't have to like the same things."

"I don't like jellyfish in the ocean!" Danny called from the water, now splashing as he turned in circles, seemingly without any say.

"Well, now," his father said.

"I get burned at the shore," Grace said. She was sitting on her new beach towel, under the trees, taking in the scent around her. Of green and shade and wood and hardened clay covered with settled grains. The cool air under the hot sun. That made her breathe. The earth that protects.

"I like the shore," Elizabeth said. She was sitting next to her father, on two of the canoe seat cushions. "I mean, I like it here, but I like the shore, too."

"Daddy, can we have Spam for dinner?" Annabelle asked.

"Well, sure," her father answered. "And we'll get sticks for cooking marshmallows later."

"Yayyyy!" you would think came from only Annabelle, but add on Grace and Danny and a smile from Elizabeth.

"Okay, time for a swim!" their father announced as he stood up, placing the remains of his soggy peanut butter and jelly sandwich on top of the cooler.

"Aren't you going to take your shoes off, Dad?" Elizabeth asked through her smile which was now staying for something new.

"What? These?" he said as he lifted his feet and looked down at his sneakers. "No, of course not," jokingly, kindly. "They're going to protect my feet from the leeches and snakes."

"Leeches and snakes!" Annabelle cried.

"Oh, it's alright, Annabelle. Just stick with me," her father teased.

"I don't think there are any leeches. And the snakes won't bother you," Grace said. "I don't think."

Their father laughed. "Come on, kids! Get your sneaks on and let's go swimming! Here we come, Danny." And with that he marched to no drummer down the bank and straight into the stream, with a plop just like his son had done minutes before. And his daughters followed, first Elizabeth, then Annabelle, and then Grace. All laughing, all raising hands to faces, arms in the air, as

they couldn't believe their father went into the water with his
shoes on and t-shirt to boot.

As Elizabeth awoke, she could smell the burning eggs outside.
Nothing charred, nothing ruined. Nothing black, nothing gone.
Simply overcooked eggs, the smell of which she will never forget.
For it goes with hearing her father out by the picnic table, lighting
the small gas stove, creating with a spatula, setting places, getting
ready for his children. The sun respectfully stopped at the outside
forest green of the tent, not wanting to interrupt the coolness of
sleeping children who think they're still under the stars. All that
peeked in was a quiet ray underneath the front flap. Elizabeth
yawned and stretched and sighed. Grace and Annabelle were still
asleep and Danny was probably still asleep in the tent next to
them that he shared with his father. Chirps dotted trees and chipmunks ran across the planks that bridged over the stream down
the way. Morning sat quietly, not minding no formal announcement, already here. And Elizabeth's father now sat outside on the
picnic bench, breakfast ready, sipping coffee, looking out at the
water. Elizabeth knew this. She also knew he had a smile on his
face. That he loved where he was. That he didn't mind waiting for
his children—they could have, deserve, a few more moments under a sliver of a beautiful moon.

CHAPTER 12

Elizabeth saw her parents kiss once. Right on the lips. Full of
love. Playful even. It reminded her of daisies.

CHAPTER 13

After a spilling out, when the cold was coming, Meggie was first touched in plaid. All fingers at once, seemingly with no pattern, but then you step back and see the thought-out lines, colors, contemplating shapes and space. She had been walking to answer the phone, you see. An innocent answer of the bells. Picked up the receiver and received a shock. No one on the other end and fingers on her back. Kneading, scratching, pulling. Oh, my, she said, turning, gasping. Racing heart. What was happening? Who was doing this to her? They scratched her until she started to bleed, making her almost prefer insanity. They kneaded her neck, not in comfort but in warning, a sensual collection of the soul, but in a dark way. At least they stayed away from her face; they left that for her, she supposed. Although the first had been the worst, the other times, a caress on the neck, a breath on eyelashes, a kiss on a lobe, all wicked, all sinful, did much more detriment by quietly letting her know they (it, who knows?) were still there, slowly, slowly, slowly. Slowly causing her pain. She couldn't see, though. Neither could anyone else. A cat caught under the moon crying about bats on his back that no one could see. That's what she was.

CHAPTER 14

Dan passed the bean salad even though Grace could see hooks shaped like red claws coming from him. Meggie took the dish in an oh so normal way even though Grace could see yellow-green muted with grey, dots of black, first stand and jut out its chest (but with cowardly eyes) then retreat within its own cloak, but all the while walking toward the claws, making sure they could see him, this yellow-green muted with grey (with dots of black). Annabelle was in the middle of telling a story of how her third-grade colleague had decided to stick paste up his nose. Elizabeth was piercing her beans with a fork and a smirk and Danny pretty much was just sitting there eating his dinner (to an outsider). They were all pretty much just sitting there eating their dinner (to this outsider).

"He just did," Annabelle said. "Right up his nose. Gross," she said as she plopped another tiny piece of meat her mother had cut for her into her mouth.

"Oh, that is," Meggie said in agreement. "That is gross."

"Did he get sick?" Danny asked.

"Can we talk about something else?" Elizabeth asked, told. "This is stupid. It's just third grade." But, no one had any "Oh, Elizabeth, stop it" tonight. They were an accepting family, after all.

"Please pass the French dressing," Dan said, and in response, Grace handed the dressing to her father, and in response, the piano they didn't have started playing in the living room.

Meggie's hand did twitch a bit, but she pretty much just kept on eating her dinner.

Dan's eyes did look over quickly to the left once, but he pretty much just kept on eating his dinner.

Elizabeth did lose her smirk, but she pretty much just kept on eating her dinner.

Danny did secretly bless himself, but he pretty much just kept on eating his dinner.

Annabelle did swallow, past her own paste in her throat, but she pretty much just kept on eating her dinner.

Grace did see the hands (through the walls), but she pretty much just kept on eating her dinner.

The piano was joined by other instruments, a trumpet, trombone, clarinet, and drums (its beat causing fuzz). A Dixieland band, it was, with music from where voodoo dolls are created, spells are cast.

"Please pass the sliced tomatoes," was said as the tune ended, eyes were cast down.

CHAPTER 15

Meggie followed Maureen. Past dead limbs and a sky that looked like it had been smeared with charcoal. "I don't know about this," Meggie said in her mind. "I'm here. I'm here," she said out loud as Maureen would look behind, making sure her friend was close by even though she could feel her breath.

What was she doing? Maureen thought. About herself. And I guess about Meggie, too. What *were* they doing? Coming here. To this house that looked normal enough next to dead trees and what looked like a soldier dying in the sky—just a dark cloud against a darker one, though. But can you trust something that looked normal against death? Wasn't it supposed to fit in somehow? Wouldn't it be more honest if the paint was chipping and the shutters hanging?

Well, perhaps she was wrong. Maybe someone named Liza who lived in a middle class home in a middle class neighborhood bringing its fingertips to its palm because winter is coming, you know, *can* tell you how to rid yourself of a ghost. And it didn't hurt that Maureen's friend Lucy's friend Jane had already visited Liza and reported back to neighbors, relatives, and whoever else cared to listen, that, yes, Liza *did* tell her that she had had two children and a recent miscarriage to boot (how could she have known *that?*) and that old Aunt Gert who had died 15 years ago had said hello and wanted to know if her silverware was being put to good use. Frighteningly accurate, everyone agreed. Frightening. We must go, everyone agreed. To see what she sees about our lives, those who have died in it, and those who have simply gone. But most of them clicked their heels and turned, unwidened their eyes, and came back, when they heard one of their children crying or their husbands asking where the latest issue of Field and Stream had gotten off to. Only the truly needy need apply. Only those who lay awake at night counting stars they couldn't see, saying prayers they barely remembered (and some made up new), asking for and asking of. Please Jesus. God. Along those lines (not to diminish but to open for all divine help). Help. Please.

Maureen got to the front door first, but stepped aside so Meggie could ring the bell. It was her call to be answered, after all. Might as well start things off right. In a straight line. Honestly. (Honestly.)

"Come in. Come in," the bright woman said. Clothes. Smile. She was wearing orange slacks creased down the middle of the road and a green knit top. Her hair was short and cropped firmly around her face. She looked younger than her 52 years but you could tell her age. It was behind her eyes.

"Maureen?" she asked Meggie.

"Oh, no, I . . . " Meggie began to answer.

"I'm Maureen. I'm the one who made the appointment," Maureen said.

"Yes, yes," the woman said. "Have a seat." She pointed to the dining room table. It had a half-filled napkin holder and a salt and pepper shaker set on it, as well as a picture of Jesus and a statuette of his mother with her palms facing the heavens. But, of course, you saw the *as well as* first on the way out. As expected. As well as any exit mixed with entrances. As well as.

"Liza?" Maureen asked as they sat down. Just to be stalling sure. Liza smiled.

"I have been to a psychic once," Meggie said, offering proof of something. "Well, it was a long time ago," she added quickly, trailing off in apology, more in response to the doubting of herself than that of any other. "Right after I got married," she added, filling up space so nothing else could. Nothing that pressed. Nothing that peeked out with cartoon white eyes from underneath a bed while hiding in the dark.

"Meggie, it's alright," Maureen said in a hushed tone, but more for effect because Liza could hear everything, you know.

"Ah, it is," Liza offered. "Did she tell you much? The psychic?" she asked while shuffling the cards. Ace of diamonds. Two of clubs. There's a Jack. Hmm. He was smiling. There goes his Queen. The diamonds seemed to go by quickly, but a heart got caught on a spade.

"Well," Meggie said, at a loss, now that she was actually supposed to come out and deliver. "I . . . " while deciding whether the memory was the business of only her mind.

"Alright," Liza said, marking the end of her task rather than of response. After all, there was a reason. She slid the cards over to Meggie. "Now, Meggie, take the cards and shuffle them three times." Meggie did as she was told. "Think about what you want to know while you're shuffling them," Liza added.

What she wanted to know? Well . . . hmm . . . that was . . . maybe . . . well . . . that's like . . . her life . . . all she could really offer were her hands. When she was finished, she brushed them together as if wiping off imaginary chalk. Liza took the deck now familiar to its dealer's goings and comings, fate and providence, soul and heart. And even of others in and around. This dealer's hand.

"You've been robbed," was said before anyone even looked at the cards.

Meggie and Maureen both were startled, as if someone had just ran in and announced a recent crime. A purse snatching. A tug of string of pearls. A life gone wrong. What Meggie and Maureen showed was increased attention to the announcer. A locking of eyes. A realization that this was serious.

"Boy, you've been robbed," Liza said again, looking at Meggie again, but this time it was a dull thud of a butter knife rather than any sharp, surprising edges. "Really," she added as if her listener did not believe. But Meggie believed. She said so with her eyes, her frown as if trying to make out small print in a newspaper, and her nodding. A sigh and then, "Yes," quietly while looking down, still frowning, but this time accepting, claiming, what the type had to say.

"Alright, cut the deck three times," interrupted any stabs at pity, self or otherwise, with a clean slice of its own.

"Ah, one . . . " eyes scanning the hand(s). "Three daughters," and a smile.

"How did you know that?" Meggie asked. "I mean, yes. Yes. Three."

"And a son."

"And a son." And a swallowing of own saliva. "His name is Danny," to help along, to show at least an effort of taping fear inside cardboard flaps.

Liza looked over at Meggie with patience, but facts only stood in the way.

"I'm sorry. Go on," Meggie said. And then, "Does it help or hurt if I tell you things?"

"You can tell me whatever you want," Liza answered, but back to scanning crowns and staffs and swords and might. The mighty and the lost. Found among the meek. Their inheritance . . . let's hope it's not squandered.

Meggie kept quiet.

"Your car needs to be fixed."

"Oh," in surprise.

"Did you know that?" Maureen asked.

"Um."

"A blue station wagon, right?" Liza asked.

A gasp from Maureen.

"Well, it *has* been making a funny noise lately. Dan said he'd look at it this weekend," Meggie said.

"It needs to be fixed," again from Liza. "Something with the transmission. Something like that."

Meggie made a mental note to tell Dan. But not the source. That wouldn't do.

A cloud came upon them shown through the face of a sooth-sayer.

"Your daughter . . . "

"Which one?"

"Your daughter." Waiting, them for her. A few starts, her for them. "Your daughter?" A hum in the air. "Has she seemed not well?" What a formal way to put it.

"Which one?" Meggie asked. "They all seem fine," she answered herself.

"The oldest."

"Elizabeth?"

"Elizabeth."

"Why, she's fine," Meggie said. And after thinking about it, "She's the strongest person I know."

"She's going through something."

"What? What is she going through?"

"I just see darkness. And lead." A puzzle coming apart. "You should make sure she gets out more," the soothsayer says.

"Elizabeth goes out all the time. She's always out with her friends," Elizabeth's mother defended.

"I'm sorry. I'm just telling you what I see."

"No, that's . . . I mean, I want to hear. Is there anything I can do?"

"Watch. Watch her. And pray. Prayer always helps."

Elizabeth needed her prayers? Elizabeth is the strongest person she . . .

And Grace, and Annabelle, and Danny. They needed prayers, too. Apparently. Just a telling of the sayer that soothes. Tries to, anyway. Maybe not of now, but of what is coming. Pray to God that they'll be alright. Pray to God. And what of Dan? Anything seen? Oh. He's a hard worker. Up for a promotion at work, I see. Okay, from the other, ready to move on. But what about the house? What's in that house? Oh, from the sayer, following leads, but then from her own, it's a dangerous thing. In that house. A dangerous thing. Is it a ghost? They want to know. It's a ghost, the soothsayer sees. A few times before, even. With others. Sent them home with the same instructions. A blessed element, the burning

soul of an Asian tree, and music that heals. That should do it. And
pray while . . . Always pray.

* * * *

"Are you sure we're doing this right?" Meggie asked as she
dipped her fingers into the holy water and sprinkled it above the
white mantel, making sure not to get any on Uncle Ezra, and on
top of the ashes that lay in the fireplace below. Maureen consulted
her notes.

"It says to do this three times a week for two weeks," she said.
"Yes, we're doing this right. Okay, let's go do the upstairs now."

"Should we bring the incense?" Meggie asked as she looked
toward the burning frankincense, the smoke of which slowly dissi-
pated as it floated above.

"Yeah. And I'll get the radio." Maureen was right, alright. She
double-checked her notes, remembering the scratch the psychic's
voice had made. Sprinkle holy water, burn frankincense, and play
soft pleasant music of any kind (preferably classical). That should
do it.

"I don't know," Meggie said as they headed upstairs. "I'm feeling kind of silly."

"Meggie," Maureen said. "Nobody has to know we're doing
this. It's best to at least try."

"I know. You're right. It's just that . . . Do you really think this
will work?"

"Meggie. What are you afraid of?"

"I don't know," Meggie said. "Maybe if we start fooling around
with this kind of stuff, things will only get worse."

"Don't you think you're already there?" Maureen asked. And
with that Meggie dipped her fingers once again into the cleaned
out mayonnaise jar that held the last remnants of holy water. "I
command you," she said. "Spirit of moves," she added, choking a
bit on her words. And then, "Leave this house," clearly.

CHAPTER 16

Meggie lay on the couch motionless, almost not having the energy to breathe, let alone move. She had been this way for weeks, ever since she saw the saucer spin by itself in the cupboard. After Maureen had done her thing with the holy water and soft music, assuring Meggie that she knew in her heart this would work, the house *had* become still, for a few days anyway. And the kids had seemed to notice, too. Elizabeth was actually nice to her, asking Meggie her opinion on a new blouse she was going to wear on a blind date; Grace seemed to be smiling more, the apprehension softening somewhat in her eyes; Danny even stood by his mother and watched as she took out the oven cleaner and sprayed fumes that traveled in little circles above his head; and Annabelle didn't seem to be on the defense so much anymore, going a whole week without silently challenging someone to a staring contest. And Dan and she had never gotten along better, with him sometimes planting a kiss on his wife's forehead when no one was looking, causing Meggie to retreat in such surprise that she almost dropped the pan of meatloaf she was holding. But then, the holy water must have evaporated and the frankincense must have withered away, because before you knew it, the water bill came and Dan and Meggie fought like old warriors, only needing the simple excuse of anticipation to draw their swords.

"Oh, Maureen, it just didn't work," Meggie had said when she walked to her neighbor's house the next day, specifically to tell her this. Her navy blue knit top had a large pull across the front and the thread hung down haphazardly, as if no one really cared if it was there or not. Maureen guided her friend to the kitchen table and poured milk into her coffee out of a ceramic cow's open mouth.

"Tell me," Maureen said.

"I'll tell you," Meggie said.

And she told of the fight and of the slamming and of the breaking and how later, after everything had been cleaned up, she opened the door to the cupboard and found the saucer spinning, as if it didn't need a child to be part of a child's game. And all accompanied by the smell of rotted wood. And the feel of maggots when she reached in her hand to stop it, still clinging to her even now, although she couldn't see them. No one could. Bats on the back. Maureen took a breath.

"We could do it again," she said.

"I just can't," Meggie said. "I just can't."

"We could try."

"What's the use?" Meggie asked, and as she closed her eyes Maureen could actually see a funnel of hope leave her heart.

And everyone (a couple of the neighbors, the grocery store clerk who had to now make deliveries to the Owenses' house, a few of Dan's friends from work) said Meggie must have come down with something because all she did lately was lie on that sofa, staring at that small water stain in the ceiling that resembled a trapped mouse.

"I don't see it," Grace had said one day, kindly.

"Oh, sure you do," Meggie said. She had one leg hanging down to the floor and her right arm rested up over her head. "See its little leg?"

"I'm sorry," Grace said. Meggie sighed.

"Oh, well, that's alright."

And this was the extent to Meggie's interactions with her children—her lying on the sofa while one of them ran in to ask her where that shirt is ("I guess in the laundry basket. Did your dad tell you what he did with it?") or if they can sleep over this person's house ("Well, of *course* you can. I've never had a problem with that, have I?"). And her children accepted this, as if it were just another small rearrangement, something they had to take only a few seconds to study and then go about their usual lives of adapting to whatever came in through the front door or the cracks of the window.

"Can we get a cat?"

Meggie was lying flat on her back, with both bare heels up on the end of the sofa and her hands neatly folded on her stomach. She pondered the frame that held Uncle Ezra—was that a gold finish?—and then answered her son.

"What did your dad say?" she asked, crinkling her brow as she tried to figure out if Uncle Ezra really *was* staring at her.

"I didn't ask him yet," Danny said in a small voice.

"Well," Meggie said in a somewhat slow, chastising tone. Danny couldn't tell if that was directed at him or Uncle Ezra. Meggie turned her head and looked at her son. He had his head tilted horizontally, matching her, and his hands were also folded in front of him. He looked as if he was standing in front of a funhouse mirror, trying to decipher his true reflection.

"You should probably ask him," Meggie said.

Danny straightened his head. "But what if he says no?" he whined.

"Well, that is a possibility."

"I don't *like* possibilities. I want . . . I want . . . "

"Danny," Meggie said firmly, with her cheek flattened, pressed against the sofa cushion and her hands still folded. "Nobody likes possibilities. But we do have to live with them."

"*Mom.*"

"Go ask your father. I'm sure it won't be that bad." She turned her head back to the portrait, studying Uncle Ezra's ascot, wondering how long it took to tie such a thing.

Two days later, Danny sat at the dining room table, with his hands beneath the table nervously holding two thin books, one on how to raise kittens and the other on different kinds of cat personalities.

"Dad?" Danny asked, his voice cracking at the end. His father lifted his head and blankly looked at him, looking even more stern than how Danny had noted him to be when he had first come home from work that night.

"I was . . . um . . . "

"What is it, Danny?"

"Well . . . "

"He wants a cat, Dan," Meggie shouted from the other room.

"Why can't Mom have dinner with us?" Annabelle asked and then took a bite out of her cherry tomato, spurting its juice well onto past her plate.

"A cat?" Dan asked.

"Well, yes," Danny said. He lifted his books so his father could see. "I've been doing some reading and they're not as hard as dogs . . ."

"I don't know," Dan said, almost dismissively as he looked down at his plate and resumed cutting his meat.

"Oh, let him have it," Meggie shouted. Elizabeth sighed and then said under her breath, "I should have done what Grace did and had dinner at a friend's."

"Elizabeth," her father said. She looked up at him. "Finish your dinner," he said.

"I was," she said indignantly.

"I'd like a cat," Annabelle said.

"I think it would be good for them," Meggie shouted. Elizabeth, Danny, and Annabelle looked at their father for an answer.

"Well, you be sure to take care of it," he said as he lifted a forkfull of food to his mouth, smiling slightly after the fork slid away from his lips, and Annabelle and Danny started to cheer. And Elizabeth smiled herself, despite the annoyance she felt when she heard one last "Yay!" on the tail end, coming from the living room.

* * * * *

Meggie felt the hole in her chest—as clear as if someone had taken a trowel and burrowed through her skin, displacing all organs so the thin sheet of stainless steel could rest next to her heart. She felt the hopelessness as she would sometimes sit up and stare at the floor, wondering what use is it to move any muscle. The room was getting darker these days, with winter coming. Oh, she had read about depression. She supposed this was something like that. But, she also read how it often occurred during the spring, when people feel that much worse when their look on life doesn't match the weather. Well, matching the weather is no picnic, either, Meggie thought. There are no checks and balances, nothing there to say "It isn't all that bad, see how bright this day is?" There was nothing to warm her back the few times she would get up to go to the front door and bend over to get the paper on the step. There was only the ice in the wind and the shorter days telling her the world was a cold, dark place to be. She was in a fog now, and no matter how hard she tried, she couldn't get away. Her favorite time of day was night, she supposed. That way, she was at least where she was supposed to be, ready for bed. Oh, it didn't matter that her bed was on the sofa these days, that didn't count. It just mattered that she was doing what other people were doing—that connected her in some small, sad way. Mornings were hardest, when people bustled and hustled, getting ready for their posts, knowing they had a place to be or ramifications would be felt. Those times, when she heard her husband opening and shutting drawers and clearing his throat, getting his voice ready for good morning greetings, and her children running here and there, pulling on jeans and grabbing jackets and book bags, those times she felt the loneliest. She would become even more rigid than usual, not even allowing her body an extra boundary of an inch or two to move within, somehow punishing herself for choosing to stay here, yet not knowing what else to do. Mid-morning became easier when she would be sleepy again. She would close her eyes and tell her-

self that some people were where she was—sick children, the elderly, and women who were about to give birth, fanning themselves—they were probably all where she was, doing the same thing,
just waiting for the next phase to come find them. Late afternoon
and early evening were almost as difficult as the morning, when
her family came home and neighbors came home to their homes,
all with stories and exasperation and annoyance and satisfaction
and sometimes even delight of what the tasks found in the world
had offered them. But, mid to late evening were the best. Then,
she could roll up even more, pulling her knees to her chest, telling
herself she deserves a state of rest after the day she's had. But, she
never rested, and hardly slept (except for a couple of hours in the
middle of the night and then again in mid morning). She could
almost see Danny's point of view, fearing the particles of the world,
for she often felt as if little specks were surrounding her, threaten-
ing to turn into a blanket of something she's sure she wouldn't
want. Even Dan had said that he's seen her, in her sleep, sit up and
pick at the air around her, trying to catch, or shoo away, the very
things that seem to seek her.

"Meggie," Dan had said one day. He sat down in the Wedgwood
blue wing-backed chair next to her and put each hand on either
armrest. Meggie continued to lay on her side, facing the backrest
of the sofa, away from her husband. "Meggie," he continued. "You
can't keep this up."

"Why not?" Meggie asked, her voice muffled by its path leading to thick upholstery. He bent forward, looked around the room,
and opened then closed his hands as if not sure himself of an answer.

"Well," he said. "Christmas will be here."

"That's three and a half weeks away," Meggie said in her
muffled voice.

"Exactly," Dan said.

"We don't usually go shopping until the week before and we
don't buy the tree until a couple days before," she said in that low,
lost voice.

"But your parents are coming this year."

Meggie didn't answer. She kept on breathing, Dan could hear her, but she didn't say a word. After a few moments, she turned, again on her back, looking at Uncle Ezra. Then she looked down at her feet. After a few more moments, she swung her legs around and sat up. She looked at Dan as if he had reminded her there were some rolls in the oven and she got up and went into the kitchen as if to retrieve them, or at least start preparing for a Christmas dinner that was only weeks away and would include her parents, guests that had come every year.

* * * *

Danny couldn't stay still. The comforter clung to his sweat and he felt as if he were trying to find sleep on the hottest of July days rather than on the night before Christmas. He wished he was little again so he could attribute this extra apprehension as a response to waiting for that fat man he really didn't know to break into his house and leave gifts and presents, some of which he asked for and some he did not, like he had in past years. He needed an excuse to shake away this feeling that was crawling slowly toward his chest, but he couldn't come up with any. He turned and sighed, twisting the covers around his legs, and finally taking his arms and abruptly folding the tops of the covers down, so that he was free from the waist up. He had already heard Elizabeth say from downstairs, "Oooh, looks like Santa's been here," and wondered why some people still go through the pretense. He supposed it was for Annabelle's sake. Well, that's fine, he thought, but she's in bed. There's no need to go to all that trouble when surrounded by those who don't believe. Danny sighed and looked out through the window, and his eyes grew heavy as he watched the night grow lighter as the moon reflected the snow back up into the black sky.

* * * *

Grace finished the last notes of "Silent Night" and then lowered her flute and rested it across her lap. She breathed in the soft, faded scent of the Christmas candle she had blown out about an hour ago and then looked out into the night. She was glad her mother was feeling better. Just earlier that evening, Grace had sat next to her mother, helping her to wrap gifts, as her mother sang "Silver Bells" under her breath. Annabelle and Danny had helped their father finish decorating the tree, and Annabelle left out three chocolate chip cookies and a full glass of milk for Santa Claus. Christmas was in the air, but it was such a bittersweet feeling that even Grace couldn't completely feel calm as she passed the lighted tree and stilted gingerbread house. She had smelled the evergreen and heard the carolers two doors down. She had put the gifts under the tree and eaten two cookies to prove that Santa had been there. And she had helped her mother make room in the refrigerator for the two pumpkin pies from the bakery and the pot of boiled potatoes that would be turned into mashed tomorrow. But, even so, Grace still felt as if she forgot something, as if out from one of the corners or behind from one of the doors the crisis for which she hadn't prepared would spring, disrupting all visions of sugar plums that dance in the air.

* * * *

Elizabeth helped her parents move Annabelle and Danny's toys over by the tree. There was a mini movie projector with slides for Danny, two new Barbies for Annabelle, a whiffle ball set, a board game that set off a loud buzzer if you didn't correctly place all of your pieces where they were supposed to go, a large stuffed frog, a new bike for Danny (as well as one for Annabelle), a puppet theater and two puppets that sat limp on its stage, a castle with its own moat and knights that were poised to defend, a toy organ, and a five-foot high playhouse, complete with a child-sized plastic table and chairs and printed curtains lending that special touch to the cardboard walls. Not to mention the mounds of wrapped boxes that held who knows what ("Well, some things need to be a surprise, even if they aren't for you," Meggie had said). And when Elizabeth had gone to bed, she knew that her parents would spend another hour or so taking in and arranging the splendor of all of the remaining gifts (which she wasn't allowed to see) for her and Grace. But, as Elizabeth climbed the stairs, she thought of her father's enthusiastic, child-like grin, anticipating the looks on his children's faces, and her mother's strong sense of self, capably wrapping this box just so and confidently placing this gift here and that one there. And she couldn't help but sigh in the inconsistency of it all. She knew that it was Christmas and that she shouldn't think of such things, but wasn't it just a couple of weeks ago when her parents were fighting over the bills, with her father screaming that Danny didn't need new pajamas, for Meggie to take them back? And didn't her mother cry and scream back that she can't live like this, that it's just too hard, that she just can't take it anymore? Maybe it was longer ago than that. Maybe it was.

* * * *

Annabelle lay in her bed, slightly shivering. Tomorrow's Christmas, tomorrow's Christmas, tomorrow's Christmas, she told herself, repeating the words to assuage her excitement, but which had the opposite effect. She stayed awake as long as she could, lying still and trying to listen for sounds on the roof, knowing that if she dared to leave her bed to look, that the light of the stars and the moon might give her a little more than she bargained for, actually allowing her to see what she sought. No, she wouldn't chance it, she thought. She'll stay in her bed and hope that Santa comes before she falls asleep; that way, she at least may be able to hear a hoof or two on the roof. That she could handle. Her mind strayed to other thoughts as she waited. Christmas is almost here. Christmas is almost here. The tree looked so pretty today. Everyone seemed so happy today. And amidst it all, Annabelle had gone to her favorite place. Her mother had gone in the other room to get a pair of scissors and Annabelle stepped over the rolls of wrapping paper and bright self-adhesive bows and sat in the rocking chair that was almost completely in the corner. She looked outside, through the windows of the door to the screened-in porch, straight through to the backyard. The pine trees, their needles, and the white ground against which they cast their shadows made her breathe a little bit easier, as if winter's cold oxygen traveled right to her lungs. She sat and rocked and breathed and remembered, or, more accurately, dreamed. As every year, her father had come in earlier that day, holding the gingerbread house he had made (with all of their help) and put it right over there on top of the marble-top washstand. At first it was too beautiful to touch, with its perfectly placed miniature candy canes, gum drops, M&Ms, and white frosting on the roof. But, eventually someone, usually Elizabeth, would come by and pluck a gum drop from one of its walls and plop it right into their mouth. But it didn't matter. The magic was still there. Even if the walls of this house were being eaten away one gum drop at a time.

There was the Christmas tree. How beautiful it looked with all of its lights and tinsel and ornaments, some handmade and some store-bought. She loved it when her father would turn out the lights in the living room and then plug in the multi-colored lights on the tree. And sometimes he would even call Annabelle over as he sat by the stereo next to the tree and place the headphones over her ears. She would sit on his lap as the bulky headphones weighed down her head and be lulled into a beautiful daydream as the tapping of her father's heel moved his leg up and down, up and down, so that her whole body moved with the music. Sometimes it was big band music and sometimes it was Christmas carols. But, it always, always made her feel part of something special.

"Okay, sweetie," her father would say. "Time to get down. We have to get the house ready for Santa tonight."

"Yay!" Annabelle would say. "Santa! Santa's coming!"

"Yes," her father would laugh. "Santa's coming. Oh, but wait," he would say as he took the earphones to his own ears. "Uh, oh," he would say with a lighthearted mischievousness. "There's a news report on. It looks like Santa got a flat."

"No, Daddy!" Annabelle would say in a child's small shout. "Santa doesn't have tires. He has reindeer! He can't get a flat!"

"Well, now," her father would answer, with a slight smile on his face. "But, that's what the news says. Maybe the reindeer got another job."

"No, Daddy! They would never leave him. Rudolph would never leave him. They all live together. Up at the North Pole! You know that! You're just kidding me!" Annabelle would say, pulling on her father's shirt, smiling toward the end herself.

"Wait, hold on," her father would say as he listened to the headphones again. "Well, you're in luck. It wasn't a flat tire, it was one of Rudolph's hooves, but it looks like a tow truck came by and fixed it. Apparently, the guy had a hoof-fixing kit in his truck."

"Daddy, you're kidding!" Annabelle would giggle. And then Danny would come in and they both would beg their father to play horse one more time and their father would get down on all fours and neigh and buck at the right times as his children held on to his shirt with small clenched fists and laughed and screamed. And Elizabeth and Grace would come in from other rooms to see what was going on and laugh as they saw their father stand on his knees and pretend he was a wild horse trying to gently throw his riders. And Meggie would come up from the basement, where she was doing the laundry, and put her hand to her brow as she screamed, "Oh, Dan, be careful!" but as she laughed, too. She then would unfurrow her brow and lean back against the doorway. And she would fold her arms, smile, and feel the pulse of her blood slow as she watched her children laugh and play and scream with glee—all proof of happy times, of happy childhoods. Yes,

Annabelle sat and rocked and breathed and remembered, some-times filling holes with dreams.

* * * *

The sun shone in through the glass, melting the frost that had gathered in the center of the window. Meggie stirred as she heard the footsteps above and then opened her eyes, which turned into a quick squint because of the bent rays that had found their way to her face. She turned and looked at Dan sleeping. She nudged him and then said, "Dan, I think the kids are up." Dan grunted as if protesting his journey out of sleep and then turned from his side onto his back, quietly staring at the ceiling, needing more time. Meggie held still, feeling the back of his hand pressed inconse-quentially against the small of her back. The side of his leg met the back of hers all the way down past her foot, continuing on its own. He was getting heavier and his pasty stomach stretched the elastic band of his briefs. Oh, well, Meggie thought. It's not like she looks like she's twenty-three. She'll be forty-two in October. Oh, she knew that her forty-first birthday was only about two months ago, but that didn't matter. She much preferred of thinking in terms of what's coming. Always had been that way—*she* thought at least. No, she had a few more sags, bags, creases than she had had a couple of years ago. And when she had been in her mid-thirties, my how she was fat. At the time, she blamed herself, thinking she had no willpower to say no to the man at the deli counter who offered her a slice of cheese when he was preparing her order or to Elizabeth (only about ten then) who had baked cupcakes by herself for the very first time. But, then she realized that it would have to take more than a piece of cheese and one cupcake with colored sprinkles on top to make her gain fifty-three pounds. Yes, fifty-three pounds, up from one hundred and ten pounds to one hundred and sixty-three, a heavy load for someone only five-foot three. And that's when it dawned on her that it had been her husband's hand that had directed what had happened. When she would have her head turned, he would serve her more potatoes, with more gravy of course, and place an extra serving of key lime pie next to her first piece she hadn't even taken a bite out of yet. On the way home from work, he would stop at convenience stores, stuffing his pockets with candy bars he bought so that he could take them home and stuff his wife. And she didn't even consider she had the power to refuse, strengthening the case that it had been all him. When she grew, so did his smile, and that did make things easier—and harder, because he was more attentive to her in bed more now than ever, a delicate phrase that doesn't nearly describe the repulsion she would feel when he would do the disgusting things he did to her. But, then she grew tired of the attention and the peace (it still had not totally found them, they just had longer episodes of it then), and she grew tired of feeling the rolls of flesh around her jar in their own unsettlement every time she took a breath, and so, she went on a diet. She counted calories, cut the fat off her meat, and said no to the man at the deli counter. But, more importantly, she pulled her plate away before Dan could serve her any more than she wanted. And she made sure she was more aware these days so that Dan couldn't feed her a chocolate bar without her knowing and so that she wouldn't just stand there in the aftermath anymore, confused, as Dan looked content, holding an empty wrapper with bits of chocolate smeared in his hand.

Of course, Dan didn't like it. Who would like their wife withering away right before his very eyes? That was Dan's take on it. She was leaving. And he would have none of that. He hollered and screamed and threw a jar of spaghetti sauce onto the new white sofa he had bought for her. But, none of that worked. She fretted and furrowed and wrung her hands, as always, sometimes throwing her body in front of him, announcing his course, something he hadn't even considered until she had pointed it out to him. But, she did all this while becoming thin as rails, with her skin becoming so close to her bones that they, at times, looked as one. Where were her breasts? They were gone and with them went the little respect Dan had felt for his wife. Oh, he had been attracted to her once, when he had first met her, but not in a physical way. He couldn't explain in what way, really. If someone had shown him a photograph of his future wife, he would have said, no, they must be mistaken, she's much too skinny. If someone had described her personality, he would have said, no, they must be mistaken, she's much too passive. If someone had described her demeanor, he would have said, no, they must be mistaken, she's much too child-like. But, when he had seen her from across the room at the dance, he couldn't explain what had happened as anything else but meant to be. His head had felt light and his eyes had seen sparks, igniting a life he was sure must be waiting for him. So, he ignored the pleas of his parents to find a more educated and suitable mate, vowing to stay with the unsuitable suitable forever. And little by little, without even his own knowledge at times, he succeeded in turning his wife into the woman he knew he was meant to be with all along, even if it was only the shell within which she came. But, she had to go ahead and ruin it. She had to become even more passive, allowing him to make any decision he wanted and questioning her own the few times she dared to make them; she had to become even more child-like, playing with and understanding her children as if she were their age, blurring the line between child and adult; and she had to starve herself to death, losing the curves every woman should have. Oh, that was it. He lost the little patience he had had and he turned and looked at his world, frustrated that he could lose such control over his unsaid plans.

"Dan," Meggie whispered. "Dan?"

"Oh, for God's sake, Meggie," Dan said. "I'm here. Can't you see that I'm here?"

"Well, I thought maybe you were asleep," Meggie said hesitantly. "I didn't want to *wake* you."

"Meggie, if you didn't want to wake me, then why . . . Oh, never mind," he said as he sat up in bed with a grunt, swinging his legs over the side. "Let's go get the kids," he said and then reached for his sweatpants, disappointing himself by putting only one leg in at a time.

"Mom, can we come down yet?!" they heard Annabelle shout from the stairs. Meggie and Dan walked faster, now getting caught up themselves in anticipation while remembering the excitement of pieces and bits of their own Christmas pasts. They stood at the bottom of the stairs and saw their children waiting expectantly at the top. Annabelle was fidgeting excitedly, pulling herself forward and back as she held onto the railing. Danny was sitting on the top step, jiggling his right leg up and down and looking down the stairs with hesitantly bright eyes and a slow smile, a look that betrayed his effort not to believe in Christmas anymore. Grace stood behind her brother and sister, with her grey eyes wanting to observe and record the magic, knowing that it would have no choice but to pass through her. Elizabeth stood furthest away, but still close enough to be part of it. Her arms were crossed and her expression bland, but she was leaning forward and her eyes did flicker now and again, as if her body was pulling her to a place where it had all been once true for her, too.

Meggie looked at Dan. He answered her expression by saying, "Okay, kids, come on down." And each of the children ran and pushed, feeling the thrill of a race they hadn't even known they wanted to be a part of until the starting pistol went off.

"My bike!" Danny couldn't help but exclaim.

"Is this other bike for *me*?!" Annabelle cried, and then, "And look, a Barbie airplane! And my frog. And . . . and . . . and a humongous *playhouse*! And . . . and . . . " as she ran to this toy and that, picking each one up and hugging, twirling, inspecting it, running into the playhouse and then back out again, readying herself for more gifts.

"Wow, my own TV!" Elizabeth exclaimed as she bent down to turn the knobs of the unplugged, large black-and-white television set. "My own TV," she said again, sitting down in her pajamas.

"Elizabeth, look," Meggie said with a smile. "There are more for you over here. Come over here." And Elizabeth stood and joined her mother, looking at all of the boxes that held her name.

"A stereo," Grace said with her eyes wide. "I can't believe I got a stereo," she said, filling up with emotion that couldn't possibly come more than once a year.

"Grace, you have more over here, too," her mother said, lifting her happy shoulders up to her happy ears. Meggie gave out a tiny laugh and pulled her robe around her tighter as she watched her children quickly sift through the boxes, determining which ones are theirs, with the tearing of paper and the crinkle of tissue leading to joyful cries of "Oh, my gosh! It's what I asked for!" or "I didn't think I'd get *this*! How did you *know*?" And Dan stood at a participant's periphery, watching his children through a lens, sending quick flashes of light whenever he saw a moment much too precious ever to give up.

When all of the presents had been opened or seen and the children were now settling, starting the inventory all over again, but this time more slowly and deliberately, allotting more attention and a longer time for each gift, Meggie went with a smile into the kitchen ("To get a cup of coffee," she said). And Dan followed his own smile through his bedroom and down to the basement ("To get a screwdriver to tighten that door on Annabelle's Barbie plane," he said). And the children were left with bright sunshine pouring in through the bay window and the cold flakes of snow settling on the branches. Now they were showing each other their gifts, with proud smiles and short-term generosity, letting this sibling touch that or that sibling play with this.

And then each child froze—

Annabelle while she was putting on Barbie's new evening wear

Danny while he was studying how the knights' swords work

Grace while she was perusing the new sheet music she got as a stocking stuffer and Elizabeth while she was trying on her new mohair sweater, caught mid-way between taking it off and putting it on.

"NO, . . . , . . . , DAN! NO!"

"OH, STOP IT MEGGIE! STOP BEING SO GODDAMMED DRAMATIC!"

They heard the pounding of the escapee's footsteps and the running after of the one everyone knew whose fault it was.

"KIDS! HELP ME! HELP ME!"

their mother screamed as she ran into the living room, her bare heels bruising themselves against the floor. She accidentally knocked over a small glass gnome Grace had given her, its colored pieces on the floor giving no clue as to what it had once been.

"MEGGIE! I MEAN IT, MEGGIE!"

their father screamed as he charged into the living room, causing the tree to shake and drop three ornaments which now mixed with the remains of the gnome.

"OH, DAN!"

their mother screamed as she threw her back against the wall by the sofa.

"MEGGIE!"

their father screamed as he pounded his own feet toward her, raising his large hand, grabbing the neck of her nightgown, pulling his force down and ripping the material so that one breast could almost be seen.

"DAN!"

their mother screamed, contorting her face and pressing her fists against the wall, making no effort to cover herself.

"YOU'RE NOTHING!"

their father screamed as he took their mother by the shoulders and threw her down on the floor, with her knees knocking down Danny's carefully placed knights and her hands crashing in the box of the latest board game.

"ALRIGHT, I'M NOTHING!"

their mother screamed as she spit her words out into the world, the victim's venom ricocheting off of her captor back into her own soul.

Their father turned and his steps pounded, pounded, pounded, past the tree, the gingerbread house, and the broken gnome, slamming the door to his bedroom, with the final shake causing the tinsel to dance like icicles caught in a storm.

Why didn't you fight back? Elizabeth thought. Why didn't you just fight back? You should've fought back. You should've fought back. You should've fought back, she thought as the rage against her father now turned against her mother. And as she watched her mother lay on the floor sobbing, wearing her torn nightgown like a trophy for the afflicted, the bile rose, eating away at her own throat.

Don't cry, Grace thought. Just please stop crying. It makes things more off-center, the sobs. That's all they do. And her soft eyes took in the sight of her mother as they reflected the memory of her father standing over her mother, raising his fists and grabbing her shoulders and tearing her clothes and following where his raging, pumping blood told him to go. Why didn't he listen? Grace thought. Why didn't he listen to the tree he had decorated with his children only a day ago, to the house made of gingerbread with licorice-bordered walls and a roof full of white frosting he had displayed himself, to the stockings he had hung by the chimney with care, as if all savior spirits of Christmas soon would be there. Couldn't he hear them?

Why can't this be like other houses? Danny thought. What had he done to be born into such a house? Maybe he hadn't been born into it after all. Maybe it happened after he came. After he came.

Oh, now I see, Annabelle thought, paving her future. But does anyone see me?

Their mother turned so each of her children could see her, with her eyes swollen from tears and her face streaked and red from their salt. The prints of her husband's fingers still marked her flesh from where he had pulled her nightgown. "He's a monster," she sobbed to her solemn children, frozen in their posts. "He's just a monster."

Two hours later, Annabelle brought her new doll into the dining room. "Look, Mommy," she said. "See how long her ribbons are?" She cradled the doll in one arm as her other hand gently traced the soft pink ribbon between its fingers. Her mother sat at the table, her eyes still wet and still wearing the ripped nightgown, but with the left side pulled up behind the shoulder so the tear revealed only the top part of her back.

"Mommy?" Annabelle asked.

"Yes, sweetie, that's nice," Meggie said in a choked voice, crumbling the chocolate-covered doughnut between her fingers.

"Santa brought it."

"Oooh, that's nice," Meggie said as her mouth pulled back toward her ears and she started to cry again. Annabelle looked at her doll's lace nightgown, continuing to play with its ribbon. She then turned to go back into the living room because she didn't know what else to do. She heard her father clearing his throat in his bedroom and she looked at her brother and sisters for signs of what to do, but she didn't find any. Danny was setting up his knights again, for the seventh time in the last half hour, annoyed with himself that he couldn't get it right. Obviously, that knight was too close to the clawfoot of the sofa and that one over there was much too close to Grace's pile of gifts. He would have to start over. Elizabeth was taking up the whole sofa, leaning against one end while her feet pressed against the other. The blank journal she had gotten from Grace lay open in her lap as she held a pen absent-mindedly and looked out the bay window. Grace had collected all of her boxes from the tree and was now carefully piling them up close to her new stereo. Their father opened the door, and although their movements did stiffen somewhat, everyone pretty much kept on doing what they were doing. His heavy steps took him past, across the foyer, and into the dining room.

"I don't care," they heard their mother say in a hushed, croaked defeat. They heard their father's steps again and kitchen sounds traveled back to them through the open doors. Their mother appeared in the doorway between the foyer and the living room. "I'm going to take my shower now, kids," she said, her eyes still foggy and bleary. "Who needs to go first?"

"I do," Elizabeth said, putting her journal aside and quickly standing from the sofa. She maneuvered past the games, dolls, paper, boxes, and bows and then brushed by her mother with a clip that told the mistletoe hanging from the brass arm of the light fixture that she just didn't care either.

* * * *

He felt Dan's rage. He sat on the edge of the windowsill and opened his soul to all brimstone and fire. He felt the splintered paint melt beneath him and its toxicity creep up inside him, poisoning his soul. *That wife*, he thought. *That house. That life*, he thought. *Those kids.* Well, he did love those kids, but he couldn't help but feel annoyance at her tears and sobs and crooked eyebrows and those pathetic "Why me's," which reached forth and grabbed those children, pulling them by their limbs, ensuring their loyalty to space within only her boundary—all pulsing his inhuman heart that much harder, so that his blood flowed straight to and from hell. *Look at her. She's pathetic. Still sitting there in that ripped nightgown, crying, two hours after the fact, as if telling the world what a fucking hard life she has. Fuck that. Fuck that. What about him? He works hard. He's fair. He's kind to the kids. When does that get noticed? Never, that's when. Not this side of hell. Well, enough of that. Don't give in*, he thought, sending him messages. *Don't give in. Then she and her ways, more wicked than yours, really, will win. And it will all be taken away from you. No one may see that now, or ever. But that's what's going on. It is. This isn't how you grew up. You came from a fine family. Without these problems. You don't deserve this. You came from a fine family.*

He felt Elizabeth's anger. *That's it*, he thought. *Get mad. Because you're the only one who sees things how they truly are. No one else will accept it. They turn the other way or they have the nerve to wake up the next day, smiling. How dare they. How dare they smile and laugh and go on after all this. After your veins and organs get stretched and ripped. Oh, I see*, he thought. *I see what you see. And what it's doing to you. Don't they know that you will never let a man love you because of this? Don't they know that when—hopelessly, really—you try, you will choose ones just like him? Not in obvious ways, but like him nonetheless—maybe not like he will be then, older and softened and most times kind, even, but like your worse memories of him. So that you spend the rest of your life fighting a battle that's long been dead, not resolved by any means, but by the time you fight it—dead. And there you will be, in a graveyard full of old warrior's bones, those of your father poised against the tallest headstone, his right arm raised high, ready to strike stones and his jaw open, ready to spit and those of your mother in a crumpled heap on the ground, with her eyes still in the socket of her skull, closed, already accepting defeat and not looking for any escape. And there you will be with the bones of an old war, watching your friends, and even your siblings in some ways, live their lives on green hills while you stand at a distance in the land of the dead.*

He felt Danny's fear. His flesh shook and his bones on loan rattled. He hugged himself while the snow grew deeper, hoping that no other spirits could see him because he feared them, too. His grey teeth clattered while his skin turned pale as he turned his head from here to there, looking for unseen poison in the air. *Oh, I know, Danny,* he shivered. *I know. Of course you see the other dangers out there, in here. How could you not? When in the middle of sleep dreams come—visions of rocking horses on clouds and the soft blue above oceans with singing seahorses, telling you to relax, to breathe evenly in their safety. When they come to you with their lies, the truth exposed when the spear of your parents' dance slices through the safety, without warning. Even on soft summer nights. Even on soft summer nights, when you thought the air was clean. Even then they scream at each other, waking you. They break, slam, throw, causing you to shiver like I am now. They hurl their rancor and hatred and venom and spite until the walls bleed. They try to kill each other, until you can't help but wonder what else is going to happen, what else is out there. MEGGIE! See? Of course there is danger everywhere, right down to the atom of things. NO! Without warning. HELP ME! KIDS! HELP ME! You have to save her, but he's your father. You have to save her, but he's your father. She's looking at you, but all you can see is dust. Of course it would seek you before anyone else. Of course it would. And it's different for you than for your sisters. You're the boy. Are you supposed to grow up like him? MEGGIE! Of course not. But in your fight, dedication to anything but that, your own molecules will fold back upon each other, afraid of their own growth because who knows what they would turn into? Watch out, Danny. The air is getting thicker, more polluted these days. The fact that others walk and live and breathe as if it was as pure as yesteryear, as it used to be before these types of things occurred, only makes it worse, the fear that is, because now you know not to be afraid just for yourself, but for the rest of the world as well.*

He felt Grace's unsettlement. *I know, Grace,* he thought. *There's a shift in the world. I know it's unfair, even though you may never admit this, or even feel it. You were born on a cloud. A soft, beautiful cloud. You were born with clear eyes. Soft, beautiful eyes. And you could see the silken threads that connected everything. From babies' first smiles to what they would see last in their life, precious visions of their precious grandchildren, while they lie dying in a hospital bed set up in their living room. And you can see the thread that weaves in and out of each life. From beginning to end. From the middle on outward, traveling both back in time and then wrapping around forward again, following a path as thin as a pinpoint through the clouds, toward the future. I know, Grace. I know you can see. I know you can see me. The others can, too, but you're the only one who believes what she's sees. You're the only one who holds onto herself, knowing there is kind strength in all grace. But, I'm sorry, Grace. In time, you will let go, too. As your bones lengthen and your skin stretches, you will become unsure of yourself, of your gift. Don't feel bad, Grace. It was bound to happen. No one will blame you for not holding onto the beauty you saw when you first questioned your mother about the leaves that turned color with another sun ("Well," your mother had said. "The leaves fall, well they fall in the Fall."). My beloved, all of the spirits cherished you. You were so precious, with your child eyes taking in only beauty, wondering what other wonderful surprises were in store for you. No one in this world will blame you for not seeing as much these days, for questioning yourself, for wondering if maybe it would be easier if you just became common. For giving up, stepping back, and watching new ashes streak all appari-*

tions with strong-felt heat. The air is bending with waves of heat com-
ing from below, Grace. How could you win? You're just a child.

He felt Annabelle's . . . he felt Annabelle's . . . where is
Annabelle? He looked through the window searching for her. No,
she wasn't there. Or there. He traveled around the house, searching each room once again. No, not there. Not there. He raised his
right hand up to his brow, shading his eyes like those who walk
the earth do, hoping that this mirror gesture would bring him
closer to the soil, in a better position to find her. But he was disap-
pearing. Where were his hands? He panicked when he saw the
tops of his sleeves empty and made things worse by waving them
back and forth, like a clown in a graveyard. His eyes became blood-
shot and his face streaked with veins. *This is what worry does,* he
thought. *This is what it does. Annabelle? Annabelle?* Here I am, she
said. *Annabelle?* Here I am. Oh, he knew she wasn't talking to
him. She has never really seen him, except for those couple of
times (shadows in the trees?). She was talking to the rug, the chair
by the window, the window itself, the floor beneath her bones,
and the roof atop her crown. She was talking to things she could
see, hoping they would reciprocate, for it was obvious that those
made of skin and breaths looked past her. Why else would they act
like that? Like demons with a debt to settle? Who else would give
their souls, their bodies up like that in front of a six-and-a-half-
year-old? Who else would? *It's alright, Annabelle,* he thought, *I see
you, here I am.* He looked down and noticed that he had no legs.
Where had they gone? he thought. His right arm was completely
gone and now his left one was starting to disappear. *It's alright,
Annabelle,* he thought. *Here I am. Here I am. Here I am.*

He felt Meggie's helplessness. *Oh no,* he thought. *What am I
going to do? Why did it find her, me? She hasn't done anything to
deserve this. Nothing. Why, then? Oh, she must have done something,*
he sighed, the very same time she did. He felt her worth seep out
from the leaks within her skin into the cracks of the dining room

table. *Go on, go ahead, see what I care*, he thought. *I'm not worth anything. I am where I deserve to be. Chained. I'm not going to even try. Oh, I have, but I get nothing but punished when I do. I get nothing but punished when I don't. I don't deserve love. Maybe because I settled. Maybe that's it. I shouldn't have settled. But I wanted those children. I wanted those children. It would have been too late if I hadn't. Nobody else would have wanted me. That's not it, really. I don't care about men and how they feel about me. Just my children. Just the children. They're all I have. They're all I've wanted. Just the children. My children. They're here with me, you know. Those poor, poor, little souls. Oh, I see. They think I don't. But I do. I just don't know how to stop it. I just don't know how. Oh, I deserve this. I must have done something. How I drink my coffee, how I slip my feet into my shoes, how I hesitate, second-guess, question, spit, how I pull the covers up over my head at night. I must have done something. Here I am, here's where I'm hiding.*

He watched that family as they reached up and picked their own thoughts from the air, putting them back inside their heads, and as they walked to and from each room, trying to hang on by rituals. He watched as they grunted and breathed and coughed and cried with a bump of a laugh in between. He watched through his own soul and then quietly backed away as he saw the strangers get out of their car. They gathered their belongings and were now using ruffled movements to cover their heads from the snowflakes as they made their way up the front stone path.

* * * *

"Hey, ho there," Dan said as his father-in-law, mother-in-law, brother-in-law, and their dog, Dutchess, all piled in from the snow.

"White Christmas," Meggie's mother said in her elderly voice (which was saved for guests and holidays). "We're having a white Christmas," she said as she clopped her walker across the foyer. "What a beautiful tree!"

"Grandmom, Grandmom!" Annabelle yelled enthusiastically. "I got Barbie's airplane!" She caught herself and then made sure her grandmother could see her talking. "I got Barbie's airplane and a puppet theater," she said in a softer tone, but with more exaggerated syllables.

"Oh, let me see, let me see," her grandmother said. "Let me see what you got for Christmas," she said as she followed Annabelle, walking crookedly behind her granddaughter, putting even more support than usual on her four-legged crutch. Annabelle sat down and began to sift through the open boxes, wanting first to show her grandmother the puppet that had orange-red yarn for hair.

"Your pipes freeze yet?" Meggie's father asked Dan gruffly.

"No, no. Not yet," Dan answered, amused.

"Daddy," Meggie said as she came down the stairs. "Merry Christmas," she said and she kissed him on the cheek. She was wearing black slacks and a soft, green sweater trimmed in red.

"Yeah, you too," he answered uncomfortably, but offering his cheek. "Those unruly grandchildren of mine around?"

"Hi, Grandpop," Grace said as she came from the dining room. "Thank you for my gloves."

"Oh, you're welcome. You open them already?"

"Yes, we opened all of the presents this morning."

"Hi, Grandpop," Elizabeth said, who was right behind Grace. "Thank you for my blouse."

"Oh," their grandfather said, clearly not comfortable with this much direct attention or gratitude. "It's Christmas . . . " he trailed off, and then, "I'm glad you liked them."

"Did you hear I got a letter back?" Alfred asked Dan as he took off his coat, shaking it in his hand once he had it off, dropping tiny icicles onto the carpet.

"Wow, gee whiz," Dan said, trying to be polite, but failing at sincerity.

"His letters, Dan," Meggie said. "The ones he sent to movie stars."

Alfred became distressed and his face was even now more red than when he had first walked in the door. "I'm not just writing to movie stars. These aren't fan letters . . . "

"Uncle Alfred smells like smoke," Danny said.

"What?" Alfred asked, brushing off each shoulder. "Oh, that's from the guy who has the route next to mine. He always smokes in the back of the office. We tell him not to, but he lights up anyway." Alfred started walking toward the living room, where the others were going.

"Doesn't he wash his clothes, Mom?" Danny asked, only a couple of feet away from his uncle. Alfred turned and looked suddenly at his nephew and then at his sister.

"Oh, I'm sure he does," Meggie said, following her son's lead and ignoring that her brother was right there, trying to smooth things over, but making them worse. Alfred looked at his sister and nephew again, with wide eyes and an indignant mouth.

"He probably just had to work today. Isn't that right, Alfred, you had to work?" Meggie asked.

"It's Christmas," Alfred said.

"We have a washer," Danny said, straightfaced.

"Danny," Meggie said. And her son looked at his uncle and then slowly moved away, all the while eyeing the shirt as if it were going to excrete some toxic fume at any minute and freeze chemical smiles on celebrants far and near.

"Here you go, Grandpop," Grace said as she handed her grandfather a festively wrapped box of red and gold. Her grandfather mumbled, "Thank you," trailing off at the end, and sat down next to his wife. She was just finishing opening her box Elizabeth had handed her.

"Oh, my," Addie said as she examined the "Best Grandmom" stocky plaster figurine. The small, animated grandmother stood frozen in Addie's hands, looking at her with a proud but impish smile, as if exchanging a secret with the recipient of this award. "I *love* it," Addie said. "Thank you."

"I don't have these," Norman said as he turned over each of

the two mystery novels, reading the backs of their book jackets, and then, "Thank you."

"See what I got my mom?" Annabelle asked. She walked over almost behind the tree, bent down, and then turned back holding a rectangle of plastic carnations that spelled out "MOM."

"Oh," Addie said somewhat taken aback.

"They're flowers, Mother," Meggie said too loudly. Annabelle proudly set down the flowers and then traipsed off upstairs to get her Ken doll who has yet to see his arranged girlfriend's new plane.

"They're for the grave," Addie said when Annabelle was out of view. Grace and Danny quickly looked up, Elizabeth just smirked toward the porch door, and Norman said, "Oh, Addie."

"Well, they are," she said. "I think that's bad luck."

"Well, I know they're for the grave, Mother," Meggie said in a hushed, annoyed tone. "But she was so proud of them."

"They were on sale at the florist on the way home from her school," Grace said. She remembered how excited Annabelle had been when she had come home from school that day, saying that the day before Christmas she was going to go back there and get those flowers, that they were just the right price. And when Grace had seen them, she hadn't known either that they were meant for those who have already been laid out and put to rest, with the only proof of their existence being memories and maybe some photographs.

"The grave?" Danny asked.

"Oh, Danny, stop worrying," his mother said. "Just stop *worrying*."

Dan kept quiet during this whole exchange, occasionally reaching over to fiddle with the volume of the stereo that emitted low, soft Christmas carols.

"I'm going to go check on the turkey," Meggie said and she stood up and walked out of the room.

And the dinner had gone like most of the others, with the crystal pickle dish holding cranberry sauce that still held the markings of the can and the new plastic tablecloth with ringlets of ivy and tilted bells printed on it lending an extra splash of color to the holiday meal. And when it was all over, and the bird was nothing but a scrap of bones and the table held crumpled napkins here and trails of crumbs there, Meggie started to clear the table, getting ready for dessert.

"What a lovely meal, Meggie," her mother said, taking her torn and dirty paper napkin to her mouth, delicately dabbing at the corners.

"Yeah, Mom, thanks," Grace said.

"A lovely meal," her mother repeated again, as if talking only to herself. "And Meggie," she started, including others back into the conversation, "You look lovely as well. A little peaked, but lovely. Have you lost more weight?"

Meggie continued to gather the plates, but her face was drawn and tight, and her eyes weren't focusing on anything. Grace and Annabelle looked at their grandparents with wide eyes, and Elizabeth and Danny stole quick glances at their father, waiting for his reaction. And Dan just smiled, with his elbows up on the table and his head resting on his folded hands, as if waiting for the next piece of polite conversation.

"No, no, I haven't," Meggie said after clearing her throat.

"Well, you look lovely."

"Thank you. I'll go get the pie now."

"I don't need any," Danny said anxiously.

"Oh, sweetheart, that's okay. I'll go get it," Meggie said, feeling a little nervous herself.

But, the worry and anxiety didn't last long. Oh, it tried. It tried to seep further under Danny's skin and it tried to crawl behind Grace's eyelids. It tried to anger Elizabeth and make Annabelle disappear, but the only thing it accomplished tonight was its own frustration, for didn't it know that when strangers are present, boundaries are rebuilt and customs are to be followed, dissipating the echoes of all previous calls of war, erasing the line that had been drawn in the hardwood floor. And so, after the children, and Meggie, and Dan realized this, the pressure of their blood dropped and their breaths were less constricted, and they dared to think that maybe the magic of Christmas had found them anyway, albeit late in the day and for only a couple of hours.

CHAPTER 17

The winter was noneventful (nothing out of ordinary), slippery with ice. One cold, cold day, after the carols had been long sung and merriment long gone and the earth seemed barren, lost in white bare branches dipped in, covered with, frozen glaze, Grace sat by the window, extending her arm out and then drawing it in, conducting her own experiment, comparing the feel of cold by the window with that of the heat coming from her own chest. Her mother shopping for new sneakers for Danny and Annabelle (with Danny and Annabelle), her father downtown doing his own shopping (for nails, wood, and food), Elizabeth upstairs under the covers—something she has taken to doing these days—this all lent to the cold, empty house whose echo was welcomed, albeit a bit unsettling. Grace opened and closed her hands, watching her fingernails leave their mark on her palms. She looked out the window at the slush that was spreading in the gutters, the deep, wide gutters that were always collecting what the earth was trying to get rid of. One year, after the rains had come . . . (that's how Old Mr. Kane next door had put it, standing there in his yellow fisherman rain jacket, matching hat, long after the clouds had gone. "The rains sure did a number on us, this year," he had said, squinting at the sun, synthetic rubber squeaking with creasing elbows, a twisting torso. "Aarrh, aarrh, ruined my basement, it did. Pictures. Memories. Mrs. Kane kept her sewing down there. Old books. I would have gotten around to reading them, I'm sure. Sure. The rains." And he had stood, watching the sun in his new gear as if telling the sky next time he'd be ready.) Well, that year, after the rains had come, they had all lifted the red plastic boat their father had bought one of them (for a birthday?) out from the garage and took turns riding the river of the gutterbanks, imagining a cool lake ahead rather than just old Second Avenue strewn with fallen acorns and shallow puddles. And now it was slush, icing over again.

What did John Anderson want with her anyway? Well, silly question. She knew. She wasn't disgusted. Not like you'd think. She wasn't offended. She knew she meant more to him than just a kiss, a feel, a getting off. (Isn't that how Marcy at school had put it? The terminology, not the sentiment.) It did feel good to kiss him. But, why did he need to touch her breasts? I mean, why *now*? Couldn't he wait a bit? She just wasn't ready. She's only fifteen. She shouldn't be thinking of such things. She really doesn't have a body. That's not why she's here. The touching, the breathing, the smells. It's all just too much for her. Streaking, marking her flesh. She's too young. (That was the reason, right?)

"What are you doing?"

Grace jumped and then turned to see Elizabeth.

"Oh," she said.

"Are you just sitting here?" Elizabeth asked. She had the look of someone who had been pulled out of sleep with a pulley and rope. Her hair was matted, her skin ashen, her eyes milky. Her flannel shirt had been buttoned incorrectly and her grey sweatpants hung in a lost way, too big, deflating where there was not enough bones and meat for their size.

"Yes," Grace said.

"I was sleeping," Elizabeth said as she walked over, yawning, to her sister. She sat down next to her and looked out the window, too. "You woke me up," she said.

"I did?" Grace asked, reviewing her thoughts, wondering if it was possible that one of them had escaped from her mind and thumped on the walls.

"All that walking," Elizabeth said. "What were you doing, anyway?"

"I wasn't walking."

"Yes, you were."

"No, I wasn't. I was here the whole time."

"Back and forth. Back and forth. You were, Grace."

"I was here the whole time."

"Upstairs?" Elizabeth asked, but now getting scared, eyes watering, limbs freezing, the mind already planning what it's going to do.

"I was down here," Grace whispered.

A breath(s). They each took in one.

"Should we go over someone's house?" Grace asked, looking around, almost beginning to cry.

"What would we *say*?" Elizabeth asked, deciding.

"We could say we heard footsteps."

"No one would believe us."

"We could call the police."

But Elizabeth looked at Grace and sliced up this idea with her eyes. And Grace understood.

"Well," Grace began, trying to come up with another solution. "We could wait outside until Mom and Dad come home."

"We'd freeze."

"Maybe that would be better."

"We're right by the door," Elizabeth said.

"Yeah?"

"If we hear anything else, we can run to the door."

"Yeah."

"So, we'll wait."

"We'll wait."

And they sat by the window until the stars came, afraid to move. And when the darkness came, so did one (or two) balls of light. A little, dancing, lively ball(s) of light that played a game (or two) right outside the window, if you were to believe such a thing. That teased and floated and sometimes played dead—if you were to look at it (them) and not to and fro, inside, thinking (outside of thinking). And Elizabeth and Grace each silently thanked God as they heard a car loudly pull up in the driveway and honk its horn (a foreign sound, not sounding like either of their parents' cars, but perhaps one of them got a ride home with someone else for some reason). They heard muted, cornerless laughter from upstairs.

Ohhh. (This not from them or me.)

Of course they were paralyzed. That happens, you know (as they know). Especially when a ghost(s) abounds(take the last off). Who *was* upstairs anyway? Going back and forth. Illogical and logical. There was *something*. Upturning at the end, the notes high even in the voices in their heads. Giving in to fear does that. Constricts your voice. But then, as done in drills, shaking it off, sucking it in, wading through, jumping in, they raced, raced, racing themselves, racing each other, racing what was there before it came upon them, to the back door, to the car, to be saved by souls. Limbs too heavy and extraneous right now. Why couldn't they just be where they wanted to go? Why did they have to go through this run again? Practiced, but not really practice at the time, too many times. Finally, finally, at the door. Elizabeth opened the door. And she said, taking in, "Thank God. I am *so* glad . . . " with relief, already conserving movements.

But, black holes don't really comfort. There was no one there, you see. And it was so dark out. Not even a phantom pocket of light to distract, entertain, dissuade, persuade. The cement driveway lay before them, its empty white (the only white) path, with side icicle rocks, traveling into the darkness (it was so dark out) as if a mocking, flat ghost (really just one here).

"The car didn't sound like ours," Grace said between breaths that had just started, building.

"I know," Elizabeth said, staring out into the night.

"But, it *was* here. I heard it."

"I know," Elizabeth said.

"Elizabeth, I'm scared."

Elizabeth began to breathe deeper, with her nostrils flaring, tears running down.

"Let's go to Mrs. Angelucci's house," Grace said. "She'll understand. I know it."

"We'll just tell her we got scared, but we won't tell her why," Elizabeth said.

"Alright."

But, they had another decision to make. They were hesitant, standing in the doorway, in between worlds. Do they chance going back inside, having to go through the kitchen, then the dining room, then the foyer (placing themselves at risk at the bottom of the stairs and being able to see straight up to the second floor) to get to the front door? Or do they leave through this door, through the darkness and upon the land that had fooled them, tricked them into being here? But the latch made up their minds for them. The old-fashioned latch (no doorknobs in this house) that started to move up and down by itself on the door to the basement. Elizabeth and Grace turned in horror as they heard the noise and then ran quicker than a streak of fear, pounding the driveway with their steps, crunching leftover black snow, each thinking the blood rushing to her head must be the reason for hearing roaring laughter from back inside the house, must be the reason for hearing the horn from a car that didn't exist. "Your ride's here!" they each heard someone shout (or was that a whisper?) from behind, neither one giving up, even as they reached the steps to the Angelucci's front walk.

* * * *

The chair no one should sit in beckoned Elizabeth. There it sat with outstretched arms of blue, waiting. Oh, occasionally, others would sit in it. But, afterwards, they would stand, stretched, worn, sour, wicked. Their eyes would narrow, with a hint of rubies to them, and seek anything that would provide an excuse. For Annabelle to stomp her foot and say, "No! I will *not* go upstairs to bed now! Fuck you, I will not!" With her parents, her siblings

mildly interested in the reasons why this child chose to fray, not
stirred because this coming from such a small person could only
top the hat off an acorn, that's about all. For Danny to smile sin-
fully and catch his breath, a state he feared, but which the evil
inside him welcomed, purveying, surveying. For future stake of
the land (body). For Grace to be trapped in knots, panicking,
flailing, trying to release her hands and toes from strings. "It's
coming! It's coming!" she would scream. With her parents, her
siblings mildly confused because this just wasn't like her after all,
not stirred because the thorns in her eyes blocked her, not them.
For Meggie to breathe in moans, enjoying how they feed her, anticipating the forbidden pleasure of a force willing to wrap its fingers around her throat. For Dan to beat the walls, throw his wife,
scrape the corneas off his children's eyes.

The chair no one should sit in welcomed Elizabeth (she has a
right to sit down in her own home). She faced the fragmented
reflection found in the tiny windows of the back porch door. Her
nose had been cut off, moved to the right side of her face. Her eyes
were uneven, one almost up on her forehead, the other down by
her ear lobe. Her smile was crooked, too, like the banished trying
too hard, the freaks who had been mistaken for monsters, but who
only want love. Her clothes changed. Gone were her Adidas, replaced by black boots. Gone were her jeans, replaced by dusty
pants smudged like old newsprint. Gone was her red blouse with
buttons down the front, and gone were her breasts, replaced by
flat crisp whiteness and a necktie worn looped under the chin, its
ends laid flat, one across the other. Frightening. The fragments of
her reflection were starting to make sense. (Anyone call for me?)
Fuck this. Fuck this house. Whatever I become is not my fault.
This invasion is not my fault. Elizabeth stood up and shook her
arms, feeling as if dead leaves were being pulled from her fingers.

* * * *

The spit hung from her hair as she watched her husband crouch and push. A heave, a hoist, a boost. Pale lips smacked against dry teeth, gums. "You make me sick," he spit (again), spoiled, from his mouth. Meggie watched as her husband pushed the sideboard back to where it belonged, over there against the wall, right by the doorway. Annabelle and Danny watched from the other doorway (across the other way), as their father placed things back to where they were supposed to be.

"I didn't do anything, Dan," Meggie said quietly, with a single stem, steadfast but knowing her place, looking down at the floor, inviting by different actions, rearranged words, rearranged drawers, a top, and a mirror (belonging to someone in the family who has long since been dead). She knew. A smack. Of his lips again and the back of his hand against the woodwork, a self-bruising.

"You make me sick," he spit, the saliva this time landing on her cheek. She didn't wipe it off. Her eyes kept their color but changed their shape. They were now diamonds lying on their side, pointing to both heaven and hell.

A heave, a hoist, a boost, a straightening of the knees. A standing up, a wipe above the eyes to announce that the work was done. A tinkling of far-off crystal reminded them that it was still in the air. It (many things) would move (be moved) again. Did they think they could stop it?

"Oh, he does, he does," Meggie later told Annabelle and Danny. "Things, things that should be practiced only by newlyweds." Annabelle frowned at the ground and Danny wondered. "You don't even want to know what kinds of things," their mother added. "I told some of my friends," she whispered, coming in closer, first looking around. "And they said they didn't do such things. They didn't." Annabelle looked up and tried not to squint while confusion covered her like a sheath. Danny wondered what friends.

"Here, here," she said, holding up the magazines. "Look what I've found. Dirt. Dirt it is," she said while Annabelle and Danny's eyes were tied to a woman with too much flesh on her and exposed. A naked fat lady with her legs spread and her mouth on something (what *was* that?). With a wink and a smile toward her audience, proud of her excess, but with a hint of dullness to her eyes. Oh, scarred. It is. All scarred. "He hid them, but I found them," their mother said. "Going to have a bonfire," she added to the conspiracy (were they in on it?). "Tonight. After he leaves. I will. I will." She sighed. Annabelle and Danny still couldn't cut the strings that held them to that lady trying to entice, her breasts larger than they knew possible, the puckered brown of which the first time they saw such a thing, the hair and pink between her legs making them wonder (why was her hand fiddling down there?).

"No, no," their mother continued in a low voice, away from, but to her children. "My friends don't do such things." She sighed. "But, sometimes I do. I do," with resignation covering her one tar-backed quarter at a time, until she was covered with tarnished circles, with only the diamonds (again) with sunken-in sides in between allowing her to breathe, matching her eyes. Annabelle looked back down while her imagination taunted her with thoughts of her parents, destroying her. Danny wondered why so much cutting takes place. On small wooden boards, old picnic tables, roll-top desks, stained sheets, lives, and sometimes even marble floors (he's sure). A coming down of knives. Molecules cutting molecules. (Isn't that what he learned from that chemistry book? It's not the actual physical body (image?) cutting another, touching, slicing, but its surrounding molecules offending, assaulting. An illusion ravaging an illusion (image), with its unseen borders doing the damage.) Next to tackle boxes, open fires, caves, his mother's heart, his own eyes, his father's skin.

CHAPTER 18

Annabelle opened her eyes and felt the blood filling her mouth. She put her fingers between her open lips to double check as she sat up. But, she couldn't see. It was too dark and there were strange shadows in this house. Where was she? Her mind was unclear and she was starting to get scared. Her heart started to pump loudly and a dog barked outside, slicing the fog.

"Carly," Annabelle said. The little girl in the sleeping bag next to her made dull, wet smacking noises in her sleep.

"Carly," Annabelle said, this time in a more urgent whisper.

Carly opened her eyes and stared at the dark shape of Annabelle.

"Something's wrong," Annabelle said. "I think it might be my tooth," she said in distorted syllables.

Carly sat up and reached for the lamp next to her. "Let me see," she said in a soft excited tone, as if she were about to get in line to see some forbidden carnival exhibit. She turned on the light.

"Eeeww!" Carly said while smiling. "It looks like it's hanging from its root!"

"Yes," Mrs. Saunders said minutes later, as both Carly and Annabelle stood before her. "It's hanging from its root." Mrs. Saunders had on a frayed, dull green terry robe, tied at the waist, and six large curlers, three on each side, in her hair. "I could wake Mr. Saunders up, but I would feel better if maybe your own father did this."

Annabelle nodded her head with her still half-way open mouth, afraid to close it, and walked steadily back into Carly's bedroom, as if she were balancing a crystal vase on her head.

"Do I get to come?" Carly asked her mother.

"No, you stay here with your father," Mrs. Saunders said while putting her long coat on over her robe.

And probably for the first time in her life, Annabelle rode through her town, any town, at 3:37 in the morning. Mrs. Saunders repeatedly tried to wipe the sleep from her eyes as she stopped at ghost-town traffic lights and slowly curved around deserted corners. *All* of the houses looked scary at this hour, Annabelle thought. The Shorts' house, usually bright and welcoming with its window boxes and yellow shutters, looked even more eerie than the houses that didn't look so cheery during the day. There it sat, with its bright paint and its closely cropped lawn with tulips (it now being spring—came so fast!) by the front steps standing perfectly erect as if they were plastic. The moon was gone and it looked like this house was trying too hard, as if hoping to lure lost children to its door so that it then could show its true colors and make way for its crookedness, decrepitude, two glowing eyes that watched from the broken dark windows, and anything else that went along with shadowed haunts of the neighborhood. Annabelle wished the other kids at school, the ones who make fun of her, could see these houses now. Then maybe they wouldn't be so quick to point and exclaim that Annabelle lived in a house of terror, that it held secrets even these kids' parents wouldn't speak of in hushed tones. They would see that sometimes it was just the light, residue from a fading moon, that distorted and changed things. Annabelle shivered and Mrs. Saunders turned up the heat in response, keeping her focus on straight ahead. The other houses passed by, almost hidden more by the silence of such a time than the darkness.

"Here we are," Mrs. Saunders said, almost too cheery, as they pulled in Annabelle's driveway. Mrs. Saunders eyes flickered for a moment when she looked at the house and then she said, "I'll walk you to the door."

"I don't have a key," Annabelle said.

"Oh, well. I suppose we'll have to ring the bell."

"That'll wake my parents up," Annabelle said, worried.

"Well, honey. That's why we're here, so your dad can fix your tooth." Mrs. Saunders kept her hands on the steering wheel and looked at the garage door. Annabelle, with her mouth still open, looked at the dashboard. Minutes passed and whatever life was outside the car seemed to start to hum.

"What time does the sun come up?" Annabelle asked, holding her hand to her chin.

"What? Oh. Well, it depends on the season."

"It doesn't come up the same time every day?"

"Well, no."

"Oh."

They sat for a few more moments and then Annabelle said, "I should be getting in now."

"Well, alright. I'll walk you to the door."

"We could go around to the side, but I'd have to pound on the window," Annabelle said.

"Oh. Well, maybe we should use the front door."

"Okay."

They both walked toward the door, with Mrs. Saunders' pink slippers and Annabelle's fire red Keds crunching dewey tips of blades. Annabelle reached up to ring the bell and the sound echoed as if the house held nothing but empty rooms and faded wallpaper. Annabelle could hear the familiar heavy steps of her father walking toward them and she looked down, trying to close her mouth.

"Hi, Dan," Mrs. Saunders said when he opened the door. He was wearing boxer shorts and a white t-shirt. Black thin socks covered his feet, making his calves look that much whiter.

"Well, what's this?" Dan said with a smile as he looked at his daughter.

"Annabelle has a tooth coming out, but it's still by its root and I thought it best just to bring her home."

"A tooth! Well, that's fine. I'll just get the twine and we'll tie one end to the doorknob . . . "

"*Daddy*," Annabelle said.

"What? You don't want to do it that way?" her father asked teasingly.

Mrs. Saunders laughed. "Alright, Dan," she said as she turned and left. Annabelle walked into the house and Dan shut the door.

"Do you still want the twine?"

"*Daddy.*"

"Just checking. Okay, let's see what we have."

Annabelle opened her mouth even wider and Dan placed his large fingers inside, making Annabelle squirm.

"It's okay," he said soothingly. "Just hold still." He twisted and turned the root, all without her feeling it, and then he carefully raised the tooth back into the socket and then gently pulled, pulling back his hand that held the tooth and root and all.

"There it is!" he said. Annabelle smiled. "Upp," he said as he looked at his watch. "If you hurry you might make the deadline."

Annabelle looked at him.

"For the tooth fairy," he explained. "She has a four fifteen deadline."

And Annabelle smiled again and her father picked her up, knowing that he wouldn't be able to do so much longer, and he climbed the stairs while his daughter laughed and he sang, "Hi ho, hi ho, it's off to bed we go. We work all day and get no play, hi ho, hi ho, hi ho . . . "

"Daddy?" Annabelle asked as she climbed into bed, ignoring the fresh folded laundry her mother had put there a few hours earlier. Her father pulled the covers up over his daughter.

"Yes, shrimpkabob?"

"Is there really a tooth fairy?"

Her father grew thoughtful, one of the few times Annabelle had seen him like this, and then, after a moment, he said, "Of course there is. You'll see in the morning." He stood up and seemed to be the tallest man she had ever seen. He walked over to the door, turned out the light . . .

"Daddy?" Annabelle asked again.

"Yes?"

"Can you leave the bathroom light on?"

And he left her door ajar, walked across the hallway to the bathroom, and reached for the light. Its stream came gently through Annabelle's room, and Annabelle sighed, not caring that this night held no moon.

And when the sun was shining and all night traces were gone, Annabelle rose from amidst her crumpled old sheet and leftover blanket she found in a closet somewhere, shaking each piece of clean laundry that had been left on her bed, looking for evidence that the tooth fairy had been there. And sure enough, after she shook out three tops, two pairs of shorts, and about nine mismatched socks, a crisp dollar bill seemed to fly magically out of nowhere, landing on her foot.

* * * *

Annabelle had never imagined that another little girl would try to take her job. But, there she was, all blonde-haired and true, right outside the back door, holding an economy-sized bag of cat food. The kittens and cats were now mewing and circling by the little girl, sometimes standing on hind legs and putting forth front paws, tiny claws, showing their appreciation or, more like it, trying to grab their gift before a cruel change of the mind and it is taken away.

"My mom said I should come and feed them," the little girl said. Annabelle recognized her. She lived up the street in the house that screamed out names whenever Annabelle or her brother would walk by (they pretty much left Elizabeth and Grace alone, or maybe her sisters just didn't come back with reports like she and Danny did).

"But, they're my cats," Annabelle said. (Danny didn't mind; he had lost interest after so many had found him, scared of the power of wishes.) The little girl pursed her lips as she bent down to feed them.

"My mom says they don't get fed. Not in this house, she says. She says it's a sin."

"I feed my cats," Annabelle said.

"Not all the time. And they're always running out in the street getting killed." The little girl topped off the cat-food bowl like a bartender topping off a beer for a man who had just lost his job. She cooed something to the cats and then turned on her heels, taking the almost empty bag of cat food with her. Annabelle bent down and took the bowl of cat food, walked around to the side of the house [much to the dismay of the following kittens (how many? oh, well, there are three over there, and two by there, and three more over . . .) and the one remaining grown cat], and dumped it into the trash. She then went into the kitchen and poured her own cat food, topping it off like a bartender who had problems of his own.

Purrs and fur and tiny souls. There's something to be said for these. When they're not getting underfoot, causing pain when they get punished. Like the time Annabelle's father took Smokey, the grey, gentle cat (one of the two who had found them), and threw her up in the air so high that she became a far-off speck, like a baby pigeon foolish enough to think that just because he didn't have wax for wings he could fly to the sun, be the hero when he came home with a glow in his eyes. Annabelle had cried, "Daddy, don't!" But, he didn't listen. And when Smokey came back to earth, she landed squarely, unjustly, on her spine, offending a law of nature, disproving tales of wives.

But, Annabelle supposed her father was angry because ends of bargains hadn't been kept. He did agree to only one kitten, after all. And then hesitantly to two. ("So they won't be lonely," his son had pleaded.) But, never, never, not in this world (the corners were changing) did he ever agree to ten, fifteen, more even. He did not count on two more cats finding his home, his house, leaving their litters by the trash cans at the side of the house, as if they had been roaming the neighborhood and sensed a giving in, a small bend here. ("Can we keep them, *please*?" his children had begged.

"Well, they *are* too young to turn away," his wife had said. "We'll keep them until they're old enough to be weaned," she had said. But, four weeks soon turned into two months and for lack of a reason except failure to notice the time, soon these little kittens pranced and pounced and took advantage as if they knew they were home.) No, Dan did not count on these litters, with his own having a hard time telling who was coming and going, and for what reason.

Yes, it was true. There were too many and they sometimes did get killed. Like the time Dan was backing out of the driveway and he ran over one, with Maureen across the street seeing it before it happened, waving her arms, trying to get him to stop. Like the time Annabelle came home from school and saw a black one with a white throat split and splayed in a shoebox, looking as if it were asleep if it weren't for the exposed white intestines that looked almost fake and plastic but which were a travesty against such an innocent, sleeping face (another lesson teaching her how to keep down bile). Like the one (this one grown) found frozen right outside the basement window, curled and huddled as if it had mistaken itself for a bear and thought it could get through such times.

These cats caused another mark against the Owenses in this neighborhood (the children realizing it more than the parents), but they saved Annabelle's life. Or so it seemed. The times she sat on the side step and sung to them, lulling them to sleep and her away. The times they slept by her side, their beating little hearts soothing cells that sometimes thought of abnormal ways. The times they just returned stares, helping by offering eyes that didn't look away.

CHAPTER 19

"Strike the devil from my soul," Elizabeth prayed. She knelt by her bed, with Old Man Kane's light slanting across her forehead. She remembered how earlier that day Annabelle had gone into her room and borrowed a pen without asking. She remembered how, when she found out, she took her little sister by the shoulders and shook her, all the while screaming, "STAY THE FUCK OUT OF MY ROOM! STAY THE *FUCK* OUT OF MY ROOM! AHHHHHHHHH! AHHHHHHHH! *FUCK* THIS *FUCK!*" She remembered Annabelle's look of surprise and then her tears and their mother saying to Elizabeth, "Was that necessary?" as if Elizabeth only had taken the last piece of candy hidden in the refrigerator crisper drawer. The webs of this house finally latched onto Elizabeth's soul, its strings pulling pink tissue away from bones. And there wasn't a thing she could do about it. Except pray, she supposed. But she felt it winning. At first, her anger had been used for many things—for distance and protection and others' guilt, wonder at what they did wrong ("Why, Elizabeth, what have I done?" in eyes, sometimes words, taking whoever would wonder away. Good.). It evened things out somehow. But she couldn't control it anymore. Now it was becoming a part of her. With every sip her mother took of her Coke with the crushed ice her father had split into pieces himself, showing his love and devotion by bringing the mini mallet to the cubes with a force the countertop had never known before; with every natural shift of an eye or brow while another responded to an innocent inquiry or followed the playful path of one of the new kittens with their eyes; with every barely noticeable flare of a nostril as someone quite deservedly drew in a breath, with all these, as well as most other minor and major disturbances, Elizabeth felt the black flames of the fire she had pretended to have burn within her now snap with heat for real. This all had surprised her at first, of course, but then she got used to it. Took it on. Did she have a choice? Her eyes narrowed in injustice and her mouth scowled in lost causes. The whites around her irises bled with blended capillaries and the color of her skin turned sallow.

"If looks could kill, you'd be dead," her grandmother had said loudly to Danny during one Sunday night dinner. The rest of the table laughed, some uncomfortably and some authentically, with Danny looking perplexed.

"What does that mean?" he asked again and again. "What does that mean?"

"I think it means," Meggie began. "That you look . . . "

"Elizabeth gave him one heck of a look," Meggie's father interjected, correcting whatever it was his daughter was going to say.

"Oh," Meggie said. "I thought it had something to do with his glasses."

"There's nothing wrong with my glasses," Danny said, pushing them back up on his nose. "They're new. I just got them."

"Of course there's nothing wrong with them," Meggie said. And then "They're new," loudly to her mother.

"That's nice," Addie said in the same tone. "But, if looks could kill . . . "

"He'd be dead!" Annabelle finished.

"I would like another roll," Elizabeth said coldly.

Grace handed her sister the basket of rolls and then looked straight across the table into the china closet at her own reflection. She liked studying herself in different situations. Here she was as cool as the rust-colored water that made the lake over on Park Avenue look like it was covered with a sheet of dusty, maroon glass. No ripples could be seen in her reflection. No curls of smoke could be seen coming from her head. Not like Elizabeth. Grace shuddered. Whatever was happening to her, she wanted no part of it.

Elizabeth, who sneered and hissed and screamed and cursed, in short spurts, without warning.

"What's wrong?" Grace had asked one day as Elizabeth lay on her made bed, with her hands behind her head, glaring at the ceiling.

"Go fuck yourself," Elizabeth had said. Grace drew in a breath and frowned. She took turns staring at her sister and then the floor, half hurt and half hoping she could help somehow. Elizabeth ignored her sister for a few moments, then she turned her head, and her eyes narrowed and threw daggers straight into Grace's chest.

"I SAID GO *FUCK* YOURSELF!" Elizabeth screamed. Grace gasped. "*GO! GO! GO! GET OUT!*" her sister screamed again. Grace grabbed her notebook and ran out of the room. Elizabeth waited for the fall-out, but none came. She stayed on her back on that bed, scowling at the same small streak of paint that had dried into a long, thin, permanent teardrop. She must have fallen asleep because, later, it was the sound of her mother in the hallway saying, "Well, I think she's just disappointed," that woke her up. To whom she was talking and why she thought Elizabeth was disappointed weren't clear. Elizabeth just froze even more than she was and hoped that her mother wouldn't come in and dispense some of her light-hearted advice such as "Oh, Elizabeth, I just think this is one of your phases," or "You just need to go outside," as if tidying up the surface of an old, battered piece of furniture, whistling while knowing that all the deep, ragged scars needed was the light touch of the feather duster.

The door opened slowly, creaking and croaking as the person behind it stopped and then started again at least three times. Elizabeth shut her eyes tightly and clenched her fists, which were now down at the sides of her thighs. The person behind the door was now in the room and Elizabeth could tell by the sharp, full breaths that it was Grace trying not to breathe too hard, her full effort having the opposite effect. Elizabeth kept her eyes shut and soon

the light was switched off, so that now the darkness that filled
Elizabeth was outside of her as well.

Elizabeth climbed in her side of the car. She looked at her
father. His profile made his nose look longer than it was and it
jutted out to the front, as if it didn't trust the driver and wanted to
navigate the way itself. Elizabeth felt hopeless. Each morning it
got worse and worse. Waking up each morning in the same room
on the same dark side of the house slowed her blood and dragged
her bones. What did she really have to look forward to? Her senior
year of high school? College after that? They were too far away.
Elizabeth didn't trust them to come, even though it was now the
end of June and her senior year would start in the fall—just a few
short months away (just a long hot season away). But, that didn't
help. Elizabeth knew not to be fooled by the promise of things
that hadn't made her happy before. Why should she look forward
to school when being surrounded by fellow classmates whose worst
problem was a pimple in the wrong place did nothing but deepen
her position, so that the hole she was standing in almost came up
past her shoulders? Why had she looked forward to the end of this
past school year? Because now she had no reason at all to get up,
move, even go to the refrigerator for some orange juice, readying
for her position of eyeing those in the rest of the world who just
don't understand—or if they did, they would look away in an
almost embarrassed repulsion, causing Elizabeth to reach down
and cover herself with her own shame of from where she came.

"I don't want to be here," Elizabeth said. Her father looked
over at her, with the red from the traffic light casting a small, fiery
circle that reached out into the night.

"We're going to get you a new field hockey stick," he said, as if
she had asked a question rather than stating anything solid.

"I want to die," she said as the words spilled from her and
pulled her arms and legs down so that she now sat slumped in the
passenger seat, like a used-up rag doll. Her father looked both
ways for oncoming cars even though the light was now green. He

carefully pulled out into the intersection and then built up to a
steady pace of thirty-two miles per hour as the summer air poured
in through the vents. He wound down his window even further
and then said, "Nah," while looking ahead. "You don't want to do
that. Then you can never come back. Once you're gone, you're
gone. Can't change your mind," he said matter-of-factly. He slowed
down to let a woman pushing a baby stroller cross the street and
then cleared his throat and brushed the tip of his nose, signaling
the ascent back into open road. And the words from Elizabeth's
father did affect her. She did look at them one by one, considering
them, turning them over in the palm of her hand as if she had
never seen them before. And that was something at least. That was
something.

$$* \ * \ * \ *$$

"God, please let me stop seeing. Let me stop seeing other
people's thoughts. How they swim and swarm above. Put me with
the others. They don't seem to be going through this. Why can't I
be like them?" Grace prayed. She sat on her bed with her flute
across her lap, praying while the mouthpiece reflected a delicate
angle of light back toward her. "Put me with the others," she said
softly out loud. Grace was tired. She was tired of the mist that
followed her and circled her head, so that all she could see were
tears and anguish and laughter and hope. When people stood before her bright-eyed and new, she could see their wishes and plans
and how they had stepped over the cusp of the latest tragedy,
deciding to abandon their doubt and trust again, thinking maybe
this time it will last. Grace couldn't see into the future. It wasn't
like that. But she had seen enough to know how it works. How the
happiest of times get pricked, as if there were some unspoken rule
that the spirit can't be too full or it would float away. How, toward
the end, despondency gets lightly stroked so that the darkness
slowly dissipates, without the distressed even realizing it, so that
they open their eyes and think the spirits to which they have prayed

decided to give them their gift right then and there, abruptly pulling them out of the chasm. Not realizing it was the gradual dance. It never ended, this way or that, and Grace just couldn't take the interrupted continuity of it all.

Elizabeth with her flames, Danny with his episodes, even Annabelle with her challenges—well, *she* gets angry, irate, annoyed (more like exasperated), too, sometimes, needs an open valve, an open something, to straighten the knotted twists in her stomach.

"She's fat and she smells," Grace had said a few days earlier, trying on these words as if they were a new hat, inspecting her reflection in this mirror and that, seeing how it feels, seeing if this way would be easier somehow.

"Oh, Grace! Stop it! This just isn't you!" her mother had said. Her mother was driving her to her friend's house for a pool party. Meggie had innocently asked how Melissa was doing, trying to show some interest in her daughter's life away from them all. Grace had contemplated her mother's question, thoughtfully staring out the window at the squirrels that climbed all the way to the ends of the branches and hopped onto the telephone wires. And without ceremony, without a formal announcement to the world, Grace decided to go against her nature, just out of curiosity's sake of where that might take her.

"She's ugly, too," Grace said, not meaning it, actually visualizing Melissa's soft blue eyes Grace had always admired.

"You can't keep this up," Meggie said.

"I can try," Grace said.

Meggie put both hands on top of the steering wheel and moved her body forward, peering through the windshield as if she were trying to find her way through a storm. Grace blinked from the sun and shifted her body uncomfortably as she tried to get used to her new take on things.

"It's just not in your nature," Meggie said.

"Well, fuck that," Grace said, surprising herself by not even choking on these words, by imitating Elizabeth so well.

"Oh, Grace," Meggie said, taking her rightful place as she did with Elizabeth.

But her mother was right, for when Grace got out of the car and saw Melissa and the rest of her friends, without her control, the kindness and balance crept back into her soul, making things even again.

But Grace still took on others' emotions, problems, even if it was temporary. When Kelly Piper from her chemistry class had been diagnosed with manic depression, Grace first fell into a deep depression herself, walking around her house barely lifting her head, wondering what kind of world would strike such a nice girl. Then, when she lifted her head, the sun was shining so brightly through the dusty and smeared windows that she thought the rays were traveling from other planets just for her. She ran through the porch and out to the backyard, spinning and holding her arms far and wide, opening herself for any other wonder of the world.

"Grace, you just have to stop taking on other people's problems," her mother had said. And Grace tried. She really did. She tried to bend down and lift the boundaries so that they encased her once again (for the first time, really), but the edges kept slipping from her hands so that the walls folded like the body of an accordion, hitting the earth with a thump, leaving her bare and exposed, not knowing where her tragedies and triumphs ended and those of others began.

And when she did try to assert herself, lead her own life and view others' problems simply as an observer, the wind would somehow swirl around a maple tree in the opposite direction and pull Grace back. Like the time that girl sitting next to her in geometry class cheated off of her during a test—Grace didn't want to break her commitment to the fairness of things (a commitment she had made before she was born) in such a bad way, that sometimes she went above and beyond and threw herself into the frenzy of it all, not realizing that tormenting yourself does not make it all better. That day, Grace hadn't even realized that Donna C. was sneaking peeks at her test, passing off Grace's answers as her own. And Grace felt bad after Mr. Steineger caught Donna, knowing that Donna would most likely be expelled (since this was her fifth time, caught that is).

"Well, I don't know," Grace had said, looking at the contorted face of Donna C. as she managed to drum up some real tears as they all sat in the principal's office. "I *may* have slid my paper so that Donna could see." Of course, Mr. Steineger and Mr. Romano, the principal, did not take this how she meant. After all, Grace had meant that, in the cosmos of things, perhaps she was used, without her knowledge of course, in a way that had contributed to the downfall of another. She had to look at all sides, after all. Perhaps whatever made Donna want to cheat somehow seeped from Donna's pores and found its way across the aisle, pulling Grace's arm up just a bit, so that Donna had a clear view. Perhaps it wasn't all Donna's fault, you see. Of course, Mr. Steineger and Mr. Romano had no understanding of this kind of thinking. Who would take the blame for something they didn't do? So, Meggie wasn't about to try to explain it to them when they called her in for a conference. She just said that Grace sometimes gets confused and that she is sure that her daughter wouldn't knowingly allow someone to cheat. Look at her grades, her record, after all. All perfect. And all achieved on her own, without cheating. Well, they said, suppose we try to start all over with Grace? Just have her serve a couple of detentions, that's all, they said. And Donna C.? Liar. Cheat. Crocodile teeth, tears. Well, she seemed to recover. She didn't get expelled and never said a word to Grace. She would just pass Grace in the hallways and smile in a devious way, as if she knew she won and thank God for the stupidity of others, which helped her to do it.

Grace placed her fingers on the keys of the flute. She lifted them up and then down again, over and over, listening to the small pop sound the key pads made as they opened and then closed the holes. Was her prayer over? she wondered. Would God know when it was over, at what point to stop listening and then go on to another? But, just in case, just in case He was waiting for some sort of closure, Grace zipped up her prayer in her mind, putting it in its own little case by saying, "Please let me be normal. Just let me be normal."

* * * *

Meggie dumped each one of the potatoes into the boiling water, resulting in a plinking sound and scattered wet heat pricking her wrist. That's funny, she thought. A new smell was floating in the corners of the kitchen. It wasn't that of soft charcoal, which sometimes wavered over there by the dishwasher, and it wasn't that of dying roses, which sometimes hung bitterly in the air over here by gas stove. It was blackened earth. That's all Meggie could come up with—dry, cracked grass that had been burned and blackened the earth. Hmm, she thought as she watched the water boil again up over the potatoes. She reached for another pot in the storage area beneath the stove and then filled that up with water, too. She went to the freezer and took out a bag of cut string beans.

"What are you *doing*?!" Danny cried, his voice seeming to have come from nowhere.

Meggie jumped, dropping the bag. "Danny," she said.

"What are you *doing*?!"

Meggie reached down to pick up the bag, feeling uneasy. "Well, I'm cooking dinner," she said.

"But there's steam coming out of that pot."

"Yes, Danny, there is," his mother answered, losing patience. "That's usually how you boil potatoes."

"But you *know* that I don't like steam."

"Oh, Danny," Meggie said as she turned.

"What's that *other* pot for?" Danny asked, his face turning red with spots of deep black-purple anger creeping through.

"For the string beans," Meggie said matter-of-factly, filling the other pot with water.

"You have to use *two* pots?!"

"Yes, Danny, to cook dinner. You want to eat dinner, right?"

"But, the *steam*," Danny whined.

"Oh, Danny, I'm just tired of this! I am! I just am!" Meggie cried. She reached for the woven pot holder Annabelle had made her, but stopped just short of it to take note of the black, burning smell that now permeated the kitchen. A large crash came from behind. She quickly turned around.

"Oh, *Danny!*" she cried. Five dinner plates were now only broken pieces of fine china scattered on the floor, their jagged edges staring in surprise up at the ceiling.

"I told you I didn't like the fuckin' steam! You knew that! YOU KNEW THAT! YOU'RE JUST TRYING TO RUN ME OUT!"

"Danny!"

"YOU'RE TRYING TO RUN ME OUT!"

"I'm not!"

"I CAN'T TAKE IT ANYMORE!"

"I was just cooking dinner!"

"YOU KNEW!"

"Oh, Danny, you need help."

"FUCK YOU! FUCK YOU! I CAN'T FUCKIN' TAKE IT ANYMORE!"

"DANNY!"

And Danny ran from the kitchen out the side door and grabbed his bike, riding off in a state of hysteria that trailed behind him, its tail, horns, waiting for his return, hoping that it would own most of his normal moments from now on.

* * * *

The tape recorder looked bigger than it was as Annabelle tried to awkwardly balance it as she walked into the living room toward her mother.

"Mommy," Annabelle whispered in a conspiratorial tone.

Meggie off-handedly put the towel she was folding in her lap, crumpling all folded corners and smoothed lines. "What do you have there, sweetie?" she asked.

"A tape recorder," Annabelle whispered.

"Is that the one you got for your birthday?"

"Yes." Another whisper.

"Did you want to sing a song?" Meggie asked with a smile. She was in an especially good mood today. She didn't know why. She didn't ponder why. She did not consider herself an erratic person, but moods did come and go without her questioning them. The windows were open and the breeze swam in, filling the living room like water in a pool. She had awoken that morning with the sun warming her shoulders and Dan leaving for work. Elizabeth actually got out of bed today, saying hello to her mother before she took her bowl of peppermint ice cream (the only thing she seemed to eat these days, when she ate, that is) and went down to the cellar to watch T.V. Danny hasn't broken one thing in the past week and Grace has seemed to allow her eyes to be soft and clear again, at least it looks that way in today's sun. Meggie smiled at Annabelle.

"How about 'Old MacDonald'"? she asked.

"That's for babies," Annabelle said in her normal voice.

"Old MacDonald had a farm, eee-eye, eee-eye, oh, and on his . . . " Meggie began to sing as she picked up the towel and began folding it again.

"I don't want to sing."

"Oh. Alright."

"I did something, Mom," Annabelle said, whispering again.

"What's that, sweetheart?"

"I taped it."

Meggie looked at her daughter. Annabelle's eyes were determined, but still as round as a child's.

"Listen," she said. Annabelle pressed the "play" button.

"I WILL NOT HAVE THIS, MEGGIE! I AM SICK OF THIS! LOUSY CUNT!" boomed from the box.

Louse as a cunt hung in the air.

Meggie could hear crying and sobbing in the background, at first wincing as if she were being privy to someone else's torture, but then taking her hand to her mouth, widening her own eyes as she realized they were her own wails. A piece of wood could be heard cracking and splintering on the tape, probably a piece of some furniture that wouldn't be able to be repaired. Annabelle shut off the tape, knowing that her mother had heard enough.

"See?" Annabelle asked. "I have more. I got the whole thing. Now you can get a divorce."

After this particular fight, which Meggie thought had been about two or three nights ago, both Meggie and Dan had mentioned divorce. Who brought it up first was not clear, not even to Meggie and Dan, but the kids' had cocked their heads so that their ears could hear again, hoping that it would be said again. Dan had paced the kitchen, with remnants of anger still clinging to his clothes and Meggie was leaning against the countertop, with remnants of tears drying on her cheeks, rims reddened and jowls at an all-time low.

"We should get a divorce, Meggie," Dan said sternly.

"I want a divorce," Meggie said at the same time.

The children were all sitting at the dining room table, well after dinner had ended and the dishes put away, as if they knew their presence was mandatory or there would be no other spectators to this latest event, causing them all to disappear, which would be much worse. Elizabeth had lifted her head and looked straight into the kitchen in hope and Grace and Danny and Annabelle had done the same thing. But the subject was never brought up again. Not that night. Or other nights (to come). Dan continued to buy his wife her Coke at that special deli that poured it over fine crushed ice, the only way she liked it, or crushing the ice himself, as touched upon before, which would be the only kind gesture toward his wife his children would remember when they are grown. And Meggie would continue to accept that tall styrofoam cup, wrapping her warm hands around it and looking down into the liquid that looked as if it were filled with shards of glass, her mouth watering at the prospect of it sliding past her throat.

Annabelle hadn't known why at the time, but she reached for her tape recorder that had been sitting on the sideboard and recorded the latest . . . the latest . . . recorded it all. When it had started, it came to her. Some angel must have been floating, flying near, whispering suggestions of future preservation in her ear. "Go get that tape recorder," the angel must have whispered. "To show your parents what they're doing," she must have said. "So that they stop and leave and make the break," Annabelle was sure she had said.

"Oh, honey," Meggie said, still looking at the tape recorder. And then, "That's a shame," to the laundry that was still waiting to be folded.

"Now you can get a divorce," Annabelle said.

"Oh, honey."

"Why not? Why can't you do that?" Annabelle pleaded, her veins pulsing from her neck. "Let's just *leave*," she said.

"Oh, honey," Meggie said, realizing that somehow the living room must have been drained, for she no longer felt surrounded by summer breezes, only thoughts of how depressed Elizabeth seems to be these days, how confused Grace is, and how violent and even more tortured Danny is becoming. And poor Annabelle. Her baby. She was trying to hang on as best she could.

CHAPTER 20

Meggie stood at the front door and rang the doorbell. This didn't even cross her mind as being odd, even though it was for the first time. The other times she had just walked around back, opened the door, and went right in, casually beginning her casual visit, knowing that this was her family and she would always belong. But this time was different. She had an announcement, or was going to attempt an announcement anyway.

"Hi, Daddy," Meggie said as her father opened the door. His backbone seemed to be bending over more and more these days, but his face still looked as young as it did when Meggie had been a girl.

"Someone wants to say hello," Norman said with a smile while his dog yapped and barked and jumped up to put her front paws on Meggie's legs.

"Hi, Dutchess," Meggie said as she bent down to pet the Lhaso Apso.

"Are you saying hello?" Norman sang to his dog. "Yes, we have a visitor. Yes, Meggie came to say hello. Hello, Meggie, she says. Hello. Okay, Dutchess, that's enough. Okay, girl. Oh, Dutchess, go lie down! I said, lie down! Go! Go! Go!"

"That's okay, Daddy," Meggie said.

"Oh, she's a pain in the . . . That's a good girl, Dutchess. That's a good girl. You lie down." And then to Meggie, "She's a good dog."

"Yes, she is," she said. Meggie looked over and saw her mother sitting on the portable toilet in the living room. Her stockings were stretched and bunched at her ankles and her floral house dress was pulled up so that its bottom edge now rested on her thighs.

"My treasure," Addie said while she smiled.

"Hello, Mother," Meggie said and then went over to kiss her mother on the cheek while Addie was still sitting on the toilet.

"Best thing we ever did was put that thing in here," Norman said.

"Norman, I'm finished!" Addie yelled.

"Oh, for crying out loud, I'm in the same room as you are!" Norman yelled back, grumbling all the while he went over to help his wife. "Come on, Addie," he said as he helped his wife up off of the toilet. She wrapped her thin arms around his neck, with their sagging skin dancing back and forth with each puff and huff her husband made.

"Did you wipe yourself?" Norman asked his wife.

"I don't need to be wiped! I already did that!" his wife yelled while her dress fell back down to her mid calves and her legs swung stiffly as if made of wood while her husband started to lift her to her chair. "I can wipe myself! I'm not an invalid!" she added. After she was in the chair, she indignantly picked up the latest Ellery Queen magazine that had been sitting on the table next to her and plopped it down on her lap, giving her husband an irate look.

"Oh, Addie," Norman said. He looked over at Meggie. "You're early tonight."

"Oh, I know," Meggie said, not giving a reason.

"My bowling tournament doesn't start until seven."

"Oh, I know."

"Meggie, you're early tonight!" Addie yelled.

"Oh, Addie."

"I know, Mother."

"Norman's bowling tournament doesn't start until seven! It's only quarter of five!"

"I know."

"Addie! I just said that!"

"Well, how am I supposed to know?! I am *deaf*, you know!"

Norman laughed. "What do you want?" he asked his wife. "Salisbury steak or chicken?"

"I suppose the chicken," Addie said.

"Do you want a T.V. dinner?" Norman asked his daughter.

"Oh, no thanks, Dad. I already ate."

"We have an extra one. Pepper steak with scalloped potatoes."

"Oh, no thanks, Dad."

"Alright." And Norman went into the kitchen to put the T.V. dinners in the oven and Meggie sat in the rocking chair next to her mother, grabbing a pad and pen first so that she could write down what was going on in *All in the Family* for her. And Addie stared at the television expressionless while Edith ran to get Archie a beer every five minutes and Meggie wrote furiously—only during the commercials did Addie give in to splinters of raucous laughter as she read what Meggie wrote.

As her parents finished up their dinners, Meggie's throat became dry and her breaths more frequent. She was now sitting on the sofa and her father was in the rocking chair next to her mother. She saw mostly their backs, seeing barely a hint of their profiles.

"I like having Meggie here early," Addie said to Norman.

"Yeah," Norman trailed off while he ate the last of his cherry cobbler which wasn't even as big as a single card from a deck.

"Daddy," Meggie said, her voice croaking in the middle. "Daddy, I'm thinking about . . . Dan and I may be getting a . . . um . . . a divorce."

Her father sat motionless, staring at the television, but Meggie could have sworn she saw his shoulder twitch a little. It was her mother who turned around toward her.

"What?" Addie asked. Norman started to write on his small pad of paper. Meggie looked down at the ground.

"I want to get a divorce from Dan," Meggie said.

Addie stared at her daughter and then took the pad of paper her husband had handed her. She read the note and she sunk back further in the chair, with every muscle seeming to retract back toward her heart. "What!? What!?" she screamed.

Meggie started to watch the tail end of *All in the Family*. Why does Edith run around like that? she wondered.

"There will be no divorce in this family!" Addie bellowed as best she could with an old woman's voice, which was worse in some ways because its shriveled shriek cut through the room in uneven lines and clung to the walls like an old stubborn vine.

"Oh, Addie," Norman said softly.

Meggie began to cry. "It's awful! It's just awful!" she cried while she stood from the sofa, taking center stage. "You don't know! He's awful to me!"

"There will be no divorce in this family!" Addie bellowed again, not looking at her daughter, but announcing this to the woman who was trying to convince young mothers that Pampers were the way to go.

"He's killing me! I'm dying! I'm actually dying!" Meggie cried, falling to her knees, sobbing with her head in her hands.

"Well, now," Norman said, not sure which way to go, if he should back up his wife and stand as erect and nonflexible as her in her cause or soothe his daughter, throwing custom and dignity to the wind so that they could be carried far away, the striving for which would never hurt his child again.

"Well, now," he said again, still deciding.

"Norman!" Addie yelled. "There will be no divorce in this family!" as if he had just announced to his wife of fifty-five years that this marriage thing wasn't what he really had intended after all.

"Daddy!" Meggie cried, still on her knees. Dutchess was confused and spent her time going back and forth from Norman to Meggie, occasionally going over to Addie's feet, exploring the bolt of emotion there.

"What's going on?" Alfred asked. He was still in his mailman's uniform and was holding an opened Yoo-Hoo soft drink.

"Nobody's getting a divorce!" Addie screamed at him.

Alfred jumped. "I'm not . . . I'm not getting a divorce," he said, defending himself, feeling his heart beat as if he had done

something wrong, even though he had never promised to stay with *anyone* through health and sickness, bad times and good, for the rest of his life. "I'm not getting a divorce," he said again, not thinking of using the argument that he had never taken a wife.

"Your sister!" Addie shrieked. "Your sister is going to disgrace this family!"

Alfred started to peel the label of his Yoo-Hoo. "Oh," he said.

"I'm an old woman and I'm sick!" Addie cried.

"Addie!" Norman yelled.

"I am! I'm old and I'm sick! Look at that toilet over there! Look at those railings on the walls! I wouldn't need them if I wasn't sick!"

Meggie continued to cry and Alfred took a sip of his drink.

"I'm deaf, too! Can't hear a thing! Not a thing!"

"Oh, Addie!"

"I thought she could hear thumps. You told me she could hear thumps," Alfred said to his father.

"Addie, for Pete's sake. It's not the end of the world if . . . "

"I'm dying," Addie said. "I'm just dying."

"Oh, Addie," Norman said as he felt the swirl slow somewhat, taking away the dizzy feeling from them all. Meggie was still crying but her head wasn't in her hands anymore.

"I'm going to go home," she sniffed. "Alfred, can you stay with Mother tonight?"

"Well, I was going to work on my screenplay," he said as he shifted from one foot to another.

"Oh, well, that's alright. I can stay."

"My tournament's in fifteen minutes," Norman said.

"You go, Daddy. I'll be alright," Meggie said as she stood up from the floor, wiping her eyes.

"I'll be back around ten."

"You go, Daddy. Everything will be fine," Meggie said, taking her place in the rocking chair next to her mother. Addie continued to stare at the television, her eyes focused on the screen, but with an air of distraction wafting above her grey permed hair. Norman grabbed his bowling ball and then left, much to the dismay of Dutchess who followed him to the front door and then yelped and cried as she realized the escape plan hadn't included her. Alfred went to his room to work on his screenplay, but all he did was lie on his bed in his uniform, going over and over in his mind that comment his boss had made about how a man is only as good as what he does. Did he mean that Alfred does enough or not? Did he mean that Alfred is doing a good job for the post office or not? Did he mean that Alfred is wasting his time writing or not? Did he mean that . . .

Meggie grabbed the pad of paper and started to write down the beginning of the plot for her mother. Starsky and Hutch were looking for Huggy Bear. He was the only one who knew who might have thrown that poor innocent girl from the eighth-floor window . . .

* * * *

Norman wiped the wet mist that had somehow found its way to the inside of the windshield. He then turned on his windshield wipers even though the windshield was now clear. Something to do, he supposed, something to occupy his hands, his fingers. That's how he worked; that was his make-up. He always had to be doing something—rewiring light switches, replacing a missing shingle, clearing a pipe, fixing Annabelle's toy dog that was supposed to bark when you pulled its leash twice—that was the only way he knew and the only way he knew not to retire for real. What is this retirement, anyway? Some of his friends had taken it seriously and plopped right down into their E-Z chairs after receiving their engraved watches plated with gold. They sat to watch the birds, they said, something they had always wanted to do. But, the birds stayed only for a while, soon flying away to busy themselves with their own lives to lead, their own sights to see. But, Norman's friends still sat, determined to follow through with their dream of stillness that had gotten them through decades of hard work. And the sun would rise and the moon would swell through its hole in the sky, and the arms and legs of Norman's friends would soon be covered in upholstery themselves, forever stuck to their posts of stillness, causing these old men to turn their heads and wonder what time of night did this trick creep upon them. And their families would stumble upon them, wondering how such a large pile of dust as heavy as chalk found its way onto the old chair that Grandpa had been sitting in only moments before. And they would raise their hands to their foreheads and shield their eyes from the indoor sun and wonder where their loved one had gone, after a while finally accepting that they had lost him and it was now time to mourn. No, that wasn't for him, Norman thought. He'd rather die. Because, really, it's the same thing. But, he wasn't alone. He still had his friends at the bowling alley who felt the same way. Men with shrinking bones and white hair who still laughed like they had when they had been young husbands and fathers and even before, their eyes twinkling with prospects of the future.

It started to rain and Norman turned his wipers back on. He thought of his daughter. For some reason, sadness has always seemed to find Meggie. She wasn't like Emma, who decided at nineteen to move to Florida so that her life stretched out before only her, with only occasional visits and phone calls connecting her to her past. And Alfred, well, he may be a bit touched, but his life isn't surrounded by such trauma. Maybe it's better to not be quite right in the head but to be at least in a calm pool (at least compared to Meggie's life), slowly drifting toward this goal or that, knowing that it's not the end of the world, that you have something to fall back on if a ripple comes along and redirects your path. Oh, he's sure Alfred wouldn't look at it that way. He's sure his son would say, "But, it's my dream, my life, to write screenplays. I'm going to be in Hollywood some day. If I didn't *really* know that, I think I'd just die." But, Norman knew better. If it wasn't this dream for Alfred, it would be another. Like when Alfred was ten and he filled his rooms with rocks—everywhere—in his shoes, his coat pockets, his drawers, his hamster cage, telling his parents that someday he was going to be an astronaut and he was going to replace all of these with moonrocks. You wait. You'll see. It'll happen. But the dust of the moonrocks soon turned into clear, colored slabs of soft yellow and pink stone that had come with a chemistry set Alfred had gotten for Christmas, stones Alfred promised his parents he would make new furniture out of so that they could feel what cool, smooth things come from the earth every time they sit down. And after a few months, that turned into something else . . . what was it that time? Oh, yes, Alfred had boiled dead hamsters he had gotten from a pet store, removing all fur and skin, and then put the bones back together as God intended. Practicing for being an paleozoologist (a what?) someday, working with fossils, he said, real life bones from another time, he said. I have to know how things are put back together, he said. It didn't matter to Norman that his son had dreamed of being a screenwriter for, oh, about twenty some years now, that Alfred had two finished and three unfinished screenplays sitting in the top left drawer of his bureau and that he swore, above anything else, that this sixth one he was working on would be the one to give him the big break everyone in Hollywood talks so fondly of. To Norman, adult dreams were simply an extension of starry nights in childhood. People have to grow up, let go, and get to work. There's a lot to do. Oh, he wasn't heartless. Wasn't it just a few months ago when Meggie came crying, saying that Dan wouldn't pay for Danny's glasses, that the school had sent home a note saying that her son needed glasses and all Dan had said was "Well, *I* need new glasses. Who gets them for *me*?" Of course Norman couldn't deprive his grandson the right to see, so he went to the bottom drawer of the dresser in his bedroom and reached for the roll of cash stashed for such emergencies. "Oh, Daddy, thank you," his daughter had said, her eyes brimming with tears. She mustn't have told anyone where the money came from because that was the last he had heard of it, but that was okay by him. He was glad to help. He really was. Children should be taken care of. Especially his grandchildren. He didn't know what his son-in-law was thinking sometimes, buying a new bike (for one of the kids) at a moment's notice, but screaming (according to Meggie) that there was no money for new shoes or incidentals such as bedding and sheets the next ("It's perfectly fine for them to use their sleeping bags," Meggie had said Dan had said). But, he supposed that was his business. Norman didn't have the inclination nor the time to stop and try to delve into another man's mind. There's a lot to do.

* * * *

Meggie pulled into the driveway and turned off the car. She reached to the left to turn off the headlights and watched the shadows grow. They climbed up the garage door, over painted bricks, and across the slanted siding, trying to peek in through the heavy blue drapes that would prick your palm with their tiny sharp fibers if you were to admiringly run your hand up and down them. She stared at the dashboard and made a mental note about how that should be dusted one of these days. She didn't take her hands off of the steering wheel because that would signal the end of her short trip from her parents' house to here and she would have no option but to get out of the car like other people do. What would happen if she just stayed here? For an indeterminate amount of time? Let's say all night. What would happen? She'd probably get arrested, she supposed. Oh, she knew that it was her property, Dan's and her property, but she was sure that she'd be breaking some kind of law. "I'm sorry, ma'am, but you cannot just wile away the time like that. Not just sitting in your car like that, in the driveway, for everyone else to see," the young officer would say while holding his clipboard with one hand and flashing his light with another. "That's a means of disturbing the peace," he would say. "Oh," Meggie would say. "I'm sorry. It will never happen again," she would say, meaning dreaming publicly in her car, not promising that they wouldn't have to visit this house again. That she couldn't promise. The last time, Grace had called them. And the time before that, Annabelle. Elizabeth used to call now and again when she had been little, but she seemed to have given up on that somehow.

"Well, you know how kids are," Dan would say. "The slightest bump and they get afraid," he would say, out of breath, his face red, his undershirt hanging crooked from his rage that has since passed. The officers would smile. "Yeah, we know," they would say. "Ma'am, are you alright?" they would ask Meggie as she sat on the steps crying, with the sleeve of her blouse torn. She would look up at the sky and wonder where the afflicted go after they die and then she would look at the officers and nod her head yes, she was alright. It was over. For now. Don't bother the children. They were just trying to help. She wasn't sure which one had called this time, but they were just trying to help. The officers would touch their caps, turn to the sound of radio garble and waves coming from their hips, and then, when they reached the end of the slate path, one would lift his walkie-talkie and quietly spout, "Just a domestic," into its speaker.

"I want to die," Elizabeth said. She was leaning against the countertop, holding another bowl of peppermint ice cream, slumped as if she were melting, too.

"You don't want to die," Meggie said. She put her pocketbook on the countertop next to Elizabeth and then took off her coat. "The world is a beautiful place to be," she said unenthusiastically as she caught her reflection in the range-top stove. She needs her hair done again. It looks so limp.

"How's Grandmom?" Grace asked as she walked into the kitchen.

"Oh, fine, I guess," Meggie said.

"I want to die," Elizabeth said again.

"Elizabeth," Meggie said. "This world is . . . it's so full of . . ."

"Oh, yeah, how?" Elizabeth asked, slowly dipping her spoon

into her ice cream as if it were black, thick soup, her lids growing, folding down so that the colors of her eyes could barely be seen.

Meggie sighed. "Well, I don't know," she said to her reflection. "That's what people say."

"Is Grandmom going to get worse?" Grace asked.

"Oh, I don't know, honey," Meggie said. Grace stared at her with those grey eyes and Elizabeth stared at the floor with those dull eyes. "Maybe we shouldn't concentrate on sad things right now," Meggie said. "Elizabeth, why don't you come food shopping with me? You can pick out what we'll have for dinner tomorrow," she said in a tone mocking all cheery people without meaning to.

"No thanks."

"Oh, come on."

"No."

"Elizabeth."

"I don't want to."

"Well, then why don't you come anyway and I'll pick out what we'll have."

"I said I don't want to. I don't want to go shopping. I don't want to eat. I don't want to even be here."

"Dad already went shopping," Grace said. "He said he likes to go shopping this late because it's not crowded. He took Annabelle and Danny with him."

"Well, where do you want to go?" Meggie asked Elizabeth.

"I mean I don't want to be *here*. Anywhere."

"Oh, Elizabeth."

CHAPTER 21

Meggie looked at the body and thought, well, this is it, death has finally come. The stomach was swelled with bowels that refused to be emptied, with feces clinging on to intestines like caked mud to an old fence post, refusing to let anything as silly as nature cause its excretion. The skin was a dying green, covering the bones in a thin, haphazard way as if knowing soon that it, too, would be gone, shriveled away, like bits of cellophane that had been slowly ripped and then discarded. The eyes, when open, were the color blue of someone who is leaving, the same color of those of an infant taking things in for the first time, whose wisdom is still intact.

"Mother," Meggie said loudly. "Turn on your side so I can wipe you." Her mother turned without opening her eyes, giving in more to this type of defeat than that of which she had invited. Meggie pulled her mother's nightgown up, bunched up the wad of toilet paper, and then wiped between the two dragging, dimpled, withered cheeks, as if caring for a baby of eighty-five years. "I'm almost finished," Meggie said when she heard her mother groan.

"*Norman,*" Addie whimpered, an embarrassing testimony to what she had once been capable of.

"Daddy," Meggie called. And then, "Mother's calling you," as she heard scuffling from the next room. Her father walked into the living room.

"*Norman,*" Addie said again, with her eyes still closed, willing her husband toward her. "*I'm hot,*" she said as she opened her eyes, meeting those of her husband's like a dart to a bull's-eye.

"Oh, for Pete's sake, Addie. I just turned *off* the air conditioner for you."

"*Norman!*" Addie said, putting forth the best exclamation she could. "*I said I was hot. Can't you turn on the air conditioner in this place?*"

"Daddy, I'll do it," Meggie said. "Just let me empty the bed pan first."

"Oh, for Pete's sake," her father grumbled while walking over to the air conditioner.

"I'll do it, Daddy," Meggie said, even after her father had turned the air conditioner back on and was now walking out of the room toward the kitchen.

"*Norman!*" Addie said again, her eyes beneath paper-thin lids.

"He went into the kitchen, Mother. I'm here."

"*Meggie?*"

"Yes, I'm here."

"*Can't they turn on the air conditioner in this place?*"

"Daddy just did, Mother. It will get cool soon."

"*I'm so hot.*"

"I know. It'll be cool soon."

Addie opened her eyes. It took her a moment to find Meggie's, but when she did, she locked onto them as if she had reached out her frail hands which were nothing more than bundles and clumps of veins and grabbed onto her daughter's shoulders for life. For life. Where had that gone? It was only yesterday when she had had a baby. Wasn't it? Is that where she was now? It was too hard to tell.

"*Where's my baby?*" Addie asked.

"I'm right here, Mother."

"*My* baby."

"Oh. Emma? She's in Florida."

Images of sand and surf and seagulls permanently glued to the center of a sun on postcards climbed over and through the bumps and crevices in Addie's brain.

"*Who took her there?*" Addie asked.

"Oh. Well, she went by herself, Mother. You remember."

Addie squinted her eyes and felt her heart give an extra push against her chest at the same time. *"My baby, I said. I said my baby."*

"Yes, you're right," Meggie said, not realizing she was making things worse. "Emma's the youngest. Alfred's the middle child, and I'm . . ."

"Who the hell is Alfred?"

"Mom!" Alfred whined while he stood at the opening to the living room, holding an unopened box of tissues and a glass of orange juice. A glossy magazine was sliding out from under his armpit, out of his grip. Addie lifted her head and looked over in his direction.

"Oh," she simply said and then laid her head back down.

"She doesn't remember me," Alfred said.

"Of course she does," Meggie said while smoothing her mother's hair.

"She just said 'Who the hell is Alfred'."

"Oh, she's just giving you a hard time," Norman said as he passed his son with two pills in one hand and a glass of cranberry juice in another, his stooped spine almost causing his back to be perpendicular to the floor these days.

"Come on, Addie," he said as he stood next to the hospital bed. "Come on," he said in a voice usually reserved for Dutchess. "It's time to take your pill."

"You treat me like a stick," Addie said to her husband as she allowed Meggie to help her raise her head.

"That's it," Norman said. "Gotta take your pills." Addie allowed some extra cranberry juice to dribble down her chin in one whimpering act of defiance.

"There you go," Meggie said, gently wiping her mother's chin with the corner of a coarse paper towel, not realizing that Addie had meant for Norman to clean up this last small mess she was leaving to the world.

"She's not doing well," Meggie whispered to her father later in the kitchen.

"Hmph," Norman grumbled awkwardly.

"Maybe the kids should come tonight."

"Well."

"I'll go get them after we see if she'll eat her T.V. dinner."

"She hasn't eaten for days."

"But, we can try."

"She's a stubborn old woman."

"Oh, Daddy."

"She is. That's what the nurses in the hospital had said."

"I'll go get the kids."

* * * *

"Well, I was just wondering when you could pick her up," Elizabeth heard her grandfather say to someone on the telephone. "I was thinking of maybe having the funeral in a couple of days." Elizabeth turned and looked at her mother with wide eyes. What was he doing? She wasn't even dead yet.

"It's alright," Meggie said. "Let's go say goodbye. Come on. Annabelle? Grace? Come on, Danny, sweetheart. Let's all go say goodbye."

But she's not even dead yet. Why are arrangements being made? But,

"Come on," Meggie said again, taking charge, keeping sadness at bay, surprising it by lifting her finger to it, streaking it, acknowledging it. And there they went, like a mother duck and her fuzzy yellow babies going to their first funeral, awkwardly placing their webbed feet to the black asphalt, not sure how to react during the thin line between life and mourning.

"Mother," Meggie said, almost shouting. A body looking more like a corpse than any walking the earth shifted beneath the gray thin hair that seemed to have been sloppily pasted on by a five-year-old. "Mother, the kids are here. They're here to say . . . They're here."

Addie opened her eyes. She looked at Elizabeth first. Elizabeth had to force herself to look back when all she wanted to do was run. It was strange because all she had thought of the last few months of her own life was death. And here it was, as if proving the strength of thought, staring at her right in the face. Did it want her, too? Is that what she really wanted? She didn't know. She just wanted to leave. To go out in the kitchen and talk about the latest baseball game with her grandfather, even though she knew nothing of strikes and innings. To go outside and play with Dutchess or simply watch the dog as she ran back and forth, stopping and starting, in her fenced-in little area, barking at anything with a heartbeat. To take a walk around the block, remembering how she used to ride her bike in this neighborhood, how she knew that this, her grandparents' stake, was also her town, her house, but much safer than home. But, she couldn't. She couldn't let her grandmother down. Her grandmother, who would reach for her hands and place them on top of her own withered ones with long filed nails freshly painted with the red of Ruby Road. "You have my hands," her grandmother would say to her, proud that at least some part of her legacy would be carried on. "Oh, you're just like your grandmother," Meggie would say to Elizabeth when Elizabeth would get "in one of her moods," as they had become to be known, with Elizabeth hearing both admiration and disapproval in her voice. "Oh, your grandmother was a strong woman," Meggie would add, not being able to commit to the disapproval, smiling a bit and allowing her eyes to shine as she remembered stories of her mother's past that had been re-told and told, eulogizing a life that still breathed in that corner chair over there watching re-runs of bad television shows. And then, "She was a flapper, you know."

Elizabeth stared into her grandmother's eyes, feeling her courage build as Addie smiled, with Addie's wrinkles deepening as her soft flesh stretched across.

"My beautiful granddaughter," Addie said. Elizabeth's eyes started to water and Grace stepped closer, saying, "Hi, Grandmom." Addie's chest expanded, its shell laboring and creaking with each breath. She looked at Grace, mirroring her granddaughter's clear eyes with her own.

"Annabelle," Meggie said. "Don't you want to . . . "

Annabelle stepped between her two sisters. She stood on her toes even though she was much taller than the hospital bed. "Hi, Grandmom," she said, mimicking her sister. Addie smiled again.

"Grandmom," Danny started when it was his turn to come next to the bed. Grace and Annabelle were now across the room, busying themselves away from this, looking at the pictures of all of them on the wall. There were the girls when Annabelle couldn't have been more than a year old and Grace had been about eight. Elizabeth had been ten, smiling brightly at her future held in the camera lens, wearing her hair in pigtails. There was her mother when she was a high school senior, with her black hair waved and combed just so, a strand of pearls wrapping around just beneath her neck. And there was Aunt Emma, at the same age, wearing a fur stole and a diamond smile. Uncle Alfred hung on the wall at various stages and ages, and Norman and Addie also adorned this house, with memories of their black-and-white, old-fashioned wedding and days of marked change, holding a baby in this picture and two and three in those. Elizabeth stayed by the bed, next to Danny.

"Grandmom," Danny began again, hoping that maybe more words would come to him the second time. Her chest slowly moved up and down, stretching her skin on top and the worn, cotton fabric of her nightgown on top of that. Danny felt his throat give way to that tingly, runny feeling he gets whenever he's upset. He looked down at the bed rail, ran his finger across it, and then moved aside to go join Grace and Annabelle documenting a history that had been before them every time they had entered this house. Elizabeth stayed. She watched her grandmother sleep and even brought her hand forth to smooth Addie's wired hair. Soon, the tears came for Elizabeth and her tiny sobs came out, choked, interrupted, and strained. Meggie walked over to her daughter and put her arm around her waist.

"It's just her time, Elizabeth," Meggie said, hugging her daughter, somber in the depressed, sacred feel of it all. And then quietly, sadly, "Oh, Mother," as she herself smoothed out her mother's hair along with Elizabeth. "Just remember," she said as her hand softly stroked back and forth. She stopped and then looked down at the rug. She looked back up at Elizabeth, her face strong and sad. "Just remember," she said. "Her final thought in this world was that you were beautiful."

Was it Addie's time? Well, yes it was. But, she didn't agree. Not that day, week, or month. Her soul clung onto that body, curling its fingers and gritting its teeth, the beds of its fingernails bleeding as death whipped it here and there, using winds of such a force found only in the afterlife. But, she refused to go. She stayed in that old body, putting up with that decay rather than face something she was sure she didn't have any knowledge of. But, she also knew that the least of her advocates was time. It crawled and marched and danced toward her, so that she knew the day would come when her back would be turned and the innocent-looking spider in the shadowed corner over there would grow to be the symbol of death, pointing at her and summoning her spirit to follow his, cloaked in black and topped off with a hood, presenting himself as most had heard when legends were swapped and speculation soothed.

Three months and three days to the day her family had come to say goodbye for the first time, they looked around themselves, watching her soul fill the dusty living room for the last. (October it was, the second and last time here.)

"She's gone," Norman said gruffly.

Elizabeth broke down. Meggie went to console her, and Grace, Danny, and Annabelle looked at the floor in their own thoughts. Grace thought of the hugs her grandmother would give her, tightening her grip as each year passed, squeezing the breath out of Grace as she showed her granddaughter how love grows. Danny thought of the times at the shore when his grandparents would invite them all down to their one-bedroom rented apartment. He thought of how, during dinner, he would have to sometimes leave the table because his grandmother would eat with her feet up on a stool and her curled, yellow toenails reminded him too much of the macaroni and cheese that was being served. Annabelle thought of how she used to stand behind her grandmother's chair and quietly say "Fuck" to no one in particular, testing her grandmother's claim of deafness. Meggie thought of the last time she had had a conversation with her mother.

"I just want you to be . . . ," Addie had said. Her skin was now so tight and thin that it looked to Meggie like a skull was talking to her with her mother's voice. Grey permeated everything. Her mother's face, eyes, patches of scalp that showed between clumps of grey threads. It seeped out of her skin onto the bed sheets, causing the dusty rose they had claimed to be to wilt under the smell of death. It climbed the walls, sneaking into the pictures that boasted happy memories, causing happy faces recorded years ago to be newly somber, so that people posed on vacation, for graduation, or as first-time spouses or parents occasionally flickered their eyes here or there, trying to find the reason why. Addie, who was as white and black as they came, was now leaving in a clump of grey.

"I know, Mother," Meggie said soothingly.

"I've done some pretty bad things," Addie said.

"I know, Mother," Meggie said candidly.

"Our Father who art in Heaven, hallowed be thy name . . . " Addie started, accepting that she would soon have to follow that young girl over there who had been sitting in that corner for quite some time now. That young girl who had been waiting patiently and who reminded Addie of herself when she had been young, before the murkiness of life complicated things, confusing everyone. "Thy Kingdom come . . . I'm going to have to follow that little girl soon, Meggie."

"Alright, Mother," Meggie said, not thinking it the least bit odd that she herself didn't see anyone else in the room, not thinking it the least bit odd that she herself didn't stop to contemplate this at all.

"Thy will be done . . . " her mother continued.

You never encouraged me to follow my dreams, Meggie thought.

"On earth as it is in Heaven . . . "

You treated Emma so kindly, but you were hard on me.

"Give us this day our daily bread . . . "

You took a dog chain to my skin when I was fifteen minutes late coming home from a date when I was in high school. You broke a plate over my head when I was seventeen, just because I said, "What is this crap?" I didn't even know what it meant. You told me that I was going to be an old maid if I didn't hurry up and find a husband. You told me to stay with that husband even though he tortures me.

"And forgive us our trespasses."

You never told me the kind of woman you were. I had to hear it all from Daddy. I would have liked to have heard about the days when you were a flapper, about the boyfriends I know you must have had before Daddy, about how you loved to play the piano.

"As we forgive those who trespass against us."

You always called me "your treasure." Only me.

"And lead us not into temptation . . . "

I know you loved me, Mother. In your way. You were just acting from your times. I guess we all do that.

"But deliver us from evil."

You loved my children more than anything. You'll never

know how much that meant to me. You were such a good grand-mother.

"... happy," Addie finished in her mind, looking at Meggie.

"Hmph," Meggie said lightly, featherdusting, returning her mother's gaze, wondering what she was thinking at such a time.

Norman thought of how strange it was to find yourself in a life that had been in the making for years, its walls of clumped hard earth rising around you after the years behind circled and then went on ahead, burrowing a secure, related future, and then all of a sudden have that all taken away simply by the last breath of an old woman. Norman looked at his wife's body. You could tell she wasn't there anymore. You just could. Oh, Addie, he thought. What will take up my time now? It wasn't as if Norman hadn't loved his wife. He did, if love is waking up every morning taking for granted someone else will be there, bad or good. If love is overlapping your breaths with some-one else's heartbeat so that you aren't sure if that last blip was your own pulse or if it came from beneath another's skin. If love is busying yourself with another's needs so that, even while complaining, you thank God that you have a reason to move, scurry about, escaping the lonely, dark hole of just sitting and trying to remember the days of glory that had seemed to escape from your fingertips even while they were happening. And, of course, there were the early years. The years when his future wife would stir something in him by ignoring him every time he passed her station at the telephone company.

"Morning, Miss," Norman would say with a sparkle of mis-chievousness.

"Yes," Addie would say, business-like, quick and crisp, not interrupting her steady flow of connecting those in the outside world, so meetings can be kept, appointments made, hearts mended and broken.

"Nice day," Norman would say on other days, with a whistle at the end.

"Yes," Addie would say, not changing her routine simply because he changed his. But Norman kept at it, saying things like "Rain might be coming," "Old Sal in accounting is getting married, you know," and "Did you know I grew up on a farm? I still like to breed dogs now and again." And then adding quietly, "I can grow quite a garden," while he walked away, with Addie mistakenly mixing up two calls as she took a moment to watch him walk down the hall as if he were on a stroll in the middle of May. And two days after Addie's twenty-ninth birthday, she proved to Norman and the world that the slow knock of persistence does pay off, simply by answering, "I do."

Norman thought of how love does change. The world ages your marriage and your wife. In a blink, that woman with soft auburn hair you never knew could give you such pleasure on soft auburn nights is shriveled and old, sitting on a portable toilet in the middle of the living room. She holds onto her life by wrapping her sagging arms around you and digging her sharp, cracked nails into your shoulders, and you find yourself saying to your grandchildren, strangers who all of a sudden appeared in your life, "She wasn't always like this, you know," with each of them nodding their child heads, trying to look wise.

And in between, in between could be salvaged if Norman took the time. He could take one foot from the beginning and the other from the end and stand firm dab smack in the middle. He could open the windows and see the lines that were beginning to crease at the corners of his wife's eyes and mouth, the change in shape her face and neck seemed to be undergoing, and watch that first stirring of when she had been beautiful spread through his chest and heart, deepening his love for the woman who changed like the seasons, allowing the world, and his life, to go on.

"Is there life after death?" Addie had asked him, the last time she had spoken to anyone. They were alone in the room, with their children and grandchildren not yet there, just as they had started.

Norman swallowed. His own eyes were slowly changing, but it would take years before they were the color of Addie's. He took a breath and looked down. "I don't know," he said quietly, as inno-cently as a child at the gates of heaven.

Addie looked at her husband. It was the purest look she had ever given him. It seemed silly not to, at this point. "I guess I'm going to find out," she said.

"Arhmph," Norman mumbled quietly, trying to hold on a little to known demeanor because he was staying.

And Addie closed her eyes, still giving slow breaths to the world until the whole of her family was there.

CHAPTER 22

Readying for the funeral, Elizabeth took out the black blouse that had been hanging at the back of the closet. She unbuttoned the blouse and slipped it on. The silk felt good against her skin. She took notice of those things these days, you know—breezes that tried to sneak by the down of her skin; the powdered, fresh smell of sheets that had just been laundered; the soft fur of happy panting Dutchess at her feet—she accepted all of these gladly, silently expressing gratitude. It hadn't always been this way, of course. Oh, she had pondered (then, before the death), contemplated the feel, smell of things (then), but not these things, more like the feel of concrete against her cheek as she lay down in the middle of the sidewalk in the middle of last July (almost four months ago). She had felt the tiny pebbles embed themselves in her skin and the flat hot concrete level the one side of her face, so that if she were to stand with her face frozen that way, she'd resemble half a cartoon image of an old man, with creases and folds of skin where no real human should ever stretch and give in. She did this (then, no Jack with a candle where thoughts should be, smiling through a flame, during *this* time) because she was considering jumping out of a window. Any window would do. Preferably high enough to get the job done. But, as her mind opened to the black ooze of such an ordeal, what had first been just a fantasy became trapped inside solid walls so that she had no choice but to investigate her options (held by chains). And Elizabeth was committed to things, you see—goals, friendships (when finding friends worthy), and a state of mind. In the beginning (when it had been just a waxed surface that hadn't even dried yet), she liked standing out in a way, her mother scurrying like a bug here and there, asking Elizabeth, "But, what's wrong? What can I *do?*" Elizabeth knew fully that this wasn't *truly* how she, herself, felt, not deep inside (depressed? sunken? it just wasn't *like* her), but it was good for effect, maybe to get people to notice what's going on around here. Notice. But, soon (ahhh, soon) the cells of her brain slowed and chemicals unbalanced themselves, so that all signals pointed to, yes, Elizabeth, you really are in such a state. And Elizabeth hunched her shoulders and lowered her lids (back when . . . when?), dragging her feet as if they were uneven clumps of clay. But, there's something to be said for exploring choices, for right then and there (back in the seventh month of the year, containing 31 days—let's honor Julius, shall we?), while her skin had become punctured and streaked with stones and dirt (during consideration), a stick of light had pierced through the haze and she thought, maybe this isn't the best way to go. Too painful, she thought. Much too dramatic. A gun to the head? Even more painful, and where would she get a gun? Knife through the throat? Much too messy. And what happens if she changes her mind after the sharp steel has already punctured her larynx and the rivers and streams of blood have already escaped, staining her panicked, heaving neck and shoulders? Sleeping pills? Maybe not painful, but who knows what really happens when the soul is put to that kind of rest?

Oh, she had been in a fog, alright. It pulled her down with all one hundred of its arms, knowing that she had given it permission when she refused to get out while she could. She just had been thankful that the shades would sometimes lift and she could actually see what was going on. She forgot pieces, moments of, sometimes whole conversations. When in the mood to talk, she would unknowingly repeat stories, thoughts she had said earlier. When others would tell her things again, on purpose, reminding her, she was just as surprised as when they had told her for the first time. My, what a selfish point of view, she thought. How can I snap out of this? She felt her soul slipping away, holding on by one thin, twisted line of red, tinged with a pinch and a thumbprint.

"We have to get her out of this, Dan," Elizabeth overheard her mother say to her father, back when swelters heat. Elizabeth had peered around the wall, still in her pajamas at five-thirty in the dusk and saw her father look full steel ahead. His jaw was fixed in determination and his eyes were wide, but concentrating, as if looking at another life, the one he was supposed to live, with other children, another wife.

"Maybe we should send her to go stay with Mother," Meggie had said, back when rivets sometimes did poke, clinching it.

And Dan stared. And Meggie watched. And nothing else was said.

And so it was decided.

They would cheer Elizabeth up by sending her off to live with a dying woman. But, strangely enough, Elizabeth welcomed that. A change of scenery, a change of venue, situation, whereabouts— that would be good, the one healthy part of her brain told the dark, decaying rest of her. That would be good.

Back when swelters heat, this all came.

* * * *

The day Elizabeth moved in with her grandparents, she met Jesus. She had dusted where her mother's teenage prints seemed to still be, opened the drawers, and then placed her clothes into the waft of scraped cedar that emanated from the dresser. It was strange being in the room where her mother had grown up. Oh, she had been in here before, but those times had been only in passing (and when she was alive), like when she had been little and she would crane her neck just so (before the tar had found itself inside her brain) as her mother explained, "Elizabeth, this is where I stayed when I was a little girl," as if Elizabeth were a visitor to a museum that held relics and re-creations of times long gone. But, now it was different. Now Elizabeth was on the other side of the red rope, actually filling the antiques with her own clothes, although with viscid movement (that, from her brain?) and displacing the stale air with her own displaced breath (partial oxygen found, she'll take that temporarily).

That's when He saved her (does one moment count even if it lasts only that long?).

She looked at the small picture of Jesus hanging by the bed and then moved closer, feeling her courage build. At first, she had been afraid, you see, as if you surely weren't supposed to look at a picture like that on purpose, actually studying halos and light and calm magic that came from such spiritual eyes. The thorns that wrapped his heart (holding it?). That surely would almost be considered blasphemous—analyzing something like that so closely and objectively, as if on display (Elizabeth at first, while turning her back). No, you were supposed to take in a picture like that only in side-way glances and just knowing through the back of your head. That's how it worked. And then He would protect you, if you just accepted him that easily, as if He were an extension of yourself (you of Him). But, then, right there on that first day, with Jesus behind her, Elizabeth had grown strangely calm and thought, well, what are pictures for if you can't step close and bring your eyes to theirs? I mean, Jesus wouldn't mind. So she did. She turned back, stepped forward and innocently stared at the face that launched a thousand miracles, and then some. And no lightning scorched through the roof, no wails came from The Other Side, and no angels trumpeted their warnings from above. Jesus just smiled slightly and stared back.

CHAPTER 23

Dinner was when Elizabeth felt the most out of place. That's when her grandfather would set-up dinner for his wife, on a tray next to her bed, and then get his own tray and set it by the T.V., knowing Alfred was at work or with his own dinner in his own room. He then would turn toward Elizabeth, as if surprised each time he saw her and say, "Oh. Well. We need to get your tray, don't we?", trying to include her, trying to be polite, but not so rude (counterfeit) as to pretend she had become as part of his routine—as taking Dutchess out for a walk every hour on the two hours, as checking the eleven o'clock news for the latest scores of sport, as shining his ball (and sometimes shoes) to walk down the alley and drop a couple of pins all were. Elizabeth would have been able to see right through that, and that would have been worse. She stood around the edges of her grandfather bending to give his wife her juice, of him mumbling sharp words of the tongue while in the pantry looking for instant soup, and as he gently but quickly lifted his wife to a sitting position, compact and dense in the secure way things were run around here. But, as the hands passed (on the face), she didn't mind being at the rim, the margin where all loose buttons, stray bottlecaps, extra bobbypins, and fringe collect.

"When I was a young girl," Addie had started three years earlier, before the sickness, before it had touched either of them. Elizabeth had sat in the rocking chair next to her grandmother, who was sitting in her usual padded, corner chair, its flowers faded by the sun's rays that had bent through the smudged glass of the window. "When I was a young girl, I saw two fingers tapping on a saucer by themselves." Elizabeth relaxed her fingers around the pad and let the paper slide out from her grip and onto her lap. She started to rock back and forth slowly while looking at her grandmother.

"I could have only been around thirteen," Addie continued, content with the attention from her audience. "I was setting the table and I heard this noise. 'Tap, tap, tap,' it went. 'Tap, tap.' I looked up at my father and he was staring, concerned, at my mother. I looked at my mother and she was staring, scared to death, at one of the empty chairs. 'Tap, tap,' the noise went. And then I saw. I saw two fingers, just like this," Addie said as she held up two of her long, already aged (how time flies!) fingers. "Tapping on the saucers. By themselves. That's all I saw." Elizabeth smiled kindly, slowly and closed. "Next thing I knew," Addie continued. "We were all sent to our rooms. I asked my father later what had happened and he said that my mother had seen old Uncle Henry sitting at the table, looking as if he were ready to be served some hot rolls." Elizabeth now rocked while she stared at her feet. "Old Uncle Henry had died two weeks before, you see," Addie said. "Oh, I believe in ghosts," Addie had said. Elizabeth was surprised, not even knowing herself how this topic came up. She hadn't relayed any experience with such a thing, because she hasn't had any. Grace had said a couple of times here and there how she had seen, heard something, someone. But, how can you put faith in such a story that comes from someone who hears the past, sees things, simply by picking up an object and cupping her hands around it, warming it with her blood as stories, visions are exchanged? Elizabeth had rocked back and forth that day, offering her grandmother her hand when Addie had moved forward and reached for it, taking it in her own, saying, "You have graceful, beautiful hands. Just like mine. You get that from me." From her.

Three years later, when Addie was in the midst of finishing, everything, two weeks after Elizabeth had moved in, the slow, soft scent of lilacs started to fill each room, starting with the frayed carpeting, building up to the flat climb of the walls.

"Take this bell," Norman said to his wife, as Elizabeth stood by the edge of the living room, with her arms crossed but with her eyes open and her soul lighter, looking on, always looking on. "Take this bell and ring it when you need something," he said. "In case Elizabeth and I aren't in the room," he added. And Addie did. She rang it when she needed colder water, when she wanted the window opened or closed, or when she just needed someone to sit next to her, to break the cloud that was coming closer simply by walking through the room. And she must have even rang it in her sleep, for one night Elizabeth heard the tinkle of a bell break through the darkness in small stripes.

Elizabeth had groaned the small inconvenience of those not happy to be aroused, half-way between the thick of the night and that of her dreams. She sat up in bed, holding herself still while the flashes of light beneath her own lids and rushes of blood within her own head calmed to be even with her breath, which was now part of the hot night that had seeped in through the cracks of the window frame. She got up out of bed and reminded herself where she was as her bare feet crossed a strange floor, picking up a soft layer of foreign dust on her soles.

"Grandmom," she whispered, less for her deaf grandmother than for loam-filled spirits of the night, announcing she was in the room, hoping to break all shadows. The whir of the air conditioner traveled, with peaks, moments of clacks and clicks, padding all corners and crevices, making Elizabeth wonder if maybe she had dreamed the sound of the bell. Her grandmother lay still, her eyes closed, her mouth slightly open, her soul in other, temporary lands. Elizabeth stayed until her eyes grew adjusted to the dark, until she (the rim around her—her rim?) wasn't so afraid of those shadows anymore, and then turned and left the room, as if knowing removing mystery is comforting, yet dull, a signal for the time to move on. When she was back at her bedroom door, however, the bell was picked up and rung again, its sound bumping through the rifts in the artificial air. The shadows came again, snuck right up behind her, and she stood frozen, looking at her door, her back to all things. The next morning she had told her grandfather about it, saying that she thought that maybe her grandmother had rung the bell once, that she had even checked on it (afraid to admit to the second time, when she had climbed into her bed and hid under her covers, shivering on such a night).

"Nuhp, nuhp," he grunted. "I would have heard," he said.

"No, no," Addie answered later, drawn out and weak. "I slept . . ." so weak, were they coming to get her soon? " . . . through the night, yes," she said a moment before she decided to sleep through the day, too.

But, as with most rituals, this one was made without reason or permission, or at least not with both at the same time, and Elizabeth learned to accept the tiny tinkling that was made (most nights) with a round piece of metal the size of a pea. Was something trying to mock the system set up for the call for help? Or was it simply trying to participate, reaching its hand from an invisible grave, in a warning, perhaps, or just a gesture to be? Elizabeth didn't know and she wasn't one to ponder such things—that had been assigned to Grace, or to her own mother, or perhaps even to Annabelle or Danny, to parts of their personalities she hasn't yet seen (or never would, if the rules are followed). All she knew was that she was better here. Her lids were now lifting without hardly any effort at all; her ankles weren't weighed down with their own bones, feeling like prisoners of the very earth; and her soul wasn't as dense anymore, like a mesh screen that had been covered with black tar to ensure no air, no oxygen, not even through small pockets that seemed to hold no harm.

Oh, Elizabeth had to work at it alright. It took more than the smell of lilacs and a ghost's bell to bring her back (or take her ahead) to someplace safe. But, on those nights (when they visited), although somewhat still frightened, she managed to look past the hills and the grass, into lands that beckoned her, and stronger ones, which told her to stay.

* * * *

"Oh, your Aunt Emma and I never really got along, I suppose," Meggie said as she picked her slacks for invisible, imaginary lint, anything to allow the snip of her fingers to have a purpose. "She just, well," sighing, "she just was the cutest, I suppose. She got away with things. Was given more things," was spoken as a soft sour smell with a hint of periwinkle drifted through.

"I think you're very pretty," Elizabeth said, comfortable in giving compliments here in her grandparents' house, amongst new, impartial scenery, where the dust that had settled was from other people's wars.

"Oh, no, I'm not," Meggie said slowly, trailing off at the end. And then with a sigh, the end of which brought back a new breath of purpose. "I should wash these sheets," she said. "Have to get ready," she said. Elizabeth stepped back and allowed her mother to pass. Meggie stopped at the edge of the kitchen, bundled the dirty sheets closer to her body, cocked her chin toward the windows, turned, and then said, "It does smell like lilacs, Elizabeth." And then simply, "My," as she walked out of the room with dream-filled eyes on her way to the washer and dryer in a cluttered, old basement.

* * * *

"I suppose I was just raised that way. That was what was expected," Meggie said. She wanted more coffee, but she didn't stand to get it. The small lamp between them glowed in a memory, making a new one. She liked the feel of the kitchen, the yellow walls, what was coming out now. A slowness had overcome them both, and when their eyes met, outlines of bodies and roles turned fuzzy, and clear beings from clear times abounded.

"But, why?" Elizabeth asked slowly, kindly.

"Well," Meggie sighing. "That was what was expected," again, slower, but with no will that was ill.

"You're much stronger than that."

Silence.

"You are."

Just a sigh.

"You are."

"Maybe," with sad eyes, already thinking the past is the future.

"You are."

"Thank you, Elizabeth," with watery eyes, as appreciation to the effort of those who bear encouragement, although kind in thought, based on false adjectives, verbs, descriptions.

And Elizabeth grew angry but in a tired way, for how can you jump in another's soul and make them see what you see?

"How is everyone else?" Elizabeth asked while helping her mother change her mother's diaper. Addie let out a quick vocal streak of soft agony and then turned on her side with her eyes closed.

"Oh, they're fine," Meggie said, with a noncommittal note of music to her voice at the end, habitually reaching for the clean, damp washcloth after she habitually answered such a question.

"Grace?"

"Oh, fine. She misses you."

"I'm sure she doesn't."

"Well, she's a quiet one."

"Annabelle?"

"Oh, she still runs around, you know. Up the stairs, through the hall, still hides in the trees, that sort of thing."

"Why does she do that?" Elizabeth asked, more as filler while she handed her mother the talcum powder than authentic curiosity.

"She's just a child," Meggie said as she tickled and dried her own hands with the powder before she patted it on her mother's skin.

"Danny?"

"Well, I worry."

"What's wrong with him anyway?"

"Oh."

"What's going to happen when he gets older? Is he going to get worse?"

"Oh, I worry."

"It's okay, Mom," Elizabeth said as she watched her mother place the covers back up over her mother, taking in for the first time actions, soft worried and unworried words, thoughts read in the eyes, in the lines around the mouth, how much she does.

* * * *

"I think we have a ghost," Alfred said. His eyes darted to the front door and back, as if worrying some entity would enter through customary means or someone else would hear, shrinking Alfred simply by not believing him.

"Ohh," Norman grumbled, throwing dried hide to the dog.

"I heard it," Alfred said. "Last night. Didn't you hear it?"

Elizabeth raised her eyebrows and drew in her lips, innocently, looking down, as a gesture of not wanting to be involved. It wasn't so much the ghost she was afraid of (at least not now, not with the drapes warm with the sun and the bustling and sitting and taking up room that was now occurring all around her), as it was any drama, little or tinier, that involved Uncle Alfred. Oh, when she had been a baby she hadn't known any better. She had raised her pudgy arms to him and smiled her whole spirit through, not picking up on, or caring about really, what the adults thought. But then she got older and observed what those grown did. They pretty much stayed away from Uncle Alfred. Oh, they would sit next to him on the sofa or pass him the pepper at dinner, but a half-way roll of the eyes and then a steady gaze into another direction, a slight smile or a curt, quick smile (not even), or a small, shallow sigh, not feeding any of the internal organs, would occur—an-

other thin, flat block building the case that nothing Uncle Alfred had to do or say could be taken that seriously.

"Did you hear it, Elizabeth?" Alfred whispered while his father was grumbling again, looking for the green plastic caveman's club he used to discipline Dutchess by harmlessly smacking what was around her whenever she misbehaved.

"Well, I . . . " Elizabeth started.

"Dutchess, get off of there!" with a slam of the club against the chair. Elizabeth looked at her grandfather and then looked back at Alfred.

"I . . . I heard a bell," she said in a tiny voice.

"This house is haunted, Dad," Alfred said.

"Oh, for Pete's . . . " his father said. "All you kids are nutty that way. Ghosts. For the love of Pete."

"No, I'm not."

"Oh, for crying out loud."

"Maybe Meggie's ghost followed Elizabeth here."

Elizabeth looked up sharply, not anticipating that she'd be brought into this this way.

"I didn't mean to . . . " she started.

"Oh, for the love of . . . " her grandfather said as he raised his hands and then the volume of the T.V., drowning out all things impractical, insubstantial, imaginary, things that don't even have the clout to appear during the day.

But, these exchanges, with Alfred insisting and Norman putting so much effort into trying to swat his son's words away, didn't really affect Elizabeth. Or Meggie when she came over, which was more often these days. Meggie and Elizabeth were in their own soft cloud of grey, just like Addie was, maybe even with a hint of a rainbow.

CHAPTER 24

The viewing was more for the living. That has been said and will be said again. Especially where Addie is concerned, for when she had lain in that coffin carefully lined with everlasting silk red and had worn baby blue chiffon—an outfit she never would have believed she'd be caught dead in—she flew and floated, roaming through tunnels and grass, following the everlasting silk light. She was worlds away from mourners who mourned, spectators who watched, and the polite who came because it was the proper thing to do after all. No, she left them to mill among each other, where they will lend a pat on the shoulder or rub another's nose into an old, hurtful pile of family history. That's where they were, after all, and she just didn't have to go through that anymore. Thank God. Oh, hello God.

* * * *

Cousin Lillian was one of the middle ones to pay their respects. She had cat's-eyes glasses and was wearing a beret.

"I'm so sorry, Uncle Norman," she said sadly, the right way. Her husband, Cousin (by blood) Murray, stood behind, with an eternal half-grin on his face which was obviously not being wiped away even by a funeral.

"You're still living at the house?" she asked Alfred. Alfred nodded his head uncomfortably and she then moved on to Elizabeth. "You're there, too?" she asked.

"Yes," Elizabeth said.

Cousin Lillian then smoothly took in each of the children,

sweeping them all under one glance, stopping before she got to Dan, finally resting on Meggie.

"You're not all going to move in there, too, are you?" she said smiling, jolly in her own joke. "Oooh, there's Uncle Mo," she said to Murray. "I've been calling him forever for the book, but he never returns my calls." Lillian, intent on completing her tree of her husband's blood, connecting twigs and uncles and aunts and their fruit, raced up to Uncle Mo as he knelt by the casket, interrupting his goodbye to Cousin Addie by marriage, twice removed.

Emma and Alvina had flown in two nights before, too late to farewell to the soul but in enough time to stand by the body, showcasing it for the rest of the world. Emma stood high and sad, proud that she had to return home only for a funeral, not for lack of will to stay away (failure), not because of remorse for starting over twenty-odd years ago by moving away and up up (nope). She stepped into her place, as if following painted footsteps on the parlor's red rug, and her daughter stood in tow, holding her preteen head in lofty air.

And the rain outside bounced off of sidewalks and streets and the rain inside bounced off of these familial strangers, back onto those who were still and always would be, intertwined, tangled, belonging.

Meggie looked at her mother's shell. That's all it was now. She couldn't even call it a body. Bodies held things. Encased things. This did nothing but lie flat, almost rise to the ceiling in its emptiness if it were not for the quilted dust of pink that had been placed, covering from the toes to the folded hands holding a rosary.

"Meggie," Dan said, dutifully, husbandly, kindly. What did funerals do to people? she thought. People moved slower, looked longer, and less, said things they normally wouldn't and some they didn't mean.

"Did you have enough time?" he asked. Enough time? Who has enough time?

"With her?" he asked. Meggie looked at the coffin and then at the empty room except for those still caught in its web—her children, her brother, her father, her sister even and her sister's daughter, her family. Family.

"I'll be able to see her tomorrow," Meggie said. "At the funeral."

"I know," Dan said, still quiet, still kind, truth kernels growing, almost popping. "But it might not be the same," he said. What would change? she thought. "You might be distracted," he said. "With the day."

"Oh," she said. "Well, then maybe I better . . . " as she moved, walked, over toward the casket. She stood, being finished with kneeling from before [when the mourners (only visiting) had been there] and lifted her hand to her mother's new sleeve, coarse in its decorative swirls about the transparent wrist of still veins.

"Goodnight, Mother," she said. With soft tears. None that remembered harsh words. Not at this time. Family. A part of it was leaving, tugging, plucking at patches of skin of those who remained, of those who roamed the carpet of everlasting red.

Black, pecking crows. They were everywhere. And they matched the sleek black of the mourning limo that rode over wet leaves, its journey startled by a few slips and slides. Elizabeth and her mother, Aunt Emma and her daughter, Uncle Alfred, and Elizabeth's grandfather all sat in the long, dark car, appropriately pensive and somewhat sagging as they watched the drops of rain streak and fog. Elizabeth's father and her two sisters and brother followed in the family station wagon, which looked awkward and self-conscious, its boat of navy blue familiar with only canoe trips and rides to the shore as out-of-ordinary outings. After following curved streets that bordered curved, styled lawns, the limo pulled up in front of the house on a hill.

"Looks like you got a few visitors," the limo driver said, and then immediately looked out the window on the other side of the

car and then down at the seat, busying himself back into profes-
sionalism where the hired simply do not impose upon such times.

"Crows," Meggie said. And she was right. There they were, at
least forty-five of them, covering the lawn like a Halloween blanket. They picked and pecked, occasionally looking up with the
quick, nervous movements of those who constantly live in a state
of immediate self-preservation. But, they didn't fly away. Not when
the car doors opened and stiff, tired legs emerged and not when
the car doors slammed shut and these tall, immense beings came
forward surrounded with a quilt made up of uneven patches of fog
and grief.

And Elizabeth shuddered because she knew that they had been
meant for her. Long ago. When she had still been there. When she
couldn't get out. When she had almost given in and didn't think
about future pockets she was meant to fill. When she had thought
about knives and guns and rope, hoping to leave no clues for the
comfort of others. When she had been caught up in that evil.
Then, the coil had found her neck, wrists, ankles. Then, she wasn't
able to struggle, for the wires had been too close to her skin, threat-
ening to slice it. She remembered standing at her window one day
(back in Caeser's month), and how something had been kind
enough (or had an ulterior motive) to move the curtain ever so (for
her arms were pinned to her sides by her own doing), so that she
could see out onto the lawn. And there they were. Crows. Almost
gnawing at the grass and dirt with their beaks, scurrying and flapping and breaking and pulling, sometimes looking up at Elizabeth as if they were human enough to wear miniature black top
hats and corn cob pipes, with grins that did not reach the eyes.
They were sent, of course. To take her up on her offering. But,
before she had the chance to leave this gash, mutilating, offending
the world, the universe, really, her mother had come and saved her
life. Either with knowing or without knowing. By sending her
away so that small streams of oxygen laced with violets and prayer
could enter her darkened lungs.

And she had reclaimed her life by watching her grandmother

lose hers. By watching her grandmother fight and pull and give in. By watching her grandmother's eyes turn sweet and young while Addie reflected upon, relived. By watching them turn bitter and sour and old and accepting, then back to baby blues. And she had stepped back and felt the wire uncoil as her brain uncoiled away from the unnatural bent of things.

With her fingernails into the earth, she had held onto small things. Somebody smiled at her. A dog licked her ankles. A friend called. She allowed herself to ponder the corners of emptiness, the stopping of continuity, the redirecting of purpose, of all, her untimely absence would cause. Tragic. Unfair in the most of ways. Such a shame. Waste. Waste. Waste. And, she'd have to start over, somewhere she's sure, after spending an eternity in that funnel that would whip her around as she was shown scenes of what her life would have been like had she not given up. More smiles. A husband, maybe. Children. But, in better ways than she had known. Victory. A purpose. Work (but it wouldn't seem like it!). Dreams known as true. Love. And then after climbing out of that hell (of seeing what was *supposed* to be), with remnants of what could have been pasted to her skin, tattooed for others to see what she had given up, how weak, how faithless she had been, she'd forever have to live many lives, here or elsewhere, trying to regain, make up for a decision she had had no idea of what had been entailed.

She had allowed herself to wonder about moments that already happened and how they would have fit in the world had she left that much sooner, before them. Would the person who had smiled at her still feel the impulse to grin, looking foolish as they turned their head this way and that, wondering themselves what they were smiling at? Would the dog who had sat in her lap pace aimlessly, feeling lost, knowing that she had wanted to do *something*, she just wasn't sure what? Would the friend who had called pick up the phone anyway, dialing the time, the movie line, directory assistance, anything, just to hold onto her linear place in the world even though someone else had to go ahead and ruin the scheme of things?

That settled it. Elizabeth wasn't about to play with those kind of forces. Those kinds of games. Better to stick to the agreement, the one made up by spirits of light who were much more knowledgeable. And so, as sure as the frost that was starting to come (by now, seeing things in Grandmom's house), the sun that would always be, even when the earth is cold and dark, and as sure as her grandmother's last breaths, an earned exit, an appreciated pulse, Elizabeth decided to live.

Backthenaftershehadlefttheholeandwenttolivewithanotherghostand hisbellandhissmellwhenthelilacsfoundherandJesussmiledandcontinuity wasrestored

* * * * *

Meggie walked past the crows. She didn't give much credence, attribute credibility to, small, black creatures. Wasn't it just the other day when Annabelle had come crying to her, saying that all of a sudden cobwebs were everywhere? Poor Annabelle, she was overreacting a bit. Oh, the cobwebs were there, alright. On the walls, binding pages of books together, sewing up the open end of a pillow case, sometimes even closing Annabelle's own lids, with Annabelle squeaking with fear as she ripped the soft white sticky strings from her eyes. But, that was to be expected. Nothing out of the ordinary there. "It's just spider season," Meggie had said. "Quite normal," she added and she thought of her own webs, those that ran from the refrigerator to the stove and to the top lock of the window above the sink. Those that hung from the ceiling, draping passersby with veils made up of grey threads of glue, spreading upon, claiming any life that was silly enough to think they could just walk through. But, Meggie didn't concern herself with such things. She would just brush her hair with one casual sweep of the hand, not worrying that any microscopic progeny may have still lingered looking for threads of a different DNA to combine with their own. And now, she just walked past the crows, tiptoeing over them when they purposely stood in her path.

Meggie accepted the murmurs of others, not realizing she broke the softness of their sympathy with a too-loud "Thank you" or an out-of-place "Did you get enough mustard for your sandwich?" She flitted and busied, just like her father, filling up condiment dishes and breaking apart rolls with a butter knife. And when the doorbell rang and a ghost and death stood at the door, holding forth hands for more gifts, she didn't look nearly as surprised as the rest of them.

"I'll tell them to go away," Emma said, taking charge, self-appointing as always (it's easy when you're usually somewhere else).

"No, no," her father said, going back into the kitchen, stepping over a toddler who must be Cousin Agnes' new great-granddaughter. "I think I have . . . I do. I have something for them." And he came back holding a ripped-open, almost empty bag of Milky Ways, looking out through the front door when he realized they had been sent on theirs.

"They're down there by the corner, Daddy," Meggie said. Norman squinted and then took off, as best he could, as if a whistle had been blown for a senior citizen foot-race, with his one foot quickly (in terms of other imaginary participants), sloppily, whisking to the left and the other to the right, all the while stooped, with time winning in its sloughing of the bones. "Here, here," he called out as death and the ghost walked back toward their waiting, smiling, middle-in-the-class-of-things parents. The parents stopped their children and told them to turn around and wait for the old man. And they did. And they held open their bags as the old man offered the only thing he had left.

"Oh, that's right," Grace said back in the house. "It's Halloween." And then, "Grandmom. She was buried on Halloween."

And so, the myths, stories came from both sides. And Dan

raised his eyebrows, slightly annoyed that this way of thinking followed them even here, on supposedly neutral (well, inactive anyway) turf.

* * * *

Nobody had really taken notice when Danny had started walking. Some say it was the funeral, the first death he had known, that had caused him to roam, but yet, oddly, with a purpose. Others say it was *at* the funeral, in between the roast beef sandwiches and pound cake, when plans were being made, with the newly created finality of "it's now time to go back to how things were" responsible for cells jumping, flittering, needing a journey. They say they remembered him getting up off the sofa in his ill-fitted suit and walking to the door, pausing, hesitating before going outside, wondering (only for a moment) if he was ill-fitted for the steps. But, he went down them and took them anyway. Down, down, down, forward, forward, forward to the next set, down, down, down, forward, forward, forward over cracks and bumps in the sidewalk, forward, forward, forward, looking down, sometimes straight ahead where shadows were beginning to chase away the light of even the street lamps.

* * * *

Grace had lost her voice. Couldn't say a thing. Only scratches, the scraping of the pharynx and larynx, the peeling, paring of the esophagus came through. "Aihr . . . " she would begin. "Ehr?" she would ask. Some say it was the funeral, the first death she had known that caused her to struggle, to lose her sound. Others say it was Normal, who had a face, a wicked memory, who was coming back, waiting for all of the pieces, that had caused her to lose.

* * * *

Annabelle . . . Where was Annabelle? She always seems to be off somewhere, doing her thing. Well, that's good. Independence. It's always good to start young. Oh, there she is, they would say, see the trail of vapors?

* * * *

"But, I don't want to go home," Elizabeth said. "I like it here."

"I know. I know you do," Meggie sighed. "You enjoyed it here," she cooed, stroking her little girl's hair. "It was special. I know." And soon her mother's meant-to-soothe words got under Elizabeth's skin, passing through a cut on her forearm she hadn't even known was there. And the foreign matter aggravated, inflamed, causing emotions to heighten and patience to wane.

"Stop it!" Elizabeth shouted (but in a small way, really).

"I'm just trying to . . . "

"I'll go pack now, is that what you want?!"

"Elizabeth, we *miss* you. We're your family. You can't escape us," Meggie said seriously, innocently, not realizing that such words are usually meant for threats. "And besides, you're all better now," she added like a cherry on top.

Elizabeth sighed. "I'll go pack now," she said, emotionless, not wanting to win or lose.

"Oh, good," Meggie said cheerily. And then, "Won't this be fun?" as she shrugged her shoulders up like a child, worsening the frayed, annoyed tips of Elizabeth's nerves and causing her own to pause a bit. What was that, she thought. Was that fear? How strange. For she does want her daughter back.

When Elizabeth had left, saving herself, something, a rusty nail, an important piece of splintered wood, something, had gone with her, causing the rest of her family to swing and stretch (involuntarily), as if they had been glued onto the inside of a giant rubber band, falling victim to its whims and ways of redefining. At first, they all had been too polite to each other, visitors in another family's home. They would say, "Excuse me," and "If you don't mind," and "Only if you care to" and give short, nervous sprouts of laughter after saying such things as, "No, we had steak last night so tonight we're having ham," and "Are you almost finished in there? I need to take a shower soon," and "Yes, the flowers do look a little perkier now that we've had the rain." All ending with an inappropriate laugh. Checking themselves. Making sure it was alright. They were careful not to step too hard, for what else would that result in? But, they also knew it was temporary, and they anxiously looked ahead with worried eyes and familiar frowns, feeling almost secure in a strange way.

CHAPTER 25

The house had that stale, musty feel to it of a property revisited, yet now foreign, the only thing in common it has to offer is a shared past.

"Come on, come on in," Meggie said excitedly, swinging her arms to the side, pointing the way, with the same proud smile she had when this new addition had been a bundle in her arms, wrapped in soft pink.

Grace and Annabelle stood on the staircase, watching, cordial, quiet, as if a long-lost aunt had come to visit, had come to stay. Two cats stared from the upper landing, another from the living room, formal, watchful in its post. Danny peered in from the dining room, where he and Vinnie were holding a funeral for a flower, one of the few times Danny allowed himself to remain still these days, and Dan was just inside the doorway, now next to Meggie.

"Let me get these," he said as he picked up Elizabeth's two suitcases. He walked up the stairs, lifting the suitcases up over Grace and Annabelle with a huff as he passed them, winking as he twisted (or was that just his face straining)?

"Come on, come on," Meggie said again, feeling useful, precious in her role. "We're going to have tuna salad for lunch," she said. "And then I'll show you to your room," as if this was Elizabeth's first visit. But, Elizabeth looked around and she saw her sisters standing strangely hesitant, strangely curious, and she saw her brother looking intent, focusing almost too much on the dried, brittle leaves as he carefully lifted the dead, red corolla the color of Lucifer into an old shoebox. And she heard her father rearranging something upstairs, while a slow, faint whistle the width of a string passed through. And she felt the strangeness, she felt the newness. She wasn't out of touch, after all. It was a bit odd. I mean, it wasn't like home. Ahh, she thought, while images of saints and pleas and pacing strain and passing pain graced beneath her lids. And she smiled. Perhaps it could be, she thought, thinking of could be's, maybe's, and dreams. Perhaps it could be. She took a breath and after saying hello, it's nice to be here, to her sisters, following the stone path for visitors they had created for her, she made her way into the dining room, asking how are you to Danny and his little friend. And she even bent down to help Danny, apologizing kindly and sincerely after bumping into him acciden-tally, causing him to drop the box and startle the devil so that he jumped from his casket made for a size eight shoe. She cupped her hand and gathered all the flakes, all the dried crisps she could, telling herself that the dried crimson left there, in the cracks of the hardwood floor, would be no problem. It would decompose itself, she thought. Eventually. No sense in sticking her fingernails through the cracks to reach it, no reason to bend them back, away from the tips of her fingers, chancing that kind of pain. And she stood up, wiping her hands on her pants, placing her feet in a new position, not realizing that she had stepped into predetermined (as those forces had hoped, anyway) indentations, circled and curved grooves, permanent ditches glossed over with floor wax, filled with looking the other way. Not realizing that these holes complemented every bump and retraction, every curve and wind as the very bot-tom of her bones. Not realizing that they were even there.

And she breathed. She breathed in the air of new vacation homes, of forests on a mountain, of campsite dew and moss and early morning fire, and she smiled a bit, feeling hungry, looking forward to lunch. For no one quite cuts up an onion like her mother.

* * * * *

Norman had stood on his front step, waving. He waved to relatives who probably would not see him again until he was laid out, a stiff body in stiff, crisp clothes. He waved to his son who had finally decided to leave, taking a chance and moving to Hollywood. He waved to his daughter, Emma, and his granddaughter, Alvina, sad they were going but happy they weren't staying long enough to prick visions of perfection one often has of faraway blood. (He can still tell stories with pride, to his bowling buddies, checkout clerks who don't care, and others who are in line waiting to buy a half pound of liverwurst of how independent, how modern, how on-the-cutting-edge-of-how-things-should-be-after-all, his second-born daughter is.) And he waved to Elizabeth as his firstborn scooted her up and away, taking her back to the walls and brick she had known, which surely must be strangers by now. And he kept on waving, even after everyone was gone, until the sun was nothing but a fading edge against the earth, its light thin and stretched out, its glow almost a deep purple now. And he kept on waving, until the widows opened their curtains and peeked across the way, commenting to themselves what a shame—he lost his wife, he lost his life—commenting to themselves how a nice new companion could help him face that empty house, and how a nice new hairdo could help them get through that front door and pull the waving old man back in with them.

* * * * *

Elizabeth sat at her desk in her bedroom, new and hesitant, trying not to fall back in. "Senior year should be fun," she said to Grace, trying, which was strange of and in itself. The artificial twirls of words spiraled in caught waves toward Grace until she smiled and looked up at them, also trying (but this wasn't as new for her). And Grace reached for them with her hands, bringing them down to her lap. She looked at Elizabeth and smiled sweetly, her eyes sympathetic in what she knew her sister was trying to do. "And there's the junior and senior prom," Elizabeth added, hanging on. "Maybe we'll both go." And Grace answered with her eyes, Yes, maybe. That would be nice.

Elizabeth sighed. "It's sure strange to be back," she said. "I miss . . . " And Grace cast down her eyes, sorry for her sister, sorry for her grandmother who had to die. Sorry for her grandfather who would now probably immerse himself in electrical wiring; gas pilots; loose, slapping fan belts; and doorknobs that don't seem to be turning just right even more than he had before. Sorry for her mother because she was just acting too cheery these days (no one would be able to keep that up). Sorry for her brother because he was leaving his footsteps all over the neighborhood. Sorry for her little sister because hers couldn't be found. Sorry for her father because he just didn't seem comfortable, not even after these last few months of calm. Sorry for herself because the silence was growing and she didn't know why. Scared for them all because the point of break (reconnecting, really) may be that much louder.

"Maybe we could wear rose," Elizabeth said, breaking Grace's thoughts, bringing back her eyes to the moment. "We both could wear rose." Yes, maybe, Grace answered with her eyes. That would be nice.

* * * *

"It's very nice to have Elizabeth back," Meggie said to Maureen. Maureen stood holding onto her cart, studying Meggie. Meggie grabbed two double rolls of paper towels from the shelf and then placed one back, looking puzzled as if someone else had placed the extra roll in her hands.

"I'm so sorry about your mother," Maureen said. An old man holding coupons walked toward them and then stopped, nearly standing right between them, holding on to the bits of paper while he squinted at them and then up at the shelves, trying to make out the tiny type, trying to find his match.

"Oh, yes, well," Meggie said. "It was nice of you to come to the funeral," she answered, quickly, casually, but sincerely.

"I feel like we haven't seen each other in months," Maureen said.

Meggie gave out a little laugh, one of her new nervous ones. "Well, it has been." And then, "I'm sorry, it's just that . . . "

"Oh, I know," Maureen said kindly. "You had to take care of your mother. We all have to do that when the time comes."

"Yes."

"Are things getting back to normal now?" Maureen asked, trying to be light, trying to follow Meggie.

"Oh, yes," Meggie said, not touched by hidden irony that could be found if one had a shovel and a pick, or simply the edge of a fingernail or a breath on loose dust. "I don't like feeling unsettled," Meggie said with another laugh. "Now that Elizabeth is home, that unsettlement is leaving a bit I think."

"But, she'll be going off to school soon, right?"

"Oh."

"Right? She's going off to college."

"Hmm," Meggie said as if this was the first she heard of her daughter's plans to walk on her own.

"Oh, it will be alright, Meggie," Maureen said with a smile and kind heart. "Everything changes. Nothing goes back."

"Yes."

"It's kind of good, don't you think?" Maureen asked.

"Yes," Meggie said, looking at the old man who was still there, almost frightened now because he couldn't find the two-ply toilet paper with quilted softness that had the red label.

* * * *

Danny walked past the shrubs, trees that were losing their leaves, and neighbors that thought he was losing his mind. He walked under the moon and with the sun as it tried to heat the cooling days. He walked through neighborhoods he knew and those who, if given the choice, wouldn't have his kind. He walked until the soul of his flesh forgot why he had started and the soles of his feet wished he never had. And when it was too late and the last or first hours (depending on how you looked at it) would come upon him, he would walk to his home, marching through the front door (much more a formal statement this way—he was still working, after all) and around, around, around, sometimes lifting the edge of the circle by going upstairs, sometimes taking it down by going underground to the basement, and sometimes even pulling, extending it, by going through the porch to the backyard, so he can walk through the trees, stepping on blades of grass of his own, on top of tangled roots as thick as gristle.

* * * *

Dan paid the bills. Dan cooked dinner. Dan shook the president's hand at work. Dan went out to lunch with the most important clients. Dan was working on inventions of his own (maybe some day he could break out—but, did he really want to?). Dan played with his kids. He did a lot, you know. Worked. Played. Worked. He had his house, his suits, his canoe, his favorite chair on the porch. His family. Steak almost every night. All things he worked for. Staying on that line. All things he deserved. And if the line should bend, split in two, he would not give up his things. He would wave goodbye to those trying to balance on fragments, on unfastening ropes that even a flea circus would turn away for not being secure enough, and he would stand straight and erect on his tight line, placing a napkin in his lap while he sat down to eat well. Steak every night.

Thank God for practicality. It cut webs, closed the cellar door, saved yourself from a loosening of the mind.

* * * *

Dan looked at Meggie. She was pretty. She's always been that.

* * * *

"I've circled everything I want this year," Annabelle said. She lifted the JCPenney catalogue up off her lap, handing it to her mother as the pages flopped in their own weight, causing the book to look like a heavy, awkward horseshoe.

"That's nice, sweetie," Meggie said as she took the catalogue from her daughter. "Did you bend back the pages that have what you want?"

"Yep!"

Meggie smiled.

"Mommy?"

"Yes, sweetie?"

"How far away is Christmas?"

"Well, not far."

"Is it the next holiday?"

"No, Thanksgiving's first."

Annabelle slumped, but with a small smile on her face. "Oh," she said as for some reason her face blushed. "I want Christmas to be first," she said quietly, still with that smile, with that red face, looking slyly up as if she thought tradition just might rearrange itself if a child asked in the right way.

"Oh, honey," Meggie said. "We have to have Thanksgiving first."

Annabelle groaned. "Oh, alright," she said as she sat up straight in her chair.

"Mommy?"

"Yes, dear?"

"Um, where's Grandmom now?"

"Oh."

"Is she in heaven?"

"Hmm."

"Where is heaven?"

"I don't know," Meggie said, looking to the ceiling and then around the room as if she was looking right there and then to find the answer for herself.

"Is it up in the clouds?"

"Well, I don't think actually in the clouds."

"If you stood on a cloud, would you fall through?"

"Now, Annabelle."

Annabelle giggled. "I know. We learned the types last week in school. There's cumulus, there's . . . " Annabelle then seemed to interrupt her own thoughts. "Hey, Mommy?" she asked.

"Hmm?"

"Can Grandmom see us?"

"Maybe from time to time."

"When she wants to?"

"I think so."

"What if I'm going to the bathroom?"

"Oh, Annabelle. I think she'd stay away then."

"Good." Annabelle watched her mother sew the stained, old tablecloth that Annabelle needed for her tea parties. "I'd like to see her grave again."

"Well, we can go next week," Meggie said as she pulled the needle through, looking down at her uneven stitches with her uneven brow as she studied them.

"I'd like for her to see me then. When I go to visit her."

"I'm sure she does. I'm sure she does. Yes," Meggie said, lulling herself into this new rhythm. In, out, up, down (depending on how you looked at it), through and through. Small things. The unimportant as the important. This was nice.

"She was a good grandmom."

"Yes."

"But, you didn't like her as a mommy."

Meggie looked up, surprising herself that she still gets startled by a child's eyes. They were so clear and big. With heaven blue, whatever, wherever, that was.

"No." A breath. "But, I suppose we all just try to do the best we can." In, out, up, down, through and through, making rhythms to find new grooves, to forget old scrapes.

"I like you as a mommy."

"Oh, sweetheart. That's because you're such a good little girl to take care of."

"You're not having any more kids, are you?"

"What?" A thump in her chest.

"I don't want any more kids in this family," Annabelle said.

"Oh, sweetheart, we're not going to have any more kids." What a strange thing to say.

"Because then we'd be stuck," Annabelle said as her mother pricked her index finger, with the blood adding another stain.

* * * *

Grace was at a friend's house. (Her friends didn't comment much on her lack of words these days—that wasn't why they wanted her company anyway, for words. No, Grace brought a balance to things and her voice had nothing to do with it. So, when they would sit and talk of boys and clothes and boys, they felt an un-usual calm whenever Grace was around, sitting in the background, as if she was there to check things, to make sure no springs broke or valves loosened—which would have caused them to forever fall into holes of it doesn't matter much.) Annabelle was also at a friend's house. Elizabeth was upstairs in her room. And Danny was roaming the world of a three-block radius.

Meggie was tired, but nervous, a dangerous combination. She was noticing things more and more these days. She noticed scratches in the furniture, scratches on the wall (who had done that, with claws?), and old faint scars of scratches on her face. She noticed stray nails sticking straight out of cracked plaster and light switches covered with smudged fingerprints that must be years old. She noticed bent, rusted hangers in the corners of closets and pieces of uneven masking tape that had originally been put up to hold sheets acting as curtains. She noticed old, dead crumbs that not even the roaches had wanted and chipped Christmas ornaments in corners of the attic. She noticed stray dots, sprays of paint (from when had they painted—had they been that careless?) and floor vents filled with webs, dust, and mites. And she thought of, quickly, almost as carelessly as the splattered paint, as the running down of things, her own pull, the one that brought her forth and attracted.

How embarrassing. How embarrassing. How embarrassing. Dan thought. It has been a while since then, since those, but space broadens the time you have to think about things. His wife on her knees. That's what she did. Right down on her knees. Tears and screams. Screams and tears. Pleas. Please, please, please, she wailed. The front door wide open. His carpool waiting for him right over there. His colleagues pretending the windshield, the windows, were opaque, only giving them hazy, if any, images that would be erased as soon as he reached for the handle, opened the door, and got in with a huff and a friendly laugh, with corporate eyes, a professional grin, a wave of the hand of how silly wives can be. Sludge as thick as caramel pulling a part of his gut back to that house as the car pulls away. Damn her. Damn that house. Well, if you wish hard enough, sometimes the punishment is granted and you get what you want.

"I'm tired," Meggie said. "So tired."
"It's all that running around you do," he said. "For the kids."
"I enjoy it."
"The other parents should do it sometimes."
"I enjoy it."
"And those PTA meetings."

"Oh, I enjoy those, too. I need to go. For the kids. What else would I do?"

"Well, you could clean a little more. Look at this place."

"Oh." (Who *had* made those claw marks? Did anyone else see them?)

"You haven't missed one meeting, have you?"

"Oh, no. I wouldn't."

"Is that because Steve Kennedy is there?"

"The principal? Oh, he's always there." Nothing to fear here.

"Is that why you go?"

"For the principal? Really." Ridiculous.

"Do you stick out your tits for him?"

SIGH. *SIGHS. SIGHS. Oh, I can't,* she thinks.

"I have to go to the bathroom," she says. And he went with her, following her so closely that the toe of his shoe almost cut her heel. Following her so closely that his breath burned the back of her neck, causing her hair to singe and curl. And he forced himself into the bathroom, breaking all privacy, breaking all respect, making all rules. And she pulled down her pants and sat on the toilet anyway, for what else was she to do? And she urinated and defecated, and watched as her husband peered, with rocks as eyes, only inches away, standing, claiming, guarding, for who knew who would fly up to the window and take his wife away?

Elizabeth sat in her room and listened. She didn't want to, but she couldn't leave. Not this room, not this house, not this life. Oh, she was back alright. The piece was missing and she had brought it back. Of course they had waited until it was just the three of them in this house. This sick place. This sick, sick, sick place that was causing her to stand for no reason and shake her skin, cry out like she was covered with dead locusts that had already gotten what they wanted anyway.

CHAPTER 26

Movement

Meggie followed her son's unsaid advice, example, and went for a walk. She supposed fall was her favorite season (sometimes they changed, depending on her thoughts). The crispness, the coolness, the promise of something new, a savior taking them all away from the black tar that has been scorched. It didn't matter that every other year they were led to a place covered in frost and shivers, death and ice. Maybe this year would be different. The smoke from the burning leaves, adding just the right amount of soft, brown bitterness to the quick, long snap of this new air said as much. The crunch of skeletons beneath her feet said as much, dividing up, expanding, the autumn blanket. Her own gait, changing, with her feet not lifting as high over the cracks in the sidewalk, not overcompensating, said as much. Maybe winter would stay away, or only threaten, this year. Maybe. Meggie walked and walked and walked. Past neighbors who lifted back a curtain to see and those who didn't care (there were a few people left in the world who thought problems were problems and life was a game of fortune, its outcomes respected, its indiscriminative nature revered). Meggie walked to the park, the same park she had played in when she had been a little girl. There's the old cannon she used to sit on when she was eight. There's the path she used to walk on with her friends, Bea and the others, after school, on their way home, or better yet, to the drug store for some soda drinks. There's that bridge where she used to sit and feel—just the wind, with the corners of her mouth turning upward when seeing happiness (a young couple with a toddler, a younger couple bending toward each other for their first kiss, a stray who found its way). But, all that doesn't matter now. That was too long ago. That happens, you know. Yes, she saw the trash. The strewn about. That happens, too. Wasn't there some town committee that appointed volunteers to pick this all up? Maybe she'd make a phone call. Meggie walked and walked and walked. To the stream. Meggie walked and walked and walked. Next to the stream until it opened up to a lake. She stood by the lake and looked up into the clouds, the sky, really. What was she doing? She wanted to speak, but there was no one there to address. She opened her mouth anyway, getting her throat and tongue ready, starting them, but then remembered Grace. Grace, who hasn't said a word in weeks. She relaxed her mouth, her throat, and realized, yes, she may miss something if she talks simply for the sake of sounds. There are other things to see, after all, to hear, than notes of your own voice. If you don't realize this, then you will soon be in a tunnel of your own making, not seeing the holes, the exits, even when they present themselves, trying to help.

She then became angry and wanted to fight. Anyone would do. Maybe that woman over there, looking so serene, sitting on a hill, hugging herself while wearing that lightly filled down jacket. Maybe *she'd* want to fight. Maybe that teenage boy over there who was standing by the trash can, tilting his head back as he consumed the last drops of his soda before he threw it out. Maybe *he'd* help Meggie prove something. Meggie wanted to comfort herself. She wanted to bend down in the grass, hug herself like that woman over there and say yes, everything is alright. But then she remembered Elizabeth. Elizabeth, who wasn't nearly as strong as people thought, but who would stand and speak against, point out, the injustices of actions, words, patterns, thoughts, the striking against heaven and the saints, even if it kills her, saying, No, don't you see? It's wrong. It's wrong. It's wrong. Even as the dirt and worms and broken, frayed twigs are hitting her coffin, piling up their case against her. It's wrong, it's wrong, she would say, her injured voice still trying to sift its way up through the earth.

Oh, my. My, my, my. Maybe it would be better if I disappeared, she thought, sitting down right there and then, pulling her knees up to her chest. She felt herself grow smaller and the appendages of the earth grow larger, taller, their leaves and branches and crests and ledges growing wide and important, all veins throbbing. She saw the valleys and lakes grow deeper, offending the earth. Oh, my. This really isn't accomplishing what I wanted, she thought. No comfort here. Worse, in a way. But protected in another. Poor Annabelle. Poor, poor Annabelle. Sweet child. Probably the last one who still is. Yes, I know. I see the rips, the tears, the wreckage of what's trying to pull her out, of what probably already has. Oh, my. How much harsher, pointed, disjoined they look from down here. Oh, my.

Meggie stood and waited patiently as the blackness fell away so that she could see again. She looked up at the sky again and breathed. She saw the light and its scatter from behind and through the clouds. Was it coming from heaven? Was there a heaven? Odd that her mother, her adversary in some ways (if an adversary can exist even though its target doesn't fight back, doesn't dare to stand up), knows the answer now. She *knows*, Meggie thought. Strange. I don't miss her, Meggie thought. Not strange. Is there a heaven? She looked down at her chest, her arms, her hands, taken aback that she was manifested in such a physical way. I have a body, she thought. I've always known that I have a soul, but a body? That's a surprise, if you think about it.

Well, I'm breathing. She thought. I'm standing on a black, stone path. The water is rippling in front of me. And the sky is now throwing hues at me. I can pound, pound, pound, feeling the earth, my own steps, below. I'm here. I can lift my head up and see. I can try, I can try to smother black holes with my pounding. The world can pull apart my limbs. It doesn't matter, it can try. For one day I will also be in the ground and others, my children, really, will remember my walk.

If I so choose.

* * * *

Dan was a strong man. In intent, body, and purpose. How committed his teeth were to clenching that jaw. How focused his eyes were when studying (when he took the time), acknowledging with a bitter laugh, what was wrong. But some had him all wrong. All wrong. How light and kind he could be, up on different plains (planes), when playing, joking, with his children, when at work, with friends, with his wife even. He just knew when silence had its place. And didn't like disruption (especially when created on purpose). Or manipulation. That's the worst kind of disruption. He was made up of almost equal parts of warrior and joker. (He saw the joker, but did he see the warrior?) Just make sure one doesn't overbalance the other, that's all, it seemed as if he told himself. That's the key. Pointed hats and bells for toes go only so far if you don't fight for what's yours, if you don't fight for what should have been yours, the life that had been spread out before you like a fresh, green field, promising you few valleys and hills, promising you a steady, secure climb, with silence, with a path as ambitious as an arrow leading straight to the meadows of well-deserved, a nice life.

* * * *

The smell of lilacs. That's all it took. You would have thought something else would have been involved. Perhaps something bigger from that ghost they had been so fond of talking about. But, no. No furniture sliding, no drawers pulling themselves out oh only this far and then stopping (then back again, this is fun), no lightbulbs flickering on and off, off and on, and then on and off again. No cabinets swinging open, imitating large, thick, square, wooden butterflies. No clothes swirling about in the closets them-

selves, as if dancing in a ballroom where the only thing not permitted was flesh. No toys floating, prancing, teasing in mid air.
No music (classical, big band, sometimes rock) from nowhere,
everywhere. All of which *had* happened at the Owenses' house. All
of which they each had witnessed, individually (always alone), in
between slights and slashes, perspectives and moods, almost-but-
not-quite-yet-there knowledge and fear of other things. You would
have thought something more than a thin shade of something
would have acted as the bugle, announcing the upcoming portent
event, or as the catalyst, stirring molecules, causing composition
to change. But, I suppose sometimes a soft scent is stronger than
an iron blade, a loose cannon, a brass bell. And that's what Meggie
found out.

Meggie took out her dish rag and stood on the chair. She opened
the cabinet to the left and above the sink and began to wipe down
its miniature walls, in the beginning losing her balance and hearing the tea cups clink as she grabbed the edge for support. She
brushed back her hair, a signal for the start of determination, and
began to tackle wood grains and splinters, snagging her cloth on
more than one occasion. She was tired, after all, of thinking about
what lay behind doors of cabinets and closets, under stout furniture, and in creases, edges, the space between the countertop and
the stove. She worked and worked, occasionally gently swatting a
cat out of her way. (Where were they going, these cats? There
seemed to be fewer and fewer of them. Annabelle had said once
that a friend of hers saw one of their cats in a new home on the
other block, happy as could be, with its own clean bowl and matching red collar. Meggie at first went to console her little girl, to ask
her if she wanted the cat back, but then Annabelle left the room
with a firm chin and a clip, cooing to the couple of cats [Smokey
and one of her kittens, Midnight] that were left, not giving Meggie
any room to comfort. The others? Where were the others, Meggie
thought. Oh, well. She supposed they had found their way. Danny
didn't seem to be too upset, either. They still had Smokey and

Midnight, after all.) She worked and worked, occasionally blowing a strand of hair out of her way with a disposable piece of her
breath. Dan had walked by almost each time she had undertaken
such a new endeavor, with a slow smile and a pat on the rear end
for his wife. He meant it as a sign of affection, a mark of appreciation, for those split wires finally coming back together again. But,
it didn't affect her in that way and it didn't affect her in the opposite way, either. She didn't sigh and squint and wrinkle her eyebrows, trying to gasp in displaced air that was hers alone, her
right. She just kept on working and wiping, occasionally remark-
ing "What *is* that?" to herself and any other spirit floating by. And
soon, days, maybe weeks, later, she was finished. The dust was
gone; the dirt had been swept up; dull layers of wax had been
stripped off and then a new, better layer reapplied; clothes had
been washed and folded, so neatly that her children were almost
afraid to wear them; the mold had been stripped from the bathroom; pictures had been straightened; Uncle Ezra's frame had been
given a new shine; and all fingerprints were gone. Every last one of
them. And the smell of lilacs filled the rooms. Every last one of
them.

Elizabeth pulled the covers up from over her head and stuck
out her nose to smell. Grace stopped the humming in her mind
and listened to footsteps, seeing through floors and walls, and
watched a hint of purple follow each one. Danny stopped counting the nails in the floor, the spots on the ceiling, leaves that had
fallen, and squinted his eyes, suspicious of the new scent. Annabelle
cradled her doll, pulling the corner of her blanket to her own
mouth, and sang softly to her baby, "Don't worry, the visitor is
here."

And Dan waved his hand in front of his face, annoyed that the
flies had found him out of season. And Meggie saw that her work
was done, silently pleased that a hidden bouquet, all mist and no
flowers, had agreed. She wasn't sure from where it came. "*Mother?*

Mother?" she had even hushed, trying to trace, trying to calm, as she turned corners and lifted bones, for this was also a bit frightening. But would that make sense? She wasn't sure. Oh, no need to know the where's, the how's, the who's. She knew why. She didn't see where he went, or his reasons, like Grace did. She didn't see him standing in front of her, wearing old black boots (made of leather and high), black trousers, and a black jacket covered with dust, the only color lent by a maroon ascot that covered his throat, like Annabelle did. She didn't see him open his mouth and try to speak, his frustration lying in the thick, constant fact that the bridge hadn't included a voice. She just smelled the clouds he left behind, thinking perhaps this was somehow part of her mother's penance, thinking perhaps this was somehow part of the penance of those who had gone before, who had had things done to them and who had done things to others. She was given permission to crack.

And she did. She cracked the bricks, scraped the cement away, chiseled away at iron, steel, and metal, proving that what man had made would not keep her. Not stagnant. Not still. Not there. Not now. Not before (for realization does travel back and change the past, didn't you know that?). Not in the coming. Not in the breath, life, soul. Heart. Not in the red, pulsing, thick heart. Not in its arteries, valves, or muscles. No.

And right then, as she was turning her last corner, she stopped as if she had hit a mirror, looking into a startled reflection, frightened because it knew it was going to be left behind. She raised her hands and pushed on the glass, trying to tell herself it was going to be alright. She met her own eyes and saw the fear. She saw the lines and scars and bars. She saw the past and black stars and Satan as red as his own standing behind her looking over her shoulder. Downcast them, she thought. Just downcast them. And following the pulses, the reflection downcast her eyes, giving Meggie just enough time to pull back and escape.

She ran and slipped and caught herself. She pulled out one of Dan's old suitcases and threw in blouses and slacks that didn't match, only one pair of underwear, and mismatched socks. She ignored Dan's rumblings, his trying to pull her back into the story, the tragedy, really, and stepped back and slid around every "what the fuck do you think you're doing?" and "go! it'll never last! you'll never last"

he sounded so small

almost surprised when she saw his puzzled looks, a swallow of saliva to re-balance himself, and his voice growing softer as he realized she had moved her position, changing his.

"Come on, kids. We're leaving. Come on," she said as she walked quickly up the stairs, huffing, but not as quite in a hurry as before, knowing that rearrangement had already instilled protection in its place. Knowing that she still needed to move, but she needed her mind, her steps steady.

"Come on, Elizabeth. It's time," she said as she shook off the sleeping bag from her daughter. Elizabeth opened her groggy eyes and watched as her dulled mind formed squiggly lines that cut the room. "Mhmfhm?" she slowly, grazingly, asked.

"Yes," her mother sharply replied, forcing Elizabeth to at least focus a little more. "It's time for you to stop sleeping," Meggie said curtly. But, then she felt bad, knowing that all roots couldn't be pulled and jarred, nature changed. "You can sleep over

Grandpop's," she added. Elizabeth blinked her eyes, trying to erase the blurredness and then sat up, inching herself a little to the right to escape the slice of quickness that seemed to be eyeing her, that was definitely unsettling her.

"Is that where we're going?" Elizabeth asked, slower than she normally would have, balancing her mother and feeding herself, feeling her bed move beneath her. She was so sleepy, so tired. (She hadn't wanted to kill herself anymore, but knew there were other, more acceptable ways of leaving. I'll just sleep my way through, she had said to herself one day.)

Meggie sat down but with eyes darting, not sure if she was the hunter trying to find something or the hunted trying to hide. Not caring. She still had to move. She knew she had to move. She knew that.

"Yes, sweetie," she said. (She *was* a mother, after all.) Deep, deep breath. "We need to leave, don't you think?"

Elizabeth stared.

Pangs still found Meggie. Even during this.

"You don't have to," Meggie said. "I mean, Grandpop's isn't as big as here and you could stay here if you want." Oh, how they still found her.

Elizabeth stared.

"This is your decision, Elizabeth. But, I do need to move." That she does.

Elizabeth looked up at her mother and forgot to move away from the quickness this time. She felt its pierce, and in the future looking back, she would concur with images from synapses and neurons that she had moved in its way on purpose.

"I want to go with you," Elizabeth said clearly, her sturdy voice sliding past the hesitancy that still lingered between bones and meat.

Quick, quick, quick. Elizabeth packed. Quick, quick, quick. Meggie got her other daughters (Grace in Danny's room, Annabelle is . . .).

"Grace, come on. Let's go. Come on."

Like Elizabeth at first, Grace just stared at her mother.

The dryness cracked like dried-up wheat beneath a hissing sun and above dead toads, ants, and mantises who hadn't prayed hard enough. The croak occurred only because panic was setting in and Grace did want to survive, after all.

But where? are the words the croak is trying to create.

"What?" Meggie asks, not thinking it the least bit strange that this is the first sound her daughter has made in weeks, maybe months. (Who can keep track of such a thing?)

"Bahh . . . t . . . hwee . . . arrr . . . ," actually comes out, upswinging at the end to indicate an answer is expected.

"Oh. To Grandpop's. We're leaving, Grace. I told Elizabeth she can stay and you can, too, if you want. But we're leaving. Elizabeth and me and Annabelle and Danny. Well, I haven't told them, yet, and they have a choice, too. But, we're leaving. It's time to go."

"Aehh," Grace squeaked. Meggie wasn't sure if this was a word or a sigh. Grace wasn't sure, either. She looked at her mother, straight into her eyes. She saw sparkles and fear, a crescent and tears. She saw frayed roots that had been cut and uncertainty that grew a brave smile, shiny eyes of its own.

"Aehh hwaan . . . t . . . cmmmm," croaked in the room, hanging dense in the air, too heavy and new.

"Oh, Grace, I'm so glad," Meggie sighed. She hung her head for a second and brought her hands to her cheeks, lightly stroking them with her knuckles. She lifted her chin back up and then, back to the quickness, said, "Pack your things. I'll go get Annabelle and then we'll go find Danny."

Meggie and her daughters walked down the hall in a thick, confused line that somehow knew exactly what it was doing. Small vinyl suitcases made for only overnight parties swayed, marking the walls, and trashbags filled with comic books and stuffed animals strained and stretched, causing blood to spread in the fingers that held onto them. Annabelle held tightly onto Smokey, and

Midnight followed, his black fur getting ready to blend. Meggie looked down at the steps with her bottom lip curled back over her teeth, intent in her intentions. Her girls followed, looking up, around, wondering what would come of this in the next immediate moments. Where was their father? Oh, there he is.

Dan stood at the bottom of the stairs, in the doorway between the dining room and the foyer, right before the front door. He looked big and heavy and red and lost. His shoulders sagged as his eyes darted, and his fists kept opening and closing as if he had known he was supposed to hold onto something, he just wasn't sure what.

"Girls," he said as Meggie walked to the door and they started to follow her. "It will be alright, girls. It will be alright."

Annabelle looked up at him and smiled kindly, not loosening her grip on Smokey or her stuffed koala bear, both of their claws hanging onto her hip. Grace looked at him with sad eyes, seeing the blurred lines that were now causing his skin to mesh with this house. She looked at him with sad eyes, seeing for the first time actual tears forming in his eyes, admitting to herself that this had been the most unexpected of all her visions. She looked at him with sad eyes. This was her father, after all.

Elizabeth looked at her father. It was too late to pull down, pull close, wasn't it?

Meggie was now outside the door and her girls followed her. They readjusted, balancing things with upper thighs and lifting them to better positions, under an arm or held close to the chest. Once on the stone path, they didn't look back. Once on the stone path, Dan shouted (was that a shout? it was in a funnel of some sort), "She brought the devil out in me, girls!" They kept walking, shuffling, picking up a fallen pillow, a lost shoe. "And she'll bring the devil out in you, too! Watch! She will, girls! She will!" His voice lost now, its notes not even noticing the other soul left in that house, watching from an upstairs window, black in its outline, black in its core.

Danny had been walking by an old scarecrow when they found him. Its old flannel shirt hung on its rake for a spine, its sleeves half-heartedly spread on the piece of scrap wood nailed horizontally to the tree. It had only a torso—no legs, no stance to scare away, only hanging and dripping posture that caused more of a smile than fear. A joke, that's what it was. All a joke.

"Come on, Danny."

Danny looked to the street and saw his mother and sisters in that old Chevy that was so faded you hardly felt trustworthy if you described it as a true blue. His father had gotten it for his mother last year. "So you can do your errands, take the kids where they need to be, not worry about taking me to work and picking me up," he had said. He had said. Not realizing prophets can be in strange places. Under rocks, balancing on twigs, at the bottom of a cold, dark well.

"Come on, Danny," his mother said again. He was still walking and his mother drove slowly next to him. "We're leaving."

Danny stopped.

"Where are you going?" he asked.

"No, all of us. You, too. To Grandpop's."

Danny felt his cheeks sting, his stomach become hollow, its twinge travel to his legs.

"But . . ."

"I have to get you kids out of there. Before it's too late."

Damage has been done. Done to damage. Done damage. Damaging done. Done. Done. Done. What were his thoughts doing to him?

"But who will be with Dad?" he asked.

"Oh, honey," his mother said.

"He'll be alone."

"Oh, honey."

"I need to walk," Danny said, beginning again. Meggie started driving the car again next to him.

"You don't need to do this, Danny," she said out the window.

"Yes, I do."

"Come with us," his mother said.

Danny stopped again and turned so that he was completely facing his mother and sisters. "I'm going to stay with Dad," he said, cutting more strings.

"Oh, Danny," his mother said, Meggie said.

Danny turned back and walked. Past colored flags hanging next to doors, past painted shutters that matched painted gutters, past more old scarecrows that hung as if they knew the frost was coming.

"I have to go home," he said, only to himself and the fearless crows because by now his mother and sisters were way up there by the stop sign.

She sat in the car and watched as they left their brother, remembered how they had left their father only moments before. She tried to talk to her father now even though distance erased sounds. But, she still believed, amazingly so, in magic. How could she not? Sometimes it's the only thing that's real. So, that's why she talked to him now, even though she was in a car traveling toward another edge. Wait, she said. I remember, Dad, she said. I remember how you used to give me a dollar a day for candy. I remember how you used to lift me in the air and let us ride you like a horse. I remember how I couldn't wait for you to get home from work so that I could jump up and try to reach the gum you hid in your pocket, so I could be close to you. I remember how you bought me a new bike whenever I wanted one. I remember. I remember going on camping trips, just us, when Mom wanted to stay home. I remember our canoe rides and how we would laugh and splash in the rusty water above the pebbles that felt so good beneath our feet. I remember your jokes, how you could make others laugh and me, too, when I was old enough to understand. I remember sometimes seeing love in your eyes. I remember how we danced, with my feet on yours. I remember soft words. There were some. I remember. I remember all those things. And more. But, I won't remember for long. I'm sorry. I won't remember anything.

I'm so sorry. But, that's the only way I can block out the bad. And
that I will need to do simply to take a step.

And who had this come from—Elizabeth, Grace, or Annabelle?
Hmm. Don't you know? You really don't? All three.

Dan stood on the front step outside the door and in his mind.
Kids, don't listen to everything she's going to tell you. It wasn't
that bad, kids. I wasn't that bad. Soon, I won't even remember, so
I know you won't either. It couldn't have been that bad. Watch out
for her example, kids. She'll never change. Clinging, whining,
pulling, sighing. Everything a drama. Putting herself as the loser
every time. It wasn't that way. We had quite the life. At least that's
how I'll remember it, so you will, too. But, I want you to know
something. I'm not going to help. In my mind, I may comment
about how things should be, what I might say or do if I were to
help. But I never will actually say or do . . . She'll ruin it for me.
Your mother will ruin it for me. And I simply don't have it in me
to fight for you. (Will that even cross my mind?) Maybe I'll have a
few suggestions when you're grown. But mostly, starting now, I'll
be on my way, my own. I have an image, something you don't
need right now. This is all a mess. Your mother has ruined this for
me. Oh, and visit me now while you can, during the next few
years, in the beginning of whatever this is, because after that you
won't be able to find me. Not until lines are crossed and I am
someone else.

Your mother has ruined it for me. Can't you see?

CHAPTER 27

Looking up at the sky is a prayer, you know. When you see the sun filtered by burnt orange, chestnut, and the color of butter and lemons. When you stop and let thoughts melt away, divided by roses, the smell of lavender soap. When it is so clear now how everything completes itself, showing you right above your very head, how the spectrum works. It doesn't matter that you saw it for just a blip. That you rode or walked through looking up and were touched, lightly, as a thin sleeve of hope passed through. You don't even have to verbalize it. In fact, you shouldn't—it's more pure that way. Your prayer. Clarity is your answer, you know. That's what you asked for.

CHAPTER 28

Are you afraid of ghosts? Oh. Well then. You might as well be afraid of your mother doing the dishes downstairs, of your father at his roll-top desk paying the bills, of your sisters in their rooms, dreaming, hoping for the day when they have lives of their own, of your brother who wonders. Because they're made of the same thing.

CHAPTER 29

What about the house? Are Dan and his son safe there? Are we safe anywhere? No, you mean are they safe from distorted hearth and evil spirit? You're still worried about the movement, the stranger that may (may as might) live there? Was that Uncle Ezra? No, Uncle Ezra is in his grave, his bones to dust, his soul searching for justice somewhere else. It was me, your narrator who has been in and out, mostly out, who roamed that house. Oh, I didn't mean any harm, scaring anyone, especially the children. I just had to do what I could to get them to stop destroying themselves, don't you agree?

CPSIA information can be obtained
at www.ICGtesting.com
Printed in the USA
FFOW02n1047160715
15216FF

9 780738 828466